THE GENTLEMAN TURNED AROUND....

He was tall and muscular, clad fashionably, if carelessly, in a dark brown frock
coat, sage green kerseymore waistcoat, and
gleaming Hessian boots. His hair was
auburn. Eyes of an unusually clear shade
of green gazed rather derisively out of a
face that was a fascinating combination of
crags and hollows and planes. There was
no doubt that he had lived each year of
his adult life to the fullest. In summation,
Angelica beheld a sardonically elegant,
diabolically seductive rakehell.

"You don't look at all like your father,"
she said.

"And you," responded the gentleman,
"don't look like Haymarket-ware! Come,
tell me what rig you're running. I'll wager
that a small gift—shall we say fifty
pounds?—will make you heart-whole
again."

Also by Maggie MacKeever:

A BANBURY TALE   23174 $1.50

LADY BLISS   50010 $1.75

A NOTORIOUS LADY   23491 $1.50

THE
MISSES
MILLIKIN

Maggie
MacKeever

FAWCETT COVENTRY ● NEW YORK

THE MISSES MILLIKIN

Published by Fawcett Coventry Books, a unit of CBS Publications, the Consumer Publishing Division of CBS Inc.

ISBN: 0-449-50074-8

Printed in the United States of America

First Fawcett Coventry printing: July 1980

10 9 8 7 6 5 4 3 2 1

THE
MISSES
MILLIKIN

One

The traditional city residence of the Barons Chalmers was an elegant stone structure in a fashionable part of London. Built a century before, and incorporating within its weathered exterior all the myriad discomforts attendant upon antiquity, Chalmers House rose several stories into the air. Atop its massive cornice, rather like a rakish bonnet, was a hipped roof with dormers and crooked chimney pots. Great prominence was given to the windows on the lower floors, and greater prominence still to the decorative classical doorway.

Within, the house boasted a predominance of cedar, mahogany, pinewood. Plainly paneled walls stretched up toward plaster ceilings enriched by simple low relief ribs; polished wooden floors were adorned by the occasional rug; wooden staircases with finely moulded handrails and delicate balusters, barley-sugar twisted, climbed into the upper recesses of the house. The doors were wood paneled, the windows of sash design.

Behind one of those doors, looking down into the street, was the current Baroness Chalmers, a title which had been the reward, and reason, for her marriage some eight months past to the gentleman who among his vast and numerous possessions numbered Chalmers House. Unfortunately, from the baroness's viewpoint, the immensely wealthy baron was proving himself of a temperament she could only call nip-farthing, cheese-paring, miserly. What cared she for wealth preserved intact for hypothetical offspring? Surely she, as one whose efforts in the production of those offspring would not be negligible, was

7

entitled from the Chalmers pounds and pence to derive some slight benefit?

In all fairness, it must be stated that the baroness had not the least appearance of a lady whose husband kept her shockingly short of funds. Lady Chalmers was clad in the highest kick of fashion in a gown of sprigged muslin with sleeves drawn at the top with colored ribbons, a high-necked bodice and a skirt edged with flounces, both vandyked, the whole trimmed with broadlace. On her feet were round-toed shoes slashed over the toecap to show a colored lining; around her slender shoulders was a Lyons shawl of flowered silk with deep borders, two and one-half yards square. It was an ensemble that would have overpowered any but the most stunning of beauties, another title to which Lady Chalmers could—and did—lay claim. At twenty years of age she was perfection incarnate, with a cloud of golden curls that clustered around her lovely face, and eyes of the purest blue. She had been, at various times and by various admirers, compared to Aphrodite, Venus, and a Dresden shepherdess, to the detriment of all three. Lord Chalmer's comments on his wife's beauty are not a matter of record, however—if comment he made.

But those who waxed loquacious about the lady's attributes might have had cause to doubt their judgment had they observed her standing at her drawing room windows, staring down into the street. Sullenness plays havoc with the most exquisite of features, and Lady Chalmers was looking distinctly petulant.

She did not do so without cause. It was a miserably dark day, if one unaccompanied by the eternal snow and hail that this April had brought, with the result that countless sheep had perished, a tidbit of information presented Lady Chalmers by her well-informed spouse, who she sometimes thought was more concerned with the condition of the country than with her own welfare. If she had married him for wealth and position—Lady Chalmers, as the beauty of her family, had had little choice but to marry advantageously, so that she might help her younger siblings—he had married her for the sole purpose of providing himself an heir. Having secured the requisite wife, he promptly and firmly banished her to the background of his life. To a young lady accustomed from the cradle to masculine admiration, such

8

conduct was incomprehensible, and made more difficult to bear by the greatest of all her follies. In short, Lady Chalmers had fallen head-over-heels in love with her stern and rather disapproving spouse.

She turned away from the window and gazed in a very gloomy manner about the drawing room. Quite the finest chamber in the house, it boasted six-paneled doors with classical motifs in the carved panel borders, a white plaster ceiling richly decorated, a massive cornice that ran around the room. Four sash windows, under each a window seat with tapering legs and scroll ends, reached from cornice to wainscot, large rectangular panels in wood frames. The chamber was furnished with pieces from various historical periods, which somehow coexisted amicably, among them a gilt suite covered in convent-worked needlepoint. Lady Chalmers crossed the room to stand before the marble-faced fireplace. Chalmers House was afflicted with unpredictable currents of cold air.

At this point in her unhappy reflections, as she was wondering if it was Chalmers House or Lord Chalmers himself who caused her to feel as if she existed in some arctic zone, she heard the sounds of arrival that she had awaited so impatiently. Immediately the petulant expression vanished from Lady Chalmers's face, to be replaced by the haughty look of a *très grande dame*. She smoothed her skirts, adjusted her shawl, cast a quick glance at her reflection in one of the sconce-flanked mirrors that hung between the windows. Every inch the baroness, she decided triumphantly, and arranged herself accordingly on a confidante to wait.

She had not long to do so, and her effect on her visitors was all she might have wished. Those visitors were three in number: a young lady who bore a marked resemblance to Lady Chalmers, possessing the same blue eyes and golden hair, and adding to these attributes a certain vagueness of expression that prompted intimates to refer to her as a lovely pea-goose; a second lady, rather more advanced in years and of an attitude which clearly indicated her practical disposition, who in such splendid company was completely overpowered; a young man who had a strong look of both his youngest companion and Lady Chalmers herself. The first two of these visitors Lady Chalmers had expected; the latter she had not. "Fennel!" she uttered, in some surprise, and then cast an anguished glance at her eldest, plainest sister. "Oh, Angelica!"

Miss Angelica Millikin, due to long acquaintance with her sister Rosemary—to long acquaintance, in fact, with a large number of siblings who possessed more hair than sense—understood perfectly that this utterance, if a trifle inane in nature, was indicative of great distress. The realization did not especially surprise her. So long as she could remember, Angelica had been called upon by her siblings to extricate them from the results of their empty-headedness. She gazed thoughtfully upon Rosemary, perched like major royalty on the confidante, and wondered what had possessed her to buy that absurd dress. "There, there, child!" Angelica murmured, as she ushered her charges, who were staring at Rosemary in a dumbfounded manner, further into the room. "What's amiss?"

But Rosemary was no child, and thus reminded of that fact, gathered around her her dignity. Was she not a married lady, a baroness, no less? Who was Angelica to speak to her in that patronizing tone? No more than a spinster of seven-and-twenty, without the slightest pretension to beauty save the blue eyes she shared with the rest of the family—the ugly duckling, not to put too fine a point on it, in a family of swans. Angelica might rule the country household from which they had all come, but Rosemary did not intend to allow her sister to similarly reign over Chalmers House. That she was not permitted to do so herself, her husband retaining firm hold of the reins, was entirely beside the point.

Rosemary patted the confidante. "Come, Lily," she said to the youngest of her callers, who was gazing in a bedazzled manner about the drawing room, "Sit here by me. Fennel, have you *again* been sent down from the university?"

The young man admitted that he had, due to an incident concerning a bearleader and a bear. It was an admission made with the unflagging good cheer that characterized Fennel Millikin; an astonishingly handsome young man of nineteen, he had not a care in the world, perhaps because a serious thought had never entered his handsome head. "Heard you was to give Lily her come-out!" he added, by way

10

of explaining his unexpected presence. "Thought I'd lend your efforts my countenance!"

To this intimation that her prestige alone was not sufficient to insure Lily *entrée* into the *haut ton,* Lady Chalmers took justifiable offense. Since it was beneath her newly found dignity to fly into a pelter, she proceeded to deliver a subtle set-down. "As you wish!" she replied indifferently, and launched into a discussion of the treats in store for Lily, chief among which were prospective visits to modistes and milliners, due to the fact, reluctant as Rosemary was to mention it, that persons of the first consideration could not be expected to clasp to their bosoms young ladies who looked like dowds.

"Wasn't so long ago," remarked the unquenchable Fennel, while Angelica pondered the transformation of Rosemary from a creature all smiles and sweet good humor into this fashionable female who was so high in the instep, "that you was a country mouse yourself. Didn't stop Chalmers from making you an offer, did it? No, don't get up on your high ropes! And don't be pitching us any more gammon, either! Because if you're saying Lily's not at the very top of the tree, even if she ain't dressed bang up to the nines—and if it's bang up to the nines you are in that rig, I'm not sure she *should* be—you'll catch cold at that!"

Sternly Rosemary reminded herself of her position and her dignity, and contented herself with hinting to her outspoken brother that he was quite ignorant as concerned the *ton.* "Let me assure you," she said repressively, "that Chalmers would be most displeased if I did not go on in the best possible style!" Unfortunately, she added silently, Lord Chalmers was not at all eager to provide the outlay necessary to maintain that highest of all styles, a failing cruelly unfeeling in a man of such plump pockets and easy circumstance. But that did not bear dwelling on. "My dear Lily, you must expect to soon be racketing yourself to pieces. It is all very dull work, I fear, but one is expected to fatigue oneself to death."

Lily was not of a temperament to be stricken by this ominous remark with dread—Lily, in whom a limited power of intellect was compensated by unbounded imagination,

11

which enabled her to see in the most mundane situations both adventure and romance, had never in her eighteen years been either fatigued or bored. "Oh, no!" she uttered, in a voice so melodious that despite the fact she never said anything of significance, everyone loved to hear her speak. "I promise you! Oh, Rosemary, you should have been with us, it was such a lark! Fennel was privileged to sit beside the coachman on the box!"

"So I was!" Fennel offered cheerfully, while Angelica wondered how Rosemary might possibly have engaged in a journey of which she was simultaneously the destination, and Rosemary stared at her brother in growing dismay. "Even tooled the ribbons myself, and don't mind saying I came coachy in prime style."

"Is that what you call it?" inquired Angelica, with a nice display of sisterly interest. "How foolish of me to have been in quite a fright! But I had no notion that your university career had endowed in you such expertise!"

"Pooh!" Fennel was sufficiently quick on the uptake to know when he was being bamboozled, and sufficiently serene in nature to accept that bamboozlement philosophically. Too, Angelica was his favorite sister. She didn't go into fidgets or ring a peal over a fellow even when he'd once again behaved in a manner that even he admitted was demonstrably bacon-brained. "You were safe as houses, on the square."

Before Angelica could voice disagreement on this point, as she might easily have done, recalling not one but several instances when she had been convinced the coach would overturn, Rosemary spoke. She did so with combined consternation and outrage. "You didn't travel here in a *public conveyance!*" she wailed.

Lady Chalmers, with her newfound consequence and dignity, was fast becoming Fennel's least favorite sibling, a position generally reserved for the youngest member of the family, a cherub prone to such gay adventures as putting toads in his elder brother's bed. "Chucklehead!" he uttered. "How else *would* we get here? *You're* the one who's well-heeled, remember? Not us!"

In point of fact, Rosemary was not well-heeled, one of the
12

reasons for her current embarrassments. "I should have sent a carriage for you," she mourned, "but I didn't think of it. Oh, dear! I hope no one saw you arrive in a hack!"

"Does it matter?" Angelica inquired reasonably. "The world must surely know already that the family is poor as church mice."

"Gracious!" Rosemary looked horrified. "I hope you don't mean to go around talking like that, Angelica! Chalmers has already promised to do well by Lily—it wouldn't do to let people think she has no dowry."

"Nor," Angelica said very sternly, while the subject of this discourse stared dreamily into space, "will it do to noise about that Lily has a larger portion than is true. I will not permit that she is presented under false colors, Rosemary!"

By this justification of her fears that Angelica meant to behave in her usual strong-minded and managing manner, Rosemary was further depressed. "Well! As if I would! Of course I never thought of such a thing! Still, it need not be common knowledge that poor Lily has no more than a pittance. Consider, Angelica! You wouldn't want Lily to dwindle into a spinster left upon the shelf!"

Since Angelica had attained precisely that unenviable position, her reponse was wry. "Better a spinster," she rejoined, "than engaged in an alliance devoid of either affection or respect." To her surprise, Rosemary flushed.

"Dear Angelica," said Lily, who compensated for a lack of native wit not only with rabid imagination but also with the kindest of hearts, "you must not worry about *that*! I mean to marry only for love, and in that case the gentleman I marry won't care that I haven't a penny with which to bless myself. Just to be certain, I shall choose a gentleman of property—perhaps even a duke!—and one with enough for *all* of us. So you see that your fears are utterly groundless!" She smiled, enchantingly.

Of the misapprehensions that Lily cherished—gentlemen of property, especially dukes, being notoriously disinclined to wed females unblessed by a single penny—she remained undisabused, her siblings being too fond of her to cause her unhappiness. Angelica sought a change of subject. "Where *is* Chalmers?" she inquired.

Where indeed? Rosemary thought resentfully. Trust Angelica to thrust straight to the heart of the matter. Lady Chalmers might not have possessed the most brilliant of understandings, but she was shrewd enough to question whether matters of government accounted for all the time spent by her lord away from his fireside, as the baron claimed. A staunch Tory, Lord Chalmers was very much involved with matters of government, made even more complex by the end of the Continental wars, an event that in some incomprehensible fashion seemed to have plunged the country into economic disaster. Rosemary thought it typically callous of her husband to expect her to concern herself with manufacturers who, without war contracts, dismissed their workmen and closed their doors, or with farmers who suffered a peacetime slump in the prices fetched by their crops. Certainly it was all very sad, but what could *she* do? Rosemary had problems of her own.

But Angelica awaited a response, with an expression that Rosemary interpreted as frankly pitying. "Chalmers?" she echoed, absently, as if caught spinning air-dreams. "He's gone to confer with Lords Liverpool and Castlereagh—the chief figures in the government, you know! I suppose it has to do with the groups of radicals who are everywhere demanding reform, though what they think to accomplish by smashing machinery I do not know!"

Still Angelica wore that compassionate face, and Rosemary laughed hollowly. "Are you thinking he should have been here to meet you? Indeed, he wanted to be! But Chalmers is an important man, my dears, and his time is not his own. Frankly I'm glad of it; to be always living in one's husband's pocket is a dead bore!" If excuses she offered, they were no more than the very excuses provided her by her lord. Resolutely Rosemary engaged Lily and Fennel in a discussion of the gaieties of the metropolis.

Angelica listened without comment. She knew herself to be in truth the oddity that her family considered her, the possessor of the larger portion of the Millikin intelligence, and the least amount of the ravishing Millikin charm. But one of

14

the family must be clever, where the rest were not: marriage had patently failed to inspire Rosemary with more prudence than she had hitherto possessed; Lily could not be expected, even with an advantageous match at stake, to desist from her usual vagaries, most recent among which had been an aborted elopement with an impecunious poet who had written incomprehensible effusions to her shell-like earlobes; Fennel, released from the restrictions of his university, was ripe for any mischief. Were not all three to land themselves in the briars, Angelica must contrive prodigiously. Such effort, she reflected ruefully, was the price demanded of her, the ugly duckling, for inclusion in their ranks. Not for the first time in her twenty-seven years, Angelica wished—oh, *how* she wished —she too might be a swan.

Two

Within the space of only days, Miss Lily Millikin had become the toast of London. Gentlemen had only to receive an introduction to begin to pay her court, indefatigable in their attentions, sighing and dying and sending her countless posies and tokens, dubbing her the Fair Incomparable—all of which gratified Lily's sister Rosemary, even as it made her wish to gnash her teeth. Rosemary was, after all, the reigning family beauty, and at twenty years of age could hardly be expected to relinquish that position without some feeling of chagrin. Still, she had had her Season, had married Chalmers with the express intention of providing her younger sisters with opportunities to make equally brilliant matches; and it was hardly admirable in her to envy Lily's success.

Despite these stern admonitions to herself, Rosemary remained envious. If only Chalmers—but he paid more attention to her sisters. Bleakly, Rosemary envisioned her future, through which paraded a steady succession of her siblings, each gayer and younger and lovelier than herself. Even Angelica, she thought bitterly, was more fortunate. A spinster of seven-and-twenty, never blessed by masculine admiration, could hardly expect other than to be left upon the shelf.

In this, Rosemary seriously misjudged her sister; Angelica had more than once studied her reflected image and questioned whether she was quite so dowdy as her glamorous family considered her to be. Yet Rosemary's lack of perception must not be held against her; she was young, and unhappy; if she was also self-centered it was because she knew no other way to be.

That particular failing was not shared by the next eldest of her sisters; Lily Millikin might be fairly called a complete flirt, but in her exquisite person there was not a single selfish bone. Furthermore, the possessor of a rampant imagination must needs also possess an avid curiosity. Lily was not only aware that Rosemary was deep in a fit of the blue-devils, she also knew why. As she pondered what might best be done with this knowledge, she gazed dreamily about the Chalmers drawing room.

That chamber was packed to its wainscoted walls with persons of rank. The gentlemen were resplendent in double-breasted dress coats and evening breeches, luxurious waistcoats and high stiff cravats; the ladies equally splendid in silks and satins and crape, lushly bedecked with flowers and jewels and the occasional plume. With a formal dinner party —the menu for which had included dishes too numerous and varied to record, all adjudged superb, which judgment, had he but been made aware of it, would have assuaged the Chalmers' superior and highly volatile French chef, currently indulging a Gallic nerve-storm in his immaculate kitchen— Chalmers House had been thrown open to select members of the *ton*.

Lily moved through the crowded room, an ethereal-looking creature in a gown of white gauze, on her golden curls an Austrian cap of satin and blonde. To Lady Jersey's reminder to present herself at Almack's, to Beau Brummel's gentle quips, Lily responded in her usual musical tones, and with her usual dreaming expression, with the result that all who spoke with her decided that Miss Lily Millikin was a good, biddable girl, a trifle lacking in animation perhaps, but a damsel who would be unexceptionable once she'd acquired some town-bronze.

These conclusions, as Lily's fond family might have attested, had they been applied to concerning the matter, were marvelously incorrect. To use the word with no bark on it, Lily was as biddable as a mule. When Lily looked the vaguest, she was most to be reckoned with; behind her bemused manner, her romantical high flights, lurked a startlingly strong will. This mule-headedness, combined with Lily's lack of what her family called horse-sense, was the reason why Angelica had abandoned the younger members of the family to their own devices while she accompanied Lily to London in the role of gooseberry.

This, too, Lily understood, and didn't mind in the least; Lily was far too kindly to harbor such emotions as rancor and resentment. Indeed, Lily hoped Angelica would succeed in preventing her from getting in a pickle, an event that would distress Angelica far more than Lily herself. Lily was accustomed to involving herself unwittingly in difficulties. She was also accustomed to Angelica extricating her from them. Lily's delicate eyelids twitched, then, as inspiration struck. Who better than Angelica to deal with Rosemary's little problems? Pensively, Lily approached her eldest sister, engaged in conversation with Lord Chalmers near the marble-faced fireplace.

"The situation," said that informative gentleman, "grows steadily worse. All over the country banks are calling in their money; some have stopped payment and closed their doors. With bankers unwilling to advance or discount, not even the rich have money to spare. I assure you, Miss Millikin, that thousands of servants are out of a place."

"Goodness!" responded Angelica, rather foolishly.

Lord Chalmers appeared to consider this an adequate rejoinder. "Conditions in London," he continued, "are no better than in the provinces. The city is crowded with demobilized sailors and soldiers, the East End districts are crowded with thousands of half-starved unemployed workers, the workhouses and debtors' prisons are crowded past capacity."

"How terrible!" said Angelica, since comment was clearly expected of her. "Surely something can be done!"

To this uninformed viewpoint—if there was a means to alleviate the country's current economic crisis, that means remained unknown to the government—Lord Chalmers responded politely with an erudite discussion of the Corn Laws passed in the previous year, designed to protect the price of home crops from the devaluation attendant upon the introduction into the country of cheap foreign corn, and also designed to restore agricultural prosperity at the cost of the consumer, which had so enraged the poor that Members of Parliament known to support the measure were attacked en route to the House.

Angelica attended his words closely; Lord Chalmers was as interesting as he was erudite. Yet, though she liked the baron very well, Angelica could not help but wonder why Lord Chalmers, whose turn of mind was demonstrably serious, had chosen to marry the frivolous Rosemary. Her sister's choice, decided Angelica, as she covertly studied Lord Chalmers, was more readily understood: the baron was a very handsome man in a stern, aloof style. He was tall, athletic in figure; his hair was dark and his eyes a chilly gray; his attitude, when not engaged in discussions of a political nature, was that of a man laboring under perennial boredom. In short, Lord Chalmers would present a stimulating challenge to any ambitious, enterprising miss.

Thought of enterprising damsels recalled to Angelica her current responsibility, and she looked around rather anxiously for Lily. "Here I am!" said that young lady, at her elbow. "Dearest Angelica, you *were* looking for me? How very fortunate, because I wish to speak to you most particularly!"

Lord Chalmers was a gentleman of acute perceptions: realizing his presence was not wanted, and additionally harboring a keen distaste for conversations of the frivolous nature habitually carried on by females, he excused himself. Lily stared after him, dreamily. "It's a pity Rosemary saw him first," she remarked. "Chalmers would have suited *you* very well, Angelica. Not only are you both very clever, you're almost of an age."

Angelica, inured by repetition to Lily's romantical high flights, looked a trifle sardonic. "Fiddlestick!" said she. "I'm quite sure Chalmers is perfectly content with Rosemary, and I am quite content to be an ape-leader. I'll have no more of your absurd attempts at matchmaking, Lily!"

Angelica was content? Lily knew prevarication when she heard it; heaven knew she was well qualified to do so, having uttered a fair share of her own clankers. It was a pity, thought the kind-hearted Lily, that Angelica had been born into the Millikin family, where a slender purse had allowed only one sister to have a London Season, that sister quite naturally not Angelica but Rosemary, and where Angelica dwelt forever in the shadow of the staggering family loveliness. Though she never said so, Lily considered Angelica poorly treated by her siblings. Of course they all adored her; if not the loveliest, Angelica was the best loved of all the Millikins—and by that very affection, by their ceaseless demands, the Millikins kept Angelica bound to them without any opportunity for a separate existence of her own. It was a very great pity, and Lily had long ago resolved to make amends. It was an effort in which she had received little cooperation, and less appreciation, from Angelica, who was currently regarding her with the beginning of a frown.

"I don't think so," Lily said simply. "I don't think Chalmers *is* content. Nor would *you* think so, had you overheard the things he said to Rosemary just before the guests arrived."

Angelica bit back a sigh. In search of fuel for her imagination, Lily displayed amazing initiative. "And just how did *you* happen to hear this conversation, miss?"

Lily looked simultaneously indignant and seraphic. "I just

19

happened to be passing by the room where they were talking," she protested. "Good heavens, Angelica, you will next accuse me of being vulgarly inquisitive, and it was no such thing."

"Doing it rather too brown!" remarked Fennel, joining his sisters in time to witness Lily's enactment of slandered innocence. "Eavesdropping again, were you, puss? Damned if *I* haven't heard the queerest thing! You know the poet Byron? You must, everyone does! It seems he's terrified of the dark and sleeps in a lighted room with pistols under his pillows, which I must say is mawkish behavior for a grown man. Anyway, his wife's going about saying he's a madly wicked person, guilty of all sorts of abominations. He may even have to leave town!"

There was on Fennel's handsome features a look of admiration for such masculine boldness, and Angelica suffered a distinct pang. Bad enough that Fennel should have set his heart on a captaincy in the Hussars, a position far above his touch and the resources of the family pocketbook; but that he should contemplate modeling himself on the scandalous Lord Byron, one of whose discarded ladyloves had just published a shocking novel in which the poet played a leading and unlaudable part, was infinitely worse. "We were talking," she said repressively, "about Rosemary."

Fennel's golden eyebrows arched. "Rosemary and *Byron*?" he said, and cast the lady a look of great respect. "Well, if *that* don't beat all! Wouldn't have thought it of her, I confess!"

"No, no!" interrupted Lily, as Angelica swallowed yet another exasperated expulsion of breath. "Rosemary and Chalmers! They had an argument."

"Oh, if *that*'s all." Fennel suffered an obvious disappointment. "So what if they did? Married people always *are* having arguments. It ain't like you, puss, to be making mountains out of molehills." He paused, judiciously. "Come to think of it, it's *just* like you! Rosemary wouldn't thank you for it, Lily."

Thus put on her mettle, Lily drew herself up to her full height, a scant two inches over five feet. "It's unkind of you to infer that I make fusses over trifles," she responded frigidly. "Even if sometimes I *do*! Because on my solemn word of honor, this time it's *not* a fudge! Chalmers was scolding poor Rosemary in the most distressing manner, and poor Rosemary looked absolutely sick with fright. Angelica, you must do something! We cannot permit Rosemary to suffer such agonies."

To this appeal, Angelica might have offered numerous responses. She might have inquired how Lily, passing in the hallway, had glimpsed Rosemary's face—but Angelica already knew Lily to be susceptible to the lure of keyholes. Also, Angelica might have pointed out that it was not a sister's place to interfere between husband and wife—but Angelica already knew that, if necessary, interfere she would.

No response seeming adequate, Angelica contemplated Rosemary, engaged in conversation with Lady Jersey. Rosemary wore a pale blue satin Empire dress veiled with Brussels net. Her bodice was decorated with three tiny bands of blue piped with white, each having three groups of points, one at each end and one in the middle; her elegant little sleeves were puffed; her skirt was embellished with two rows of double petals piped with white, the bottom a deeper tone of blue than the upper. She was breathtakingly elegant. She was also languid and melancholy and looked as if she might at any moment fall into a lethargy.

"*What* agonies?" inquired Fennel, who remained unconvinced that Lily was not once again diverting herself by weaving a Canterbury tale, a pursuit that he personally considered a very poor sort of amusement, though he was not one to spoil sport. Fennel was a keen devotee of such pastimes as came under the heading of having a bit of frolic, pastimes for which, he had begun to realize, London offered him hitherto unencountered scope. "What was this argument about?"

Lily screwed up her features. She possessed an astounding capacity of memory and could recall perfectly everything she heard or read, a feat made none the less remarkable by her failure to comprehend more than half of it. "Chalmers said first that he'd not seen that gown before, and Rosemary said

21

it had been hanging in her closet for months. Chalmers said, very politely, that he didn't believe her, since he knows the contents of her closet as well as Rosemary does, having purchased it for her, and that gown wasn't among the items for which he'd paid. Then Rosemary said the gown was part of her trousseau, and she'd never before had occasion to wear it. Chalmers said that horse wouldn't run either, since he knew very well the gown was no part of her trousseau, and she'd had countless occasions to wear it before. He accused her of running into debt, even after he'd told her he wouldn't tolerate such nonsense." Lily looked perplexed. "It is the oddest thing, Angelica! Chalmers didn't seem the least concerned about paying for *our* dresses, but he doesn't wish Rosemary to have new clothes—which is very shabby of him, to say the least!"

Angelica contemplated the cost of her own gown, a simple sea-green affair with a high waist and narrow skirt, trimmed only with a few knots of matching ribbon, and castigated by a despairing Rosemary as distinctly frumpish; and then her sister's well-known extravagance. For Lord Chalmers, Angelica felt a sneaking sympathy. "Was that all?" said she.

"*All?*" echoed Fennel, indignant on his sister's behalf. Rosemary had, after all, married for money. To do so and then be denied that commodity, in such short supply among the Millikins, must cause Rosemary a very justifiable frustration with which Fennel could easily sympathize. "By Jove, it's the outside of enough."

"There's more!" Lily was pleased to have sparked such animation. "Chalmers said it would serve Rosemary well if she found herself at *point non plus,* and if she'd spent more than her pin money, after he'd warned her against it, she needn't apply to him for help. And then he wanted to know why Rosemary wasn't wearing the Chalmers sapphires since they'd so nicely complement her dress. Rosemary said the catch was loose and she'd taken it to the jewelers' to be fixed. Chalmers said he didn't believe that either, so she started to cry!"

"And?" prompted the fascinated Fennel, while Angelica sank down upon a needlepointed chair.

Lily shrugged. "Then I came away. It didn't seem proper to stay."

It had hardly been proper to listen in the first place, reflected Angelica; still, there was no point in scolding Lily, who was by nature immune to chastisement. As did her brother and sister, Angelica stared at Rosemary.

That combined gaze had its effect; Rosemary, looking rather annoyed, abandoned Lady Jersey to cross the room and confront her siblings. "Why the deuce," she demanded irritably, "are you gaping at me?"

"A sad fix you've got yourself in this time!" Fennel responded sternly. "It's exactly what you deserve for trying to puff up your own consequence! I ain't saying the family's up to snuff, because it's plain as a pikestaff that we ain't, but none of us have ever before had to try and outrun the bailiffs. And it's no good your trying to pull the wool over *our* eyes, my girl!"

Clearly it was not, but how had they learned of her difficulties? Unerringly, Rosemary's gaze fell upon Lily, lost again in a romantic daydream—to wit, that she should somehow simultaneously marry off Angelica, relieve Rosemary's financial distress, and secure for Fennel his captaincy, in the process bringing herself to the attention of her own unknown true love. "I should have known!" Rosemary uttered scathingly. "Is this how you repay my hospitality, Lily? By listening at keyholes?"

Lily looked wounded. "Rosemary, I could not help but hear! And what I heard put me quite in a puzzle, because Chalmers has been so generous to us, and I am very grateful to him for it, so I told Angelica."

Rosemary turned pink, then white, then pinched herself to make sure she was not caught up in some nightmare. "Chalmers," she said, in a more reasonable tone, "is the highest of sticklers. Oh, dear! I admit I have done some absurd things—but I did not wish to stoop to—and I cannot help it if he has formed an unfavorable and unalterable opinion—but I'm sure he will soon come about again!" She paused for breath, and found her audience regarding her skeptically. "Pooh! You need not think I am trembling lest he denounce me publicly. But Sally Jersey is taking her leave! Chalmers will be even more displeased if I fail to attend to my guests!" She fled.

Contemplatively, the Millikins gazed after her. Lily ventured the opinion that Rosemary must be forgiven her odd behavior, obviously being a little out of sorts. This arrant understatement, Angelica let pass. "I don't understand," she remarked. "Surely Chalmers isn't so very high a stickler that he'd denounce Rosemary for a few debts."

It was seldom Fennel achieved enlightenment more rapidly than the most clever of his sisters. He was delighted to do so in this instance, a process achieved by visualizing what he himself would do in Rosemary's place. "Not for a few debts," he said wisely. "But if Chalmers discovered Rosemary had popped the family sapphires, he very well might divorce her outright."

Three

"Rosemary did *what*?" inquired the most senior of the Millikin progeny, a physician by profession, and Valerian by name.

Angelica cast her brother an anguished glance. "Popped the sapphires! Left them with a pawnbroker. Oh yes, she admitted it. And now she must reclaim the gems before Chalmers' suspicions are further roused, but she hasn't the money to do so, and has no means of getting it." Agitated, she paced the floor of Valerian's small and shabby sitting room.

"It is the most wretched calamity, and I don't know *how* I am to deal with it."

"Tell Chalmers!" Valerian responded promptly. "Why should *you* have to deal with what's-her-name's—Rosemary's!—difficulties?"

This statement gave Angelica pause in her perambulations; she regarded her eldest brother ruefully. Valerian, at four-and-thirty, possessed the same brown hair and blue eyes as did Angelica, and there was a strong family resemblance between them. Both had a look of their own mother, the first of their father's wives, a lady of great good sense, many years deceased. Why was it, wondered Angelica, that a gentleman with blue eyes and brown hair and unexceptionable features could be attractive, when a female similarly endowed was only plain? "Shame on you!" she said, with amusement. "Forgetting your own sister's name."

Valerian stretched out his long legs and contemplated a boot. "Half sister," he corrected. "Why should I remember the chit's name when I haven't set eyes on her for years? And from what you tell me, I'm glad I haven't! She sounds a mooncalf."

"She is," agreed Angelica, in whom fondness for her siblings was untainted by any blindness regarding their shortcomings. "They *all* are! Rosemary is, as Fennel calls her, a chowderhead, as is Fennel himself; Lily's a lovely pea-goose. As for the others—Hyacinth and Violet; Amaryllis and Camilla, the twins; Hysop, the youngest—they're also feather-heads. *Just* like their mother." She looked shamefaced. "Oh, Valerian, I know I should not say it, but sometimes I wish Papa had never married Marigold! We rubbed on well enough together, the three of us, until he brought her home."

Valerian greeted this mention of his stepmother, a lady scarcely five years older than himself, with an expression of profound distaste. The lovely Marigold, from whom her offspring had inherited their bedazzling beauty, was of a jealous nature, and had consequently resented all reminder of the previous Mrs. Millikin, most especially her stepchildren. So active had been Marigold's resentment that Valerian had at the earliest opportunity left home. Nor had he returned,

25

though, while his father lived, they had managed to meet, without Marigold's knowledge, albeit infrequently.

Toward his stepmother, Valerian bore no malice: with the influence of his father, and the beneficience of his wealthy godfather, Valerian had done well enough. He was a member of the Royal College of Physicians, and on the honorary medical staff of St. Bartholomew's Hospital.

It was a pity, Valerian thought, as he regarded the remaining member of his family for whom he possessed the least affection, that Angelica had not been able to similarly escape. She was looking shockingly worn down.

Angelica sighed, then rubbed her arms; the fire smouldering in Valerian's grate did little to dispel the chill of the room. "But he *did* marry her, and he wrung from me a promise to look after all of them, so there's no use bewailing what's done. Oh, Valerian, it's so good to see you again."

"So it is. I've missed you, sis." Valerian reached out and grasped her arm. "But don't think to involve *me* in this imbroglio! I haven't the blunt to buy back what's-her-name's accursed sapphires, and I wouldn't, even if I did. Anyway, I have more important things to do."

"Just like Papa!" said Angelica. "Spending all your time taking care of poor people who never pay you a blessed penny. I didn't mean *you* should buy back what's-her-name's—I mean, Rosemary's—sapphires. Why should you? After all, she is my responsibility."

With this viewpoint, Valerian saw no reason to argue; Valerian considered his own responsibility not to his father's muddle-headed younger progeny, but to mankind in general. Still, he didn't see why responsibility for those muddle-headed youngsters should fall upon Angelica either, despite a promise made under duress to their father on his death-bed. He drew her down onto the arm of his chair. "I'm not saying I won't help you," he offered generously. "You'd better tell me the rest of it."

"There's not much more." Angelica settled comfortably against Valerian's shoulder. "Rosemary swears she put Chalmers off the scent, which I doubt; Chalmers isn't one to be easily sidetracked. Incidentally, she's convinced he has a ladybird tucked away somewhere, being unable to comprehend why any gentleman should devote so much time to something so dreary as government."

"Ninnyhammer!" was Valerian's verdict. "What's the chit like, Angelica? How is it she ran into debt?"

"I fear Rosemary is a *trifle* spoiled." Angelica spoke as guiltily as if she were responsible for that failing, which she certainly was not. "She's wildly extravagant and undisciplined, and when Chalmers was fool enough to tell her how she was to go on, she quite naturally took a distempered freak and ran counter to his decrees. Oh, I make no excuses for her! To allow herself to be drawn into the hands of moneylenders, no matter how innocently, is reprehensible in the extreme, and does her no credit. All the same, she *has* made a Jack-pudding of herself, and *much* as I deplore it, I cannot leave her to suffer the consequence! The poor child is convinced that Chalmers, were he to learn the truth, would at the least roundly denounce her, and at the worst publish her misconduct to the world."

"Balderdash!" uttered Valerian.

"Perhaps. But there's no persuading Rosemary that she doesn't hover on the brink of some vile scandal, and it's true that were her indiscretions to become known the consequences would be unpleasant. Meanwhile," Angelica added somberly, "Fennel has taken it into his head to emulate Byron, is going around in the oddest clothing and trying his hand at poetry, and is yearning after a macaw. And Lily has taken it into *her* head that Chalmers should divorce Rosemary, since *they* obviously don't suit, and then marry me!"

Valerian turned to stare into Angelica's face. "Sits the wind in that quarter?"

"No!" snapped Angelica. "It does not! Lily has the crackbrained notion that I should marry *someone*, and Chalmers and I are both *clever*, you see!"

This novel notion gave Valerian food for thought. He was not in the habit of contemplating the unhappy lot of the only sister whom he held in affection, by habit directing his contemplative moments toward such weighty matters as the nesting habits of cuckoos and the propagation of eels; but on

Valerian's behalf it must be stated that he had not been hitherto aware that Angelica *was* unhappy, their concourse having been limited to terse and sporadic letters over the past several years. Now that he turned his keen intellect to the matter, he realized that Angelica could not be other than dissatisfied, their hare-brained siblings being hung around her neck like so many millstones.

A gentleman of blunt manner, Valerian made this sentiment known. "Why *don't* you get married?" he inquired.

"To whom?" retorted Angelica, irritably. "Chalmers, as Lily suggests? Fustian! I'll have you know, Valerian, I'm tired of people chattering eternally at me. Were I to develop a fondness, it would be for a gentleman who was impenetrably taciturn! Not that I shall have opportunity to do so; any gentleman who admires me need only take one look at any one of our sisters to forget my existence altogether—and you needn't say that's fudge, because I speak from experience!"

From this slightly hysterical outburst, Valerian deduced a number of things, chief among them that Angelica's patently low evaluation of herself was directly attributable to the unchristian Marigold. He moved from his chair to stand before the feeble fire, from which vantage point he thoughtfully surveyed his sister.

Angelica, huddled in the chair Valerian had abandoned, was the picture of gloom. True, she was no beauty, not in the flamboyant fashion of Marigold and, from report, Marigold's children; but she was not unlovely either, in a subdued, understated style. Tall and very slender, Angelica was blessed with the bone structure that ensured her looks would not deteriorate with age. Marigold, as Valerian recalled, and he did so with no small satisfaction, was not similarly blessed. Too, Angelica possessed an almost formidable intelligence, a quality for which Valerian had the highest respect, and another quality which Marigold patently lacked. But Angelica would never credit that her stepmother might be jealous, and Valerian did not waste his breath.

"I am being unbearably foolish!" said Angelica, with the air of one determined to be so no more. "It is hard to be the ugly duckling amid a flock of swans, because one cannot help but hanker after swanliness oneself. You will never have heard anything half so absurd, I expect! I vow I sometimes marvel at myself."

As did Valerian, who would not have expected a display of sensibility from so sensible a source; perhaps Angelica had from long exposure picked up some of the less admirable habits of her charges. "Did you tell what's-her-name that you were coming to see me?"

Angelica deemed it neither politic nor kind to inform Valerian that, for all the mention made of him by the family, she was the only one who remembered his existence. "I left Rosemary attempting to teach Lily the shawl-dance. They are engaged this afternoon to attend a harlequin-farce at Astley's, from which I excused myself."

Valerian quirked a brow, looking saturnine. "What's-her-name doesn't pay much attention to your comings and goings, then?"

"I suppose not," replied Angelica, bewildered. "You must not think too poorly of the child, Valerian! Rosemary is sadly out of curl, due to the anxieties preying on her mind, and she is not in the habit of, er, regarding any but herself. Nor must you think I am ill-treated, because I'm not! Doubtless I should not have complained so to you, but there is no one else—and I am very fond of the family!"

To these protestations, Valerian paid scant heed. "Could you slip away from Chalmers House as easily again? Could you do so regularly?"

Unaccustomed to the company of a brother who reasoned rationally, Angelica watched him with fascination. "I guess I could, but to what end?"

Valerian smiled, an exercise that he performed seldom, and executed beautifully. "Would you be willing to do so, if it helped you to haul what's-her-name's coals out of the fire?"

Angelica blinked, then frowned. Of course she would do anything within her power to rescue Rosemary from almost certain ruin, but Valerian's smile had recalled to her some of his own less laudable tendencies. Her elder brother was made up of a curious blend of indifference, deviousness and sharp, shrewd wit; and he had an uncanny knack of manipulating

29

people to suit himself, as if they were no more than chessmen on a playing-board. "Why should I?" she asked cautiously.

"All in good time!" retorted Valerian. "Yes or no?"

Strongly, Angelica was tempted to respond in the negative. But she recalled Rosemary's dilemma; the number of impecunious admirers who dangled after Lily, which gave rise to a strong fear that Rosemary had dropped several fallacious hints concerning the contents of the family pocketbook; Fennel's ominous utterances, in view of his admiration for the infamous Byron, about having a bit of frolic. "I am used to manage," she responded hollowly. "Don't tease yourself."

Valerian stifled a snort. Manage, did she? "I thought you wanted my help?" he murmured craftily. "Things have come to a very pretty pass when you cannot bring yourself to trust me. It makes me melancholy, Sis, to think that Marigold has estranged even *you* from me."

That Valerian didn't look the slightest bit melancholy escaped Angelica's attention. In a flurry of skirts she rose from the chair, ran to the fireplace, and clutched his coatsleeve. "It's not that! Honestly, Valerian! If I seemed unappreciative, it is just that I am distracted—oh, *pray* forgive me."

Slightly ashamed of himself for even briefly adding to his sister's budget of woes—but she would, he hoped, come to thank him for this piece of work—Valerian magnanimously indicated forgiveness. Angelica, anxious not to further wound this most beloved of her siblings, humbly begged to know for what reason he would have her slip away from Chalmers House in a manner, due to Rosemary's newly acquired dignities, that was bound to be clandestine.

"Stiff-rumped, is she?" inquired Valerian, with disinterest. "I'm glad it's you must deal with the chit! If it was me, I'd wash my hands of her—of the lot of them! Since you won't, I've thought of a way for you to raise the wind."

Oddly, Angelica felt no relief at this promise of rescue. "That is?"

Again, Valerian smiled. "I have a friend—one of my old teachers—who is in need of an amanuensis, being engaged in writing his memoirs. You'd fit the ticket perfectly."

"I would?" Angelica's tone was skeptical. "Why? I can't
30

imagine that such a position would be difficult to fill."

Nor would it have been, had the position existed in the first place. Not by so much as an eyelid's flicker did Valerian betray his engagement in blatant falsehood. "Sir Randall is a physician," he explained, "and deuced hard to please. Even so, you assisted Papa in his surgery, so you won't be squeamish; and if you can put up with Marigold and her gudgeonish brats, you won't mind Sir Randall's little eccentricities."

Why did Angelica feel as if she was being pushed willy-nilly in a direction she didn't wish to go? "What makes you think that your Sir Randall would wish to tolerate *me*?" she responded doubtfully. "If he's so difficult to please?"

Valerian was not put off by this missishness; when pursuing his own ends, and Valerian seldom pursued any *but* his own ends, Valerian was undeterred by even acts of God. "Oh, he'll like you!" he asserted, as he surreptitiously tugged at the bell cord that hung beside the mantelpiece. "And you'll like him. Think of the opportunity, Angelica—Sir Randall was one of the most highly respected physicians of his day. You always said if you weren't a female you'd have been a physician—well, here's an opportunity to work for one and at the same time to earn enough to keep what's-her-name's creditors at bay while we think of some way to put them off entirely."

Angelica should have been rendered highly suspicious by Valerian's sudden helpfulness, but suspicion drowned in a wave of dizzying relief. She had not dared hope that, in her wearing task of keeping Rosemary from disaster, Valerian would render aid. She had misjudged her brother, enormously —he offered not only a chance to help Rosemary, but involvement in the world of medicine that was denied her by her sex. In defense of Angelica's lack of foresight, it can only be said that she had been unexposed to Valerian's highly original methods for a large number of years.

"Oh, Valerian!" she breathed. "If only Sir Randall—I should like it of all things!"

"Thought you might, Sis!" Valerian ruffled her hair. "You just go and see Sir Randall—here, I'll write you a note of introduction."

As he did so, under Angelica's bemused eye, Valerian's elderly housekeeper shambled into the room and announced, breathlessly, that an urgent case of measles awaited the doctor's attention. Angelica had too high a regard for the art of medicine to hamper its practice; clutching the note, stammering her gratitude, she took her leave.

Valerian looked after her, then back at his desk. That he made no effort to attend the urgent case of measles is explained by the circumstance that no such case existed, this being the standard ploy he used to rid himself of visitors of whose company he had tired. Not that Valerian had tired of Angelica; but he was not a man to waste time with words when action would better serve.

For the problems of what's-her-name and spouse, Valerian had neither interest nor concern. He did not, however, intend that Marigold should succeed in her obvious intention of seeing Angelica dwindle into a fubsy-faced old maid.

Angelica yearned after a gentleman most impenetrably taciturn? Wearing a smile that was distinctly diabolic, Valerian penned yet another note, informing Sir Randall Brisbane that he had just hired an amanuensis, sight unseen.

Four

It was a very foggy day, of the sort that inspired prudent folk to remain at home by their snug hearthsides. The Millikins, however, were marvelously imprudent, and not to be deterred from the delightful prospect of visiting the shops by the minor inconvenience of not being able to see more than a few scant paces in front of them. Too, Rosemary was fast learning how to deal with impatient creditors. When one lacked the where-withal to settle one's debts, one could stave off the reckoning by ordering additional goods.

They were a gay little party, Rosemary and Fennel and Lily, and soon to that group were added Messrs. Gildensleeve and Meadowcraft, Steptoe and Pettijohn, the core of Lily's admiring retinue. Ardent young men all, Messrs. Gildensleeve and Meadowcraft, Steptoe and Pettijohn professed them-selves oblivious to such lowly considerations as the quality of the elements. What mattered an influenza when by it one was privileged to escort the Fair Incomparable?

Alas, Lady Chalmers knew the parents of these ardent young swains to be rather more practical. Perhaps Angelica had been correct; perhaps it *hadn't* been quite the thing to give out that Lily's portion was a great deal more handsome than the truth—but the thing was done. Without making herself look a fool, Rosemary could not retract the tales she'd spread before Lily ever came to town.

The party browsed through the shops that lined Oxford Street, a wide boulevard inlaid with flagstones and lighted with street-lamps enclosed in crystal glass. Since the Millikins displayed a marked determination to inspect each and every establishment, their perambulations took a great deal longer than the brief time promised airily by Lady Chalmers to her coachman, who had deposited them in Piccadilly, and received instructions to pick them up again in Oxford Street in a half-hour.

"I don't know *how* it happened!" wailed Rosemary, as she whisked her sister into the establishment of W. H. Botibol, a *plumassier* by trade. "The family never had sixpence to scratch with, and suddenly *I* did! Chalmers left me alone so much, and I wanted so very badly to cut a dash; I didn't realize everything was so expensive, and it was much too late by the time I *did*!" She sniffled. "I dare not ask Chalmers to bear the expense, or let him know my accounts are of the most desponding cast, because he is the most unfeeling man and I cannot bear that he should condemn me for my irresponsible conduct yet once again."

Reluctantly, Lily withdrew her dreamy attention from ostrich feathers and artificial flowers destined to adorn bonnets and huge gypsy hats. "How can you still be so dreadfully in debt?" she asked, with what was for her a fine display of logic. "After all, you *did* pop the sapphires."

"Hush!" Frantically, Rosemary glanced around and waved away the hopeful shopkeeper. "Do you mean to tell the whole world of my predicament?"

There was on Lily's lovely face a look of keen interest. "The sapphires!" she persevered.

"Oh, if you *must* know!" Rosemary flushed. "I meant to pay my dressmaker off, honestly I did! But on my way to do so, I stopped for just a moment in a most elegant little shop and—well, there I saw the most elegant *toilette*. You needn't look so disapproving, I *did* pay for it! And the cream of the jest is that I have had to hide it in my closet and dare not wear it, because Chalmers would be bound to read me a scold."

Lily was driven by this confession to actually frown, despite the well known detriment to ethereal complexions of such exercise. As a result of this unprecedented act, Rosemary's blue eyes filled with tears. "Don't *you* go scolding me!"

she begged. "I cannot bear to be spoken harshly to! It is bad enough that Chalmers holds me in disgust. Oh, how did I get in such a muddle? I have wracked my brains for some solution, but nothing answers the purpose."

"Come, come," soothed Lily, with infinite patience, as she patted her sister's hand. "Don't bother your head further. Remember, Angelica promised to fix it up all right and tight."

Rosemary cheered, slightly. "I don't know how she means to go about it. Chalmers is the greatest beast in nature, and he won't thank me for making him look a fool."

Lily's frown deepened. True, that one of the warmest men in England kept his wife without a feather to fly with argued a great insensibility, but that minor flaw would not weigh with the unfrivolous Angelica, for whom Lord Chalmers was earmarked. Still, there had been something in Rosemary's tone—"Rosemary! Do you *care* for him?"

"Care!" Rosemary extracted a dainty handkerchief from her reticule. "Of course I care! It is quite midsummer moon with me—not that it signifies, because Chalmers has shown himself determined to hold me at arm's length. It is not fashionable, my dear, to dote on one's spouse! So you see Chalmers would hold me in even greater disgust if he knew my affections have become fixed on him to an alarming degree." She applied the handkerchief to her reddened nose. "But this will never do! Take my advice, Lily: don't settle in matrimony with a man who's rich as Croesus because all he'll ever do is pinch at you."

Lily could conceive of no gentleman so unperceptive as to pinch at her; gentlemen were, in her experience, more likely to be stricken with admiration at her more daring endeavors, or, if not precisely admiration, a strong protectiveness. That she did not point this out to her stricken sister, nor express the viewpoint that Rosemary's continual lamentations on the topics of her unfeeling husband and her unhappy circumstances were very dull work, were further proofs of Lily's good heart.

"There, there!" she soothed. "You are going on in a very bad way. Perchance if you were to intimate to Chalmers—no, a curst high stickler like Lord Chalmers would probably think you too *coming*."

"He would likely," mourned Rosemary, into her handkerchief, "bid me go to the devil. Chalmers has a *very* strong sense of propriety."

Because Rosemary's woeful face was buried in her handkerchief, to the fascination of the shopkeeper who hovered just out of earshot, she did not see the quizzical expression on her sister's piquant features. In Lily's experience, gentlemen gifted with declarations of affection by dazzling ladies were not prone to think much of propriety. Husbands and wives, it seemed, behaved differently.

Belatedly, Rosemary recalled her consequence and her position and her dignity. "It is the way of the world, my dear!" she announced, briskly stuffing the soggy handkerchief back into her reticule. "When the gentlemen come courting, they're all posies and pretty words—but it is a very different thing once the knot is tied! Do you know the last present Chalmers made me? A book called *Take Your Choice*, by Major John Cartright, the most powerful piece of propaganda, Chalmers tells me, for radical reform. What's worse, he insisted that I read it, as if I cared for such things! And all so I may understand the danger of the Hampden clubs that have sprung up everywhere, due largely to Major Cartright's efforts, clamoring incessantly for parliamentary reform and universal suffrage and other such tedious stuff. But why should I afflict *you* with it? Come, my dear, let us rejoin the gentlemen."

In point of fact, only one gentleman remained, the devotion of Messrs. Gildensleeve and Meadowcraft, Steptoe and Pettijohn having proved inadequate to the rigors of standing for a very long time on a damp and foggy street corner. Fennel, made of sterner stuff, accustomed to the dilatory behavior of females confronted with shops and equally aware of the peals that would be rung over him if he abandoned his sisters, still waited patiently. "Your *beaux* all pleaded prior engagements," said he to Lily, when the ladies reappeared. "Dashed if they ain't dull sticks! Hope you mean to look higher, puss, because I don't scruple to tell you that if *I* had to live with any one of them I'd probably be driven to throttle him!"

"Oh, no!" Lily responded absently. "I must have a peer." And then she lapsed into a profound abstraction from which she could not be roused even by mention of Princess Charlotte's impending marriage to Prince Leopold of Saxe-Coburg-Saalfeld. Accustomed to such fits, her siblings ignored her silence.

Lily's plans had, in the past several moments, received a severe set-back. Well enough to decide that Chalmers should divorce Rosemary and marry Angelica, if Rosemary's affections were not engaged; but to scheme to set at naught the marriage of a sister who was madly enraptured of her spouse was an altogether different thing. Therefore, that course of action must be abandoned, and another potential husband found for Angelica, while Rosemary must somehow be reconciled with her spouse. Yet where was to be unearthed a gentleman of sufficient seriousness and cleverness to suit Angelica? Lily could think of no such paragon offhand. And how was Lord Chalmers's ardor to be kindled when he was by all accounts a curst cold fish, and additionally apt to discover at any moment that the wife whom he held in such scant affection had been sconcing the reckoning? Lily had set herself a harsh task indeed.

She did not despair, nor reflect that such arduous endeavor must seriously interfere in her own pursuit of a peer. She would think of something, surely?

At this point, Lily was interrupted in her ruminations by Rosemary, who urged her ungently into the Pantheon Bazaar. Of course Lily would think of something! She always did. Setting aside such arduous undertaking for the future, she gave herself up to the pleasure of rummaging amid ribbons and lace and fancy trimmings and other such delights.

It was while the sisters were comparing the relative virtues of very pretty English poplins at 4s 3d, and equally attractive Irish ditto at 6s, that disaster struck. Lily, hitherto unacquainted with nemesis in human form, dreamily gazed at the personification thereof, a middle-aged woman of haggard aspect, dressed most fashionably. Rosemary, all too well acquainted with this specter, gasped and blanched.

"Madame Eugénie!" she whispered, much less like a haughty baroness than a schoolgirl caught in mischief. "I would not have expected to encounter you here! I mean, it is a pleasure to see you, naturally! Indeed, I have intended to come in and speak with you about, er, a certain matter anytime this fortnight!"

"*Vraiment*?" inquired Madame Eugénie, somewhat ironically. One of London's most successful modistes, Madame Eugénie possessed a shrewd grasp not only of the vagaries of fashion, but of ladies who were potential candidates for that time-honored activity known as outrunning the constable. Lady Chalmers, thought the shrewd modiste, was as nervous as a cat on hot bricks. "The husband is not *sympathique* to milady's little predicament?" she murmured slyly. "Perhaps milady did not put the matter to him in quite the proper way. Milord would not wish his lady to be dunned in the streets by her creditors, *n'est-ce pas*?"

"Oh, no!" Rosemary's lovely face turned even more ashen, and her expression, as she gazed anxiously about her, was terrified. "I have not yet had the opportunity to broach the matter to him, Madame Eugénie. He is so busy with matters of government that I am reluctant to take up his time with trivialities. Of course," and she attempted to gather the tattered shreds of her dignity, "he will attend to it most promptly once I have bespoken it to him."

"*Voyons*!" Madame Eugénie spoke even more wryly. "Then I suggest you do so immediately, *ma petite*. If not, milady is likely to find herself in Queer Street—and milord would be a great deal less complacent about that, I think."

"Do you dare *threaten* me?" gasped Rosemary.

"Threaten?" Madame opened wide her eyes. "Why should I threaten? It is milady who owes the monies; it is milady who does not pay her debts. Me, I am a simple working woman with my own debts to pay. *Chérie*, I am reasonable, I do not expect payment to be immediate. *Tout de même*, I am also practical, I cannot wait forever. In your case, milady, I have no more patience. I give you only until the end of this week."

"And then?" inquired Lily with keen interest, while Rosemary trembled like an aspen in the wind. "You can't draw blood from a stone, my good woman."

"From a stone, no, but milord is rather warmer, *enfin*!" In Madame Eugénie's eyes, as they rested on Rosemary, there was not the slightest hint of sympathy. "If milady does not wish milord to learn of her extravagance, she knows what she must do."

"But *how*?" moaned Rosemary. "It is well and good to speak of contriving, but I do not know what I may do. Pray reconsider, Madame Eugénie! Chalmers will be out-of-reason cross with me!"

The Frenchwoman shrugged and turned away. *"C'est la vie."*

Even as these horrid, if not entirely unexpected, developments took place within the Pantheon Bazaar, Mr. Fennel Millikin lounged in a Byronesque manner in Oxford Street. A shop window displaying colored prints had caught his attention, and he had moved closer to inspect them. Depictions of incidents of the recent European wars, most notably a Russian landscape strewn with frozen Frenchmen, caught his attention only briefly; of much more interest was a series of fiercely libellous, and very popular, prints concerning no less than Fennel's hero. Byron and other gentlemen of fashion ogled actresses who stood in a group like so many sheep; Byron eloped with an actress, abandoning his wife; Byron dominated a promenade scene with a woman on each arm while a third woman, in a state of pregnancy bordering on the elephantine, confronted him angrily. Now there, thought Fennel with admiration, was a man who knew how to savor life to the utmost!

It must here be stated that although Fennel wished to emulate his hero, his admiration was that of an inexperienced youth, and he had no desire whatsoever to emulate the poet's much-discussed depravities. As was natural in any lad of his age and inexperience, Fennel was not without aspirations in the petticoat-line—but he knew very well that pretty opera-dancers were above his touch, their smiles and more intimate favors being reserved for gentlemen a great deal more plump in the pocket than himself. As for the rumors concerning Byron and his half-sister Augusta—well! The notion of a similarly bizarre relationship with his own half-sister convulsed Fennel with whoops.

Nor was he tempted to overindulge in brandy or laudanum, or to behave in such a manner as would cause every face to turn against him. Definitely, he didn't wish to leave behind him a trail of broken hearts. What Fennel aspired to was a certain recognition by his peers, the sort of recognition attendant upon collecting about him such notably eccentric items as macaws and silver funerary urns from Greece, and drinking cups fashioned from human skulls. Too, he would have liked to set feminine hearts aflutter, preferably from afar. Fennel had too many sisters to remain in ignorance of the wearisome high-flights of young ladies of good birth.

A gay blade he would fashion himself, a sport and a bit of a rogue—but never beyond the line of being pleasing, because then Angelica would have his head for washing, perhaps even send him promptly back to his university. Having settled this important point, Fennel studied his reflection in the shop's plate glass window.

A narrow cravat of white sarsenet with the shirt-collar falling over it, black coat and waistcoat embellished with seals and watchchain, broad white trousers—complete, Fennel decided, to a shade. But what the devil was taking his sisters so long? He had promised Angelica to keep an eye on them. Fennel turned away from his own image to stroll toward the entrance to the Pantheon Bazaar. Would a limp, à la Byron, be a trifle overdone? After due reflection, Fennel decided that while a limp might add immeasurably to his aura of brooding mystery, it might be tediously difficult to sustain. Fennel was possessed of a certain dilatoriness of memory. As he reached this monumental decision, he collided head-on with a young lady in the fog.

"Oof!" said she, and tumbled right off her feet. Appalled, Fennel quickly knelt to assure himself that he'd inflicted upon his victim no fatal injury.

"Dashed if I saw you!" he protested. "It's this accursed fog!

40

I say, are you all right? Beg you'll accept my apologies."

"It's nothing, truly! Do not concern yourself. If you might assist me to my feet—oh, thank you, sir."

Fennel not only heaved the young lady upright, he restored to her the package that had upon their collision fallen into the street. Then he took a close look at the damsel.

She was not at all the sort of female to whom he was accustomed, being neither blue-eyed nor yellow-haired. She was not ravishing or dazzling or ethereal. Instead, her figure was plumply pretty, and the face turned up to him was dimpled, rosy-cheeked and cherry-lipped, adorned by twinkling brown eyes, surrounded by curly dark hair. "I say!" uttered Fennel. "You're a deuced pretty puss. Guess I shouldn't have said that, eh? Beg pardon, again!"

The young lady did not appear disturbed by such frank manners; she dimpled even more. "La, sir, I don't know why you should apologize for coming the pretty, unless you was bamming me! And you weren't, were you? I thought not! I can generally tell when someone's offering me Spanish coin. But let me introduce myself! I am Phoebe Holloway."

What would Byron have done, Fennel wondered, in a moment such as this? Alas, he did not know. But he recalled his sister Lily's last, and most ill-fated, suitor and that individual's predilection toward spouting poetry. Fennel was not adverse to taking a great many pages from someone else's book. Therefore he informed Miss Holloway that her teeth were like pearls, her eyes like stars, her complexion the finest porcelain—and, he'd wager, though he could not see them beneath her fetching bonnet, her ears like seashells.

Highly diverted by this flummery, Miss Holloway giggled and revealed yet another dimple, then suggested that since Mr. Millikin patently had nothing better to do with his time, he might proffer her escort. Fennel promptly professed himself eager to do her bidding. Highly pleased with one another, the pair set out, abandoning Fennel's hapless sisters to the perils of the Pantheon Bazaar.

Five

As Rosemary was encountering nemesis in the guise of
Madame Eugénie, and Fennel was striking up a fateful acquaintance with Phoebe Holloway, their sister Angelica was
taking the first step upon the pathway toward her own unwit-
ting destiny. Her emotions, at this most important of moments, were distinctly mundane: she was cold and cross,
nervous at her imminent interview with the hard-to-please Sir
Randall Brisbane, and fagged half to death by worry about
her addle-pated siblings. So very low were Angelica's spirits,
as she descended from the hackney-coach and warily approached Sir Randall's residence, that she entertained an
uncharitable wish to have been born an only child.

Sir Randall Brisbane dwelt on the outskirts of London in a
rambling brick structure surrounded by extensive grounds.
All appeared in good order, Angelica decided, as she peered
cautiously into the thick fog. Valerian's remarks about Sir
Randall's eccentricities struck her in retrospect as ominous.
Angelica inhaled deeply, then raised a gloved hand to rap
sharply at the door.

Before she could do so, the door swung open. Angelica
stared at the butler, discomposed.

"You'll be the young lady Sir Randall is expecting," said
that worthy, in a manner so genial as must have seen him
immediately condemned by his fellows, butlers being as a rule
even more starched-up than their masters, experts in the art
of chilling with a glance. "If you will follow me, miss?"

Angelica did so. The butler led her, not as she had expected into the entryway, but around the side of the red brick house to a garden. He indicated a doorway in one of the high walls. "If you will enter, miss?" And then, to Angelica's utter stupefaction, he tipped her a wink.

Warily, she lay her hand upon the door latch; cautiously, she pushed. Had Angelica at that moment followed her own inclination, she would have taken to her heels. Eccentric, was Sir Randall? If he made it a habit to interview prospective employees in the garden on cold and bitter days, he was more than eccentric. But Rosemary's future hung in the balance. Angelica must persevere.

She stepped into the garden; behind her the door swung shut. Before her spread a vista so staggeringly bizarre that all powers of reflection escaped Angelica—though, had she been capable of reflection, she would have decided without hesitation that Sir Randall was definitely beyond the bounds of everyday eccentricity, was, in fact, distinctly queer.

The garden covered perhaps two acres and included all the sorts of vegetation ordinary to such spots. The weather being unfavorable to such vegetation, the garden at the present predominated with bare branches and twigs which protruded in a grotesque manner through the fog. But this fact did not account for Angelica's befuddlement, nor should it: not a garden in all of London did not suffer a similar plight. Among the barren vegetation wandered a menagerie the likes of which Angelica had never viewed, and had never hoped to view. Some she recognized—a zebra, two panthers, some sheep and a ram. All appeared to coexist most amicably.

"Gracious!" she said faintly, then gasped as a huge and shaggy shape emerged from the fog. Feeling rather foolish, and very much relieved, Angelica discovered that the ominous figure was not her prospective employer but a buffalo.

"Don't let them frighten you, girl!" came a pleasantly gruff voice, from the vicinity of a marble bench. "They're only curious. For that matter, so am I! Come closer and let us have a look at you."

Gingerly, Angelica threaded her way through the wildlife which, she was relieved to discover, were not so friendly as to force unwelcome attentions on her. On the far end of the marble bench was perched an elderly gentleman, muffled to his bewhiskered chin in outdoor attire. From beneath his disreputable hat, which was pulled well down over his ears, protruded sparse snow-white hair. On his nose sat a pair of spectacles. "Sir Randall?" Angelica inquired, timidly.

"Can't see a curst thing in this murk!" replied the gentleman, irritably. "Don't let anyone tell you it's not a wretched nuisance to grow old. 'Tis like having *ten* spanners thrown simultaneously in the works, and no way to get them out again. Although I daresay the beasts are glad enough of my infirmities! I meant to dissect the brutes, but neither my hands nor my eyes are what they used to be. Don't stand there gawking, girl; that much I *can* see! Sit down! I have quite enough people hovering over me."

Abruptly Angelica sat, unsure whether to be horrified or amused. Stunned, she watched a very queer-looking animal approach Sir Randall, drop awkwardly to its knees, and place its head in the doctor's lap. "This is a shawl-goat from the East Indies," said he. "Those sheep you see are from Turkey. I had wanted a whale but, alas! It was not to be."

With all her might, Angelica strove to restrain an inclination to laugh out loud. She diffidently suggested that, were Sir Randall to wipe the moisture from his spectacles, he might find his vision a trifle more clear.

Sir Randall did so, in the process revealing a round and cherubic countenance. He replaced the glasses and regarded Angelica suspiciously. "You don't want for sense." The admission was made grudgingly. "Nor did you go all mawkish at the notion of dissection, which is a point in your favor. Why not, eh?" Sir Randall scratched the goat's neck. The goat looked blissful and made noises strongly suggestive of a wish to purr. "Are you one of those newfangled females who think it is modern to be thick-skinned?"

Considering the temperature of the foggy garden, Angelica would not have been regretful were that indeed the case. "My father was a doctor, sir," she replied meekly. "He made a lifelong study of pathological anatomy, believing that the examination of diseased tissues and organs might lead to a clearer conception of the symptoms and appearances of disease in living patients. I was used to help him prepare his anatomical specimens."

"Humph!" ejaculated Sir Randall. "A strange pastime for a female."

"So my mother believed, sir." Surreptitiously, Angelica chafed her frozen hands. "It all came about when Papa chose to operate on my cat. I insisted on being present—Papa, when engaged in experimentation, was not entirely trustworthy. He was so pleased when I did not, er, cast up my accounts that he immediately determined to make me his assistant."

"And the cat?" inquired Sir Randall.

"The cat lived for many years, sir." Angelica gently strove to guide the conversation into more practical channels. How much had Valerian told Sir Randall of the circumstances surrounding her application for this post? "As did Papa, but now he is gone, and I must make my own way in the world."

"Dear me!" murmured Sir Randall, still scratching the goat. "How very tiresome."

"I am not without some knowledge," Angelica persevered. "In addition to assisting Papa, I have read Mr. Matthew Baillie's *Morbid Anatomy*, and Mr. William Wethering's *An Account of the Foxglove*, and Mr. Jenner's work on the causes and effects of the variola vaccine. Unfortunately, I have been unable to keep abreast of such studies since Papa's death."

"Jenner, eh?" By this admitted lapse of diligence, Sir Randall did not appear especially disturbed. "Injections of cowpox to inoculate against smallpox. What did you think?"

Angelica briefly forgot her adopted humility. "I think, sir, that for the Royal College of Physicians to refuse to admit Jenner unless he passed the usual examinations in Latin was a great piece of nonsense! And I further applaud him for refusing to take their silly tests." It occurred to her, tardily, that Sir Randall was undoubtedly a member of that august body. Would he dismiss her without further ado? Angelica eyed a panther that was similarly eyeing her, and hoped Sir Randall would.

He did not. "So I told them at the time," he said, as he intimated to the goat that it should remove itself from his lap. "That examination is so much poppycock. Membership to the college can be obtained for a down payment of fifty guineas after passing three examinations of twenty minutes each. Any man who is a good classical scholar may pass, yet know nothing of chemistry, medical jurisprudence, surgery and anatomy—as is all too often the case. To that unhappy situation, your brother is one of the rare exceptions."

Angelica flushed. "He told you."

"You need not feat that *I* shall blazon about your family difficulties." Sir Randall inched about on the bench, the better to contemplate his guest. "I give you my word that I shall be silent as the grave. Though with the busy sack-'em-ups, the grave is none too silent these days! Medical instructors are at the mercy of the rascals—but without cadavers the teaching of medicine would come to a halt. One can hardly learn to perform surgery without a subject on which to operate! I myself am a member of a committee formed to impress on the government the necessity for an alteration in the law—but that's neither here nor there. You may not be aware that my dear wife passed away some years ago, Miss—er. I think we should bestow upon you another name, since all of my household is not so discreet as myself. Smith, I daresay, is innocuous enough. To continue: mine is a bachelor household, Miss Smith. The presence of a young lady, even for a few hours each weekday afternoon, may give rise to gossip."

Angelica elevated her gaze from the panther to Sir Randall, who was regarding her no less keenly. "It is good of you to concern yourself," she replied, smiling. "But I cannot imagine who would suspect a female of my appearance of behaving improperly! My family might load me with reproaches were they to learn of it, but my family—excepting Valerian!—are all feather-heads. And since they *won't* know, it doesn't signify a straw."

Sir Randall had listened to these disclosures with an expression indicative of secret disagreement. Angelica interpreted that expression as arising from displeasure with her disregard for the proprieties. "To be blunt, sir," she added, on a deep intake of breath, "a female in my position can't afford delicate principles!"

"I did not mean to question your decision, merely to put you on guard." Stiffly, Sir Randall rose, displaying a stature deficient in inches and cozily corpulent. "The matter is settled, so far as I am concerned. Shall we retire indoors before you turn to ice?"

Upon this display of belated solicitude, Angelica raised her brows. "My household," Sir Randall explained simply, as he extended his arm in a courtly manner, "is filled with spies. Therefore, I thought our conversation would best be conducted in relative privacy. Do not look so concerned, Miss Smith! Since my watchdogs are constantly at loggerheads—in particular, my butler and my valet—I occasionally manage to do as I please." Before Angelica could question these statements, Sir Randall launched into a diverting tale of a zealous surgeon once known personally to him, who had with a single swoop of his knife removed a limb, three of his assistant's fingers, and a spectator's coat-tails.

This digression saw them into Sir Randall's study, where he seated Angelica before a blazing fire. Sir Randall, now that she could clearly study him, bore no resemblance to the ogre she had first thought him to be. Instead, engaged in divesting himself of myriad outdoor garments, Sir Randall looked very much like a plump little leprechaun. The hair that adorned his round head was confined largely to his jowls; and the eyes behind their spectacles twinkled merrily. "Gave you quite a start, did I?" inquired Sir Randall, acutely. "My apologies, but I had to discover if you would truly do. And I have decided that you will, Miss Smith. Why is it that you're unmarried? Surely all the gentlemen cannot be so deficient in good taste!"

Wryly, Angelica admitted that all the gentlemen seemed to be. "I do not consider marriage the be-all and end-all," she continued. "Shocking as it may be of me! I have always thought a female should be allowed the option of doing other with her life than raising a family. Alas, there are few such other options, but perhaps someday . . . Now you will think me a bluestocking! It is all your fault, sir, for tempting me to ride my favorite hobby-horse."

"A bluestocking?" Sir Randall's cherubic face was creased

with thought. "What's wrong with that, pray? My blessed wife was a bluestocking, rest her soul, and though she may have sometimes taken hold of the wrong end of the cow, her views were infinitely curious and interesting. Surely there's room in this vast world of ours for different points of view?" He eyed the doorway. "Apropos of which, here's Williams with our tea."

Indeed it was the butler, gazing upon his employer with a paternal eye. Behind him followed a footman, laden with a heavy tray. "This is Miss Smith, Williams," offered Sir Randall. "She is about to become one of our *happy* little family."

"Very good, sir," responded the butler, regarding Angelica with an expression that she thought oddly triumphant. "May I say that it is a pleasure to make your acquaintance, Miss Smith?" So saying he nudged the goggling footman and indicated the door. They exited.

Why triumph? mused Angelica. Had it been her imagination or had Sir Randall spoken of his happy family with a certain irony? But first things first, and Angelica was not certain of what her duties as amanuensis would involve. Delicately, she put forth an inquiry.

"My memoirs?" Sir Randall echoed blankly, around a mouthful of watercress.

"Yes, sir." Angelica's new employer was not only eccentric, but exasperating. "Valerian told me you were engaged in writing them. Am I mistaken, sir? It was my impression that you required assistance in that endeavor."

"Oh, *that*." Sir Randall swallowed and applied a linen handkerchief to his lips. "To be sure I do—more than you can imagine, Miss Smith! My papers are in such a tangle that I daresay we shall have to start over from scratch." Balefully, he glanced around the room. "If you will take my advice, you will not mention your, er, friend or our little conversation unless assured of our privacy. In this house, the very walls have ears."

Considerably taken aback, Angelica followed his gaze. Due to her sister Lily's rampant curiosity, Angelica was acquainted with the hazards imposed on privacy by eavesdroppers—but she saw only a comfortable, slightly shabby study, which offered no lurking listener an adequate hiding-place.

Sir Randall offered no further explanation, and it was hardly Angelica's place to interrogate him. Supposing he would eventually inform her of the tasks required of her, she too took a sandwich. There fell a companionable silence, broken only by the sound of munching.

Now that Angelica had opportunity for reflection, a number of things struck her as perplexing. Sir Randall feared spies? Who would wish to pry into the affairs of an eminent physician, no matter how eccentric? What might have he have to hide? Perhaps this dread of spies was merely a delusion attendant upon advancing age. If so, it was the greatest of pities. The cherubic doctor deserved to live an existence freed from such petty aggravations, real or imaginary. Covertly, she glanced at him.

"Durward is the worst," Sir Randall said gloomily. "My valet. You'll make his acquaintance soon enough, I'll warrant; the long-nosed wretch won't be able to refrain from stealing a peek at you. If Durward had been employed by Boney, the French would never have lost the war." He selected another sandwich. "I suppose I should be proud to have rendered the nation so valuable a service by taking Durward into *my* employ."

The situation, decided Angelica, grew momentarily more curious. Gently she intimated that, if Sir Randall did not approve of his valet, he might dismiss him from his post.

"Send him off with a flea in his ear? Would that I could. But the next would doubtless be even worse." Sir Randall forestalled further interrogation by popping the sandwich, in its entirety, into his mouth. Footsteps sounded in the hallway, a delicate mincing tread. Murmured Sir Randall, in garbled tones: "Prepare yourself, Miss Smith."

Six

Beneath the hipped roof of Chalmers House, a musical party was underway. A lady of opulent stature and piercing voice had been lured away from the Italian opera to perform a number of arias for Lady Chalmers's guests; Lady Chalmers herself had been persuaded to execute a piece on the piano, and did so very well; Miss Lily Millikin had made her debut at the harp, on which instrument she displayed a surprising expertise. Then came a break in the entertainment so that the guests might refresh themselves before being subjected to the offerings of lesser celebrities.

It was a pleasant evening's entertainment, the guests agreed, as the gentlemen hovered over the punchbowl and the ladies took their ease. Everyone appeared to be enjoying himself immensely, with the possible exception of the hostess's family.

This odd circumstance had brought itself to the attention of Lily, as it might be expected to have done, in light of her rampant curiosity. In truth, she could hardly have failed to note that Rosemary was out of sorts, since Rosemary was kicking up a dust beneath Lily's very nose.

"Cruelly unfeeling!" Rosemary repeated, in case Fennel failed to take her point. "It passes human bearing that you should have put us to the blush. To go off and leave us unescorted—how *could* you do such a thing?"

Fennel regarded his sisters tolerantly, not a bit abashed by these very great incivilities. "Take a damper!" said he. "No use crying over spilt milk."

Rosemary looked as though she contemplated physical violence, and was prohibited only by the presence of her guests. "Coxcomb!" she gasped, and turned smartly on her heel.

Lily gazed after her sister, who wore a satin gown with festooned trimming, bordered with rouleaux, the sleeves and bodice slashed, and on her golden curls a cap ornamented with rosebuds; and then returned her attention to Fennel. Her brother, she noted, was looking studiously Byronesque. "Poor Rosemary!" said she.

Fennel did not respond, but stared absently into space, on his handsome face a look of great and pleasurable abstraction, due to reminiscence concerning a merry damsel with rosy cheeks and cherry lips and a delightfully vulgar turn of speech. Lily, who was unaware of this damsel's existence, and who therefore assumed that her brother was air-dreaming about drinking cups fashioned from human skulls and silver funerary urns from Greece, reached out an elegant little hand and pinched him smartly.

Fennel winced. "Ears like seashells, I swear it!" he muttered, absently rubbing his bruised arm. "Teeth like pearls!"

Lily eyed her brother curiously. "Gracious, Fennel, I know that!"

Fennel grinned. He knew better than to make privy to his sisters the fact of his new acquaintance. Lily would wax rapturous about love and romance; Angelica would subject him to a lengthy interrogation concerning Miss Holloway's character and background; Rosemary was bound to disapprove. "Not you, puss. It's deuced hot in here. Think I'll have some punch!"

In turn, Lily watched her brother's departure. Unless she misread the signs, with which she was very familiar, Fennel was very far gone in infatuation, an affliction to which all the Millikins were prone, save Angelica. Simultaneously reminded of both her sisters and her swains, Lily gracefully craned her neck. Messrs. Gildensleeve and Meadowcraft, Steptoe and Pettijohn stood gazing on her at a humble distance, on their faces identical expressions of calf-love. What dear boys they were! thought Lily, and awarded them a collective smile that made all four look besottedly blissful.

51

Lily had no time, just then, in which to receive gallantries; she wished to speak with Angelica before the entertainment resumed. The eldest of her sisters, mused Lily, as she turned away—causing uniform disappointment to settle upon Messrs. Gildensleeve and Meadowcraft, Steptoe and Pettijohn—was exhibiting behavior that was distinctly freakish. Where did Angelica slip away to each afternoon in so clandestine a fashion? Rosemary and Fennel appeared unaware of this strange behavior, both being occupied with concerns of their own; but Lily's dreamy eyes overlooked little, and certainly nothing so intriguing as Angelica's disappearances.

Had Angelica an admirer? wondered Lily, as she made her way toward her eldest sister, engaged in conversation with Lord Chalmers and another gentleman near the marble-faced fireplace. Was the practical member of the family embarked upon assignations with an ineligible *parti*? It seemed a reasonable assumption. Lily could think of no more logical reason for Angelica's queer behavior, behavior that would be unnecessary were the gentleman unexceptionable. Poor Angelica! Left on the shelf without ever having had a single chance to fritter away.

As grows obvious, Lily was not particularly distressed at the notion that her eldest sister was embarked upon an unsuitable *affaire*. Had she been taxed with this lapse from propriety, Lily might have opened wide her lovely eyes and answered simply that the Millikins thought the world well lost for romance. Why should Angelica be the one exception, the one member of the family to sow no wild oats, however belatedly?

Nonetheless, Lily was distressed on Angelica's behalf. She feared that her sister's ineligible suitor would play fast and loose with her, would leave her to wear the willow—and what would happen to the rest of the family were the sensible Angelica to sink into a decline? The thought made Lily very melancholy.

Angelica bore no look of a lady thus afflicted, was in fact carrying on her conversation with animation. She looked very nice, mused Lily, in her dress of blue crape vandyked around the petticoat, and with her hair drawn back in ringlets from her face. Lord Chalmers apparently agreed with this assessment; he was regarding his eldest sister-in-law appreciatively. What a coil was this! sighed Lily to herself. If only Lord Chalmers displayed equal admiration for his wife! He must be induced to do so, but how? Deeply pondering, Lily made her way through the guests, a progress that was not rapid, for Lily was the most popular person possible with all parties. Behind her at a respectful distance trailed Messrs. Meadowcraft and Gildensleeve, Steptoe and Pettijohn.

"All the workers are hungry, angry, and loud in their protests," Lord Chalmers was saying, as Lily at last arrived. "The cotton-spinners in Lancashire and iron-moulders at Merthyr Tydfil, the Spitalfields silk-weavers, the Leicestershire stockingers and the Nottinghamshire hosiers. These accursed Hampden clubs! Heaven knows where it will end." He made an irritable gesture, and in so doing espied the newcomer. "Ah, Lily! May I make known to you Lord Kingscote, a friend in all but matters of government? Gervaise, Miss Millikin is another of my wife's sisters."

"Charmed," said Lord Kingscote, with patent insincerity, as Lily dropped a pretty curtsey.

"Lord Chalmers is a Tory," explained Angelica, *sotto voce*. "Lord Kingscote is a Whig."

"The laborers," continued Lord Chalmers, "have arisen *en masse* to destroy machinery, to which they attribute the wretched condition of the economy. In Nottinghamshire, Leicestershire and Derbyshire the Luddites have broken out again, by night demolishing stocking-frames and cotton-mill machinery."

Though Angelica found this discourse stimulating, it was clear that her sister did not. "Lord Kingscote," murmured Angelica to Lily, who wore a glazed expression, "is but recently returned to England from abroad. Lord Chalmers is catching him up on current events."

"The labor market," added Chalmers, "is additionally flooded by thousands of ex-soldiers and sailors; and the fierce competition for those jobs that do exist has forced wages down even further, a situation for which the government is held to blame. It is a deuced touchy situation, Gervaise."

"I make no doubt it is," replied Lord Kingscote, blandly taking snuff. "I hear that at St. Ives the populace celebrated Christmas by throwing a tax-collector out the window. Admirably enterprising folk! Meanwhile Weston is trying to pass even more restrictions on the exclusion of foreign produce—rapeseed and linseed, tallow and butter and cheese, at last count, I believe." He shook his head. "Oh, you Tories!"

"Lord Chalmers!" Angelica was inspired by the feral gleam in the baron's eye to hastily intervene. "I believe that a gentleman is trying to attract your attention. There, by the doorway!"

Chalmers glared in that direction. "I see no one."

"Could I have been mistaken?" Angelica energetically fanned herself, while Lord Kingscote watched ironically. "Perhaps I have grown overheated! I think, a glass of lemonade?"

Lord Chalmers regarded his eldest sister-in-law, then smiled. "Lest I indulge in dagger-drawing in my own home with my own guest? I stand rebuked! In reward you shall have your lemonade, Angelica. Do you care to accompany me?" Angelica cast a glance at Lily, who was looking very, very vague. Until she had time to reach certain decisions, Angelica had no wish for lengthy converse with any of her siblings. She agreed.

Bereft of her quarry, denied the opportunity to ask any of the questions that buzzed bee-like through her brain, Lily studied Lord Kingscote. He was a gentleman of eight-and-thirty, of medium height and wiry physique. His hair was brown, his countenance swarthy, his eyes dark and his nose hooked. He was homely, superior, understatedly and indescribably elegant.

Lily knew who Lord Kingscote was; all England did, for wherever the duke went, his reputation preceded him—and, since the duke was of nomadic constitution, that reputation had penetrated the far corners of the earth. Lord Kingscote was one of the highest-bred men in England, with a fortune to match; he was a man of the world who did everything with regal magnificence; by the countless dazzling barques of frailty by whom he had been favored, the total of whom even Lord Kingscote had lost count, he was universally adored. He was of too advanced an age and too aloof a disposition to appeal to Lily, of course, but Angelica had seemed to rub on with him well enough. Perhaps here was a gentleman of sufficient seriousness and cleverness to suit. Lily cleared her throat.

Lord Kingscote had not been unaware that Miss Lily Millikin was staring at him, but he had paid her little heed; young ladies always *did* stare at Lord Kingscote, usually with a large degree of avarice. The duke was a bachelor, and determined to so remain; when he wished feminine companionship it was readily available; when he did not wish it he was free to pursue his adventurous inclinations wherever fancy led him, without the impediment of trailing skirts. Satirically, he surveyed Lily.

Certainly she was a beauty; it was scant wonder that she had created so great a sensation on her debut. But Lord Kingscote was far beyond the age of being overwhelmed by loveliness—beyond, in fact, being overwhelmed by anything. As did all things, beauty in surfeit lost its allure. He supposed he could not deny this young lady her opportunity to attract his interest to herself without appearing rude—despite the tedium attendant upon plaguesome damsels, the number of which seemed to increase each year, Lord Kingscote was never rude. It was said of him by a long succession of Cyprians that no gentleman alive knew how to deliver a more kindly, or generous *congé*.

Since he was doomed to ennui, he would make the best of it. Lord Kingscote placed a wager with himself on which ploy the Fair Incomparable might utilize, and how many minutes it would be before she fatigued him beyond tolerance. "You wished to speak, Miss Millikin?" he inquired gently.

"Yes, sir." Lily awarded this perceptiveness the highest marks. "Would you explain to me—what *is* the difference between a Tory and a Whig?"

Here was an unusual gambit! Perhaps the duke would not grow bored as quickly as he'd expected. "Primarily that the Tories are in power," he replied. "We Whigs are great at denouncing everything the government does, but fundamentally we believe the same things."

"That doesn't help me very much," said Lily, whose
55

efforts toward enlightenment had caused her to frown most charmingly. "I am very ignorant in such matters—in a great many matters! But though I am not precisely needle-witted, I can generally understand if someone properly explains. Would you mind so much explaining to me, sir?"

Amused by such gargantuan effort—and why the devil should such a pretty widgeon wish to understand politics?—Lord Kingscote obliged. "The Tories embody the tradition of resistance to the aggressive principles of Revolutionary France—to change in any guise. Reform is anathema to them. It is the widespread belief of the Tories—of the upper classes in general!—that the only way to maintain law and order is to suppress the masses."

Certainly Lord Kingscote was clever; Lily could grasp only half of what he said. Since Lily was accustomed to grasping only half of anything that was said to her, she was not disturbed. "*Is* reform necessary, sir?"

"Lord, yes!" replied Lord Kingscote, highly diverted by the look of dogged concentration on his companion's lovely face. "There are two hundred and twenty capital offenses on the statute books."

"Then why is the government so against it?" inquired Lily, admirably demonstrating that ladies who aren't needle-witted can occasionally thrust to the heart of a matter with praiseworthy directness.

It was not only to the heart of the matter to which Lily had thrust, though she was unaware: Lord Kingscote was very much in charity with this unusual young lady, who seemed to have no other view but that of gleaning a laborious insight into political affairs. "Because the parliamentary reform demanded by the radicals—annual parliaments, universal suffrage—would greatly threaten Tory supremacy. The government is all atwitter, due to the Hampden clubs that Chalmers mentioned, the purpose of which is to demand, most stridently, precisely those measures. Fortunately—or unfortunately, depending on one's viewpoint—the violence of the radicals alienates many who might otherwise support them. The horror of the French Revolution remains painfully clear in many minds."

"Oh." Lily had only the haziest notion of what the French Revolution had entailed; something to do with heads in baskets, she believed. "What do *you* think, sir?"

Lord Kingscote's thoughts at that moment were not such as he would confide to his companion, being too comfortable in his bachelor status to announce a suspicion that he'd been stricken by Cupid's dart, and furthermore being determined to immediately wrest that missile from his chest. Puzzled by his silence, Lily blinked at him. The duke decided to let his wound fester a trifle longer. "I?" He shrugged. "Many of the Hampden clubs entertain highly unpleasant designs of seizing the property of the leading individuals in their communities. Since I am the leading property holder in a great many communities, I can hardly wish them joy of it."

"Naturally not! I perfectly see that." Lily sighed. "It must be very nice to be wealthy, I have always thought—my own family hasn't a feather to fly with, you see." She looked guilty. "Oh, drat! Rosemary would be very angry if she knew I'd told!"

"Do not distress yourself, Miss Millikin!" Lord Kingscote's voice, due to a strong inclination toward mirth, was strained. "Lady Chalmers will never hear of your blunder from *my* lips. Tell me, is it at you that those four young puppies are gaping? I cannot imagine that their attention is for myself."

Lily glanced over her shoulder, encountered the combined soulful glances of Messrs. Meadowcraft and Gildensleeve, Steptoe and Pettijohn, and giggled. "Pay them no heed, Lord Kingscote; *I* do not! Pray do not think me ungrateful, for naturally I must count myself honored that they have chosen to admire me, and I do!"

Lord Kingscote suffered a pang of disappointment that Miss Millikin should utter so ordinary a comment, then took himself to task for expecting that she should be the exception to his maxim that young ladies were invariably humdrum. "I'm sure," he offered politely, "it is not surprising that the young gentlemen should admire you."

"Oh, no," Lily replied simply. "They always do. It is because I am a nonpareil, I suppose. At all events, it doesn't signify, because I must have a peer—a *wealthy* peer, because as I have told you, our pockets are to let." Again, she frowned. "Although I have not yet decided exactly how I am to accomplish it, the only peers I have thus far encountered being either married or stricken in years."

Lord Kingscote, who as a bachelor must number among the aforementioned afflicted, could no longer restrain his mirth. He chuckled. Lily regarded him quizzically.

"What have I said—oh, dear! I did not mean to infer that *you* are stricken in years, sir! It would have been odiously impertinent! Although you're hardly in your salad days—but I daresay any number of ladies wouldn't mind *that*!"

"Due to my vast fortune, I conjecture?" gasped Lord Kingscote, who could not recall, despite his great experience with the game of hearts, having been so thoroughly entertained in many years. "You relieve me!"

"Poppycock," Lily said gloomily. "I make no doubt I've sunk myself quite below reproach. Again!"

This sad little admission had a strange effect on Lord Kingscote—strange, that is, in that he had never before experienced a sensation in his breast as if elegant little fingers had plucked at his heart-strings—a sensation that afflicted all of Lily's *beaux* at some point in time. She was a lovely pea-goose, the duke sternly admonished himself; she had admitted herself to be on the hang-out for a fortune; she was young enough to be his child. But her lovely mouth was trembling, and she looked so damned bereft . . .

Lord Kingscote regained sufficient poise to make an elegant leg and extend an arm. "You grievously wounded me, Miss Millikin; there's nothing for it but that you must atone. Perhaps if you will accompany me on a stroll around the room, I might recover my spirits. We will proceed at a gentle pace, due to my decrepitude."

"You are in a very teasing mood, I think, because you must know you're not *that* old." Incapable of resisting flirtation with any gentleman who came in her way, Lily placed her fingertips on the duke's arm and smiled up at him. "We are having a comfortable prose together, sir, are we not?"

Lord Kingscote returned that smile, ruefully. How the world would laugh to know that England's most elusive, most determined bachelor had been dealt a fatal blow by a beautiful pea-goose.

Seven

Morning had come. The watchmen who every half-hour throughout the night had informed the populace of the condition of the weather and the streets had been replaced by the dustman with bells and chant, the porter-house boy in search of the pewter pots which had been sent out with supper the previous evening, the milkman; the clatter of the night coaches had given way to morning carts. Chimney-sweeps with their brushes, crossing-boys with their brooms, emerged sleepy-eyed from their hovels; hawkers appeared with their wares, which ranged from hot buns to old clothes. Soon the air would be sweet with diverse horns and bells, the clatter of horses' hooves and wagon wheels on the cobblestones, the cries of broadsheet vendors, ballad-singers, lavender girls and muffin-men.

Of this restless panorama, the inhabitants of Chalmers House were mostly unaware. Rosemary lay still abed, reluctant to arise and embark upon a day that would doubtless present her yet further problems; Fennel too remained secluded, dreaming of rosy cheeks and cherry lips; Lily, who had arisen, studied her attitudes in her looking-glass. Lily had decided that Lord Kingscote was the perfect candidate for the hand of her sister Angelica. Now it remained only to subtly intimate to the interested parties that they were excellently matched, and then to determine how best to kindle Lord Chalmers's ardor for Rosemary. Meanwhile, Lord Chalmers breakfasted in solitary splendor, as was his habit; and Angelica—well, Angelica was not there.

Haze had settled on the city, a combination of fen-fog and smutty chimney-smoke, the sickly stench of rotting drains and horse dung. Angelica inhaled the polluted air, happily enough. From the overheated and strained atmosphere of Chalmers House, she had been glad to escape.

Angelica's various responsibilities were weighing on her heavily. She had hoped to receive word from her elder brother, Valerian, before now; she had hoped Valerian would evolve a means by which Rosemary might be extricated entirely from her difficulties. Angelica could only conclude that so trivial a matter as Rosemary's imminent disgrace had slipped Valerian's mind.

At least, with Angelica's earnings from Sir Randall, Rosemary's creditors could be held temporarily at bay. Typically, Rosemary had not asked how Angelica had come by that money, had accepted the money and Angelica's stern admonition to spend it wisely, with a very poor grace. Angelica sighed, and in her abstraction only narrowly escaped collision with a brewer's dray drawn by draught-horses as large as Sir Randall's buffalo. Perhaps she should not have scolded Rosemary, but it was difficult to think of her sister as a woman grown, especially since she did not conduct herself as befit an adult. Still, there was some excuse for Rosemary's sulkiness. Why did a man so wealthy as Chalmers keep his wife short of funds?

There was no ready answer, and Angelica pushed the question aside. She wondered if Sir Randall would be able to keep this proposed rendezvous, or if his plans would be thwarted by the mysterious Durward. Ample ground for speculation existed in that strange household. Angelica was no closer to enlightenment regarding her employer than she had been on their first meeting, more than a week past. The butler Williams was patently devoted to his er - loyer and by extension to Angelica, whom he seemed to regard as an ace in his employer's sleeve, cause for even further mystification; while the loyalties of Sir Randall's valet patently lay elsewhere. But to whom? On whose behest did Durward poke and pry? And why? The valet had an uncanny knack of being precisely where one wished he was not. Angelica would not have been surprised to learn that even then he trailed her down the street. Unable to resist a glance over her shoulder, she saw only apprentices removing shutters from bow-fronted windows, and scarlet-coated porters, and urchins leap-frogging over posts.

Angelica was aware that it was extremely reprehensible in her to lend her efforts to this morning's enterprise—which had been in its planning explained by Williams as an effort to show them as wished he wasn't that Sir Randall was still master in his own house—but she had been only too eager to grasp at an excuse to absent herself from breakfast with her sisters. Since Lily tended to wax enthusiastic about romance, and Rosemary the opposite, and it fell upon Angelica to maintain the uneasy peace, breakfast was traditionally the most uncomfortable of meals. Too, Angelica had grown very fond of her employer during the scant duration of their association. She was pleased to lend her efforts to Williams's scheme to thwart Durward, even though she suspected the butler's efforts were prompted by a desire to put the valet's long and twitching nose sorely out of joint.

Sir Randall was waiting, precisely as planned, bundled up as on their first encounter, with his disreputable hat pulled down over his ears. He espied Angelica and grinned. "Success, my dear!" he said mischievously. "What shall we do with our freedom?"

"I don't suppose," replied Angelica, as she returned his smile and took his arm, "that you'd care to discuss your memoirs?"

"No, I would not—and I must tell you that I find it very tedious of you to be forever nattering on about the same thing! Do you think I hide some great secret in my past? I assure you I do not. Now, shall we proceed? I have in mind a particular destination, and one that I fancy may interest you."

Angelica had become very fond of Sir Randall and very familiar with his household, including the menagerie, but on the memoirs that were allegedly the reason for her employment she hadn't done a stitch of work. Consequently, she felt very guilty. She explained this, as Sir Randall conducted her through streets filled with peddlers and pedestrians and carts.

"Balderdash!" responded Sir Randall, with a reproving glance. "Take heed, my dear, lest you turn into a shrew. 'Tis too fine a morning to be thinking about those dratted memoirs—and moreover, what I pay you for is the pleasure of your company." And then he embarked upon a most interesting dissertation on the temperature and weight loss of hibernating hedgehogs.

It was, in Angelica's opinion, anything but a fine morning; the air was thick and damp and odoriferous; but she resigned herself to yet another several hours being frittered away. Angelica was not accustomed to leisure, her days having been crammed with the problems of her siblings for the past many years; and she was not comfortable with unproductive idleness. Yet, as Sir Randall had pointed out, the time he purchased of her was his to do with as he pleased. And if he chose to amuse her, Angelica needs must bear it with good grace.

So thinking, she returned her attention to her companion, who was in a distinctly garrulous mood, and who had progressed from the topic of hedgehogs to animal life in general and the classification thereof, in line with which he stated modestly that he could identify the genus and species of any animal existent given but a single small bone. From bones he moved on to nerves, and the two types thereof, motor and sensory, as expostulated by his great friend, Sir Charles Bell. "A dedicated man and a great surgeon," Sir Randall concluded. "After the battle of Waterloo, Charles went to Brussels and offered his services to the English army. He operated an entire week almost without rest. If only these old hands of mine—but you are not paying attention, Miss Smith! What can you find of more interest than what I am telling you?"

Since Angelica could hardly confide to Sir Randall that she had been speculating upon whether he did or did not have windmills in his head, she sought a more innocuous response. "I beg your pardon! I had a letter from my stepmother by the last post and it has made me apprehensive, but I must not worry you about my concerns. Do continue! I promise that I will refrain from further wool-gathering."

"Piffle!" Sir Randall said genially. "I hope you have not received bad news?"

Angelica refrained from an uncharitable remark that any news proffered by her stepmother was ill. "Not precisely. Marigold writes that they are all merry as crickets—which, since my stepmother's ideas do not at all accord with my own, I find positively ominous." She glanced wryly at Sir Randall, who was looking very thoughtful. In a rush of confidence, she added: "Do you know, sometimes I am tempted to toss my bonnet over the windmill and consign them all to—to blazes! Not that I should ever really *do* it, but the notion grows more tempting each day!"

At this bad-tempered comment, Sir Randall evinced no dismay. "Tell me about this family."

Angelica did so, without hesitation; Sir Randall made a sympathetic, if unusual, confidant. She told him of Hyacinth and Violet; Amaryllis and Camilla, the twins; Hysop, the youngest of the clan; she even explained to him the estrangement between Valerian and their younger siblings, due to the efforts of Marigold. "She is the most tiresome creature," Angelica concluded. "But my tongue has run away with me. I beg your pardon!"

"Get married!" advised Sir Randall. "Let your husband take over the responsibility."

"Sir, you have not seen my sisters," Angelica responded ruefully. "Even if I wished a husband—which I do not!—to attract the attention of any gentleman to myself when my sisters are all far more lovely would be very up-hill work. Enough of my affairs! Where are you taking me?"

Angelica was correct in deducing that Sir Randall had in mind a specific destination, toward the attainment of which he had led her past the Royal Exchange, the Bank of England, and the Guildhall. "You'll see soon enough," he responded enigmatically, as he paused by a vendor and presented her with a potato baked in its skin. "For the nonce, Miss Smith, you must trust me."

Perhaps it was foolish in her, but Angelica did trust Sir

Randall. Once more she worried at the puzzle of why Durward expended such energy in spying on him. Surely Sir Randall was engaged in nothing so nefarious as made such surveillance necessary? *Could* there be some dark secret in his past, a repetition of which was so greatly feared that he must be spied upon? So absurd a notion made her smile. Given a choice between Sir Randall and his valet as potential villains, she would without hesitation choose Durward. Angelica heartily disliked the valet, whom she considered an odious little monster of unscrupulous nature. So far as she could tell, Durward cherished equally inimical sentiments toward her.

Sir Randall, engaged in consuming his own potato, had digressed into reminiscences of his own hey-day, when his eyes had been keener and his hands more steady and dissection his delight. "We teachers were completely at the mercy of the resurrectionists," he explained. "At the commencement of each new session at the hospitals, those rascals would appear, flitting around the dissecting-rooms and through the hallways, even appearing during lectures. They are simultaneously the blessing of the medical profession and its curse."

Having abruptly lost her appetite, Angelica surreptitiously disposed of the remainder of her potato. "The wretches operate in gangs," continued Sir Randall, oblivious to her onslaught of squeamishness. "Each has its own territory, and if one dares invade the domain of another retaliation is swift. The gangs will do anything to spoil the success of their rivals, even to desecrating cemeteries. Still, they need to be circumspect to a degree, lest they come to the attention of irate townspeople."

Not only was Angelica put off by this grisly topic of conversation, she was beginning to harbor a burgeoning suspicion. "You seem to know a great deal about these men, Sir Randall."

"Oh, yes!" Sir Randall replied cheerfully. "So does your brother, I'll warrant. Here we are!"

Angelica was relieved that her employer's attention had strayed from the topic of resurrectionists and graves; and eager to see where he had brought her. She was, due to the wearying nature of her various responsibilities, eager to embark upon what her brother Fennel would have termed "a bit of frolic," and curious to see what Sir Randall's notion of such frolic might be. What were these iron gates toward which he was leading her? Surely no public pleasure-spot was surrounded by so high and wicked-looking a fence? Realization burst upon Angelica, leaving her very much shocked indeed.

"Faint-hearted?" inquired Sir Randall, as he pushed open the gate. "I had thought you made of sterner stuff, Miss Smith."

Angelica did not answer; she was visited by a very vivid recollection of a certain room in Sir Randall's house, a chamber bare of all furnishings except an operating table. Coupled with recollection was a memory of Sir Randall's frequent expostulations upon the art of dissection and the valuable information gleaned therefrom. Appalled, she stared about the cemetery to which Sir Randall had led her. Could this be the reason for Durward's vigilance? Was the eminent Sir Randall Brisbane prone to undertake his own resurrection work?

So very agitated was Angelica that she might have asked these questions outright, had she not just then become aware that she and Sir Randall were not alone. Sir Randall, quicker on the uptake than she, was brandishing a fist beneath the nose of the huskier of two extremely disreputable-looking individuals.

"A pretty pair of scoundrels you are!" he announced. "At least Couch and Murphy have the decency to postpone their unsavory activities until after nightfall. Well, Bimble, what excuse have you for this despicable conduct? I conjecture next you will resort to outright murder."

Bimble, it soon became evident, had any number of things to say. First he stated that though Ben Couch, leader of a gang of four extremely capable London resurrectionists, might be a bit nicer in his tastes, he was nowhere near so successful as Bimble himself. He then explained the highly competitive nature of his business, and his own aversion to such time-consuming activities as trailing into the country in search of a corpse. "Get 'em while they're fresh, that's the ticket!" he said, while Angelica stared in horror and the second resurrectionist—Mallet by name—watched with interest. "This is a dog-eat-dog world, guv'nor, and the sawbones prefer corpses that ain't been below ground. As for the other—you'd make a nacky corpse yourself!"

"Bosh!" Sir Randall snapped. Angelica admired his courage, a quality in which she was sadly lacking. "Be on your way or I'll call a constable."

Bimble greeted this threat with the courtesy it deserved, which was none. "By all that's holy! You wouldn't dare, being as your own presence here stinks to the sky of fish!" His red-veined eye alit on Angelica, cowering behind her employer. "Who's this, your doxy? Damned if you ain't a rum one! And at your age!"

Here Mallet grew weary of this exchange of pleasantries and intervened. "Cut line!" he abjured. "Was you to slip a Ned into our crooks, Sir Randall, we might be persuaded to shove our trunks. Have a bit of hub and grub, eh? Being as you won't want anybody about whilst you conduct your little business."

To this incomprehensible speech—which, when translated into less colorful terms, meant merely that Messrs. Mallet and Bimble would, if Sir Randall paid them a guinea, retire forthwith to indulge in food and drink—Angelica paid little heed. She was stunned by the realization that Sir Randall was acquainted with these ruffians.

"One must cut one's garment to fit one's cloth," remarked Sir Randall, as he delved into a coat-pocket.

"Knew as soon as I clapped my glaziers on you—"began Bimble, to be silenced in mid-speech by Mallet's elbow in his ribs. He whoofed. Mallet muttered a single word. They took summarily to their heels.

"A *most* infamous proceeding!" remarked Sir Randall, restoring the guinea to his pocket. "I wonder what made them take fright. Odd, that, since the brutes usually fear nothing, even going so far as to snatch the bodies of those unfortunates who meet with violent death before the coroner's inquest. Did you take note of their tools? The sharp curved long-handled spades, the scoops on jointed shafts, the grappling tongs and crowbars? Naturally it is essential that in their work they leave no trace. Miss Smith, what ails you? Why are you yanking in that annoying manner on my sleeve? My dear, you are looking absolutely sick with fright! The wretches will not return, I promise you."

Certainly Bimble and Mallet had vanished, but the inspiration of their hasty departure had not. In fact that inspiration minced ever closer, an expression of extreme distaste on its pinched features, prominent among which was a twitching nose. Angelica strove desperately to compose herself sufficiently for speech. "Durward!" she hissed.

Sir Randall swung around to follow her anguished gaze. "That's put the cat among the pigeons!" he muttered bitterly. "I daren't hope Durward will refrain from pitching tales."

"But sir, to whom?" Though Angelica was appalled by her discovery for the reason underlying the surveillance kept on her employer—said reason being her employer's attraction to cemeteries and the contents thereof—she was in no way reconciled to the possessor of that twitching nose.

With as cherubic a countenance as ever graced a church-choir, Sir Randall gazed heavenward. "My dear, have I not explained? How very remiss of me! Durward is in the employ of my son."

"Your son!" Angelica gasped. Her employer had heretofore made no mention of any progeny.

Eight

It was yet mid-afternoon when Lord Chalmers returned to his elegant town house, behavior so unlike his lordship, who usually departed the premises at dawn and remained absent until sunset, that his butler stared. Lord Chalmers then added to that august individual's confusion by inquiring the whereabouts of his baroness, another unprecedented event. The butler controlled his amazement sufficiently to respond that he believed Lady Chalmers had retired to her boudoir. Lord Chalmers mounted the pretty wooden staircase with barley-sugar twisted balusters and finely moulded handrail; and the butler retired to the nether regions, there to inform the superior French chef that something had put his lordship in a right rare tweak, for which her ladyship was about to be raked over the coals, unless the butler had misread the signs.

In point of fact, the butler had done precisely that: Lord Chalmers was not in a temper but in a state of extreme contemplativeness, due to a conversation held that morning with his old friend and political antagonist, Lord Kingscote. Gervaise, it seemed, was greatly taken with Lily, to such extent that his casual remarks had sent Lord Chalmers to inquire of his wife the state of her sister's heart—if Lily *had* a heart, of which Lord Chalmers was not convinced, due to her distinctly off-hand treatment of Messrs. Meadowcraft and Gildensleeve, Steptoe and Pettijohn. Lord Chalmers could not decide whether to be amused by this development, or appalled; matrimony, in his experience, had a most adverse effect on the Misses Millikin. Who would have thought that Rosemary would with marriage evolve from a fresh and simple country girl into a fashionable lady of immense consequence? Chalmers was not sure he approved the transformation, but supposed it was only to be expected that Rosemary should try to live up to the dignity of her newly acquired estate. It did not occur to him to tell her that such effort was not necessary.

It should perhaps here be stated that Lord Chalmers was, in his fashion, fond of his young wife. That he did not expend much thought on her, or much time in her company, was due to his involvement in matters he considered to be of far more immediate import. The government and Parliament had with a lavish hand supported the Continental wars, with the result that the national debt had risen from £252,000,000 to £861,000,000, with the necessity of an annual £29,000,000 to discharge the interest alone, and the additional necessity of somehow transposing this burden from the aristocracy to the common folk. Along with Wilberforce and his evangelists, Lord Chalmers believed that it was the privilege of the poor to be patient in adversity, and of the rich to accept without question the kindly dispensations of Providence.

Alas, the poor were not inclined toward that viewpoint, and the government had been inundated with petitions from the commercial interests, even threatened by its own supporters, did not expenditures and taxation decrease. Meanwhile the old, blind, mad king was immured in a wing of Windsor Castle; Prinny was embarked on his most costly project to date, with the assistance of his favorite architect transforming the west end of the capital into a fashionable new park and a sweeping avenue; the royal dukes were deep in debt and controversy; the Princess of Wales was traipsing around the Mediterranean with an Italian courtier and a retinue of rogues and buffoons. With all these problems plaguing him, it is little wonder that Lord Chalmers had scant time for his own domestic affairs.

Still, this matter of Kingscote had perturbed Lord Chalmers sufficiently to distract him briefly from matters of state; and now that his shrewd mind was directed toward matters matrimonial, he had come to the conclusion that, in his own household, something was definitely amiss. He saw little of his wife even at the best of times, but lately it had seemed as if she was deliberately avoiding him. Lord Chalmers decided to demand an explanation of this bizarre conduct, for which no justification came readily to mind. Rosemary need not think to put him off with her vaporing; he fancied he knew just how to deal with that missishness. As becomes apparent, subtlety was not Lord Chalmers's *forte*.

Lady Chalmers was indeed in her boudoir, as the butler had taken leave to guess; clad in a pretty morning gown of lawn, lavishly embellished with ribbons and lace, she reclined gracefully on her *chaise longue*. Had it not been for the scowl on the baroness's exquisite countenance, as she stared at several sheets of papers strewn across her lap, she might have posed for a portrait of beauty at rest.

Lord Chalmers was not especially appreciative of so lovely a tableau; he allowed the door to close smartly behind him. Rosemary started and blanched. "Chalmers! What the deuce are *you* doing here?"

"You're in high bloom today!" responded her lord, politely. "As to the other, I live here—or had you forgot?"

"How could I, pray?" With what she hoped was nonchalance, Rosemary gathered together her papers and stuffed them out of sight under a pillow. "You gave me quite a start; I did not expect you."

"That much is apparent." Lord Chalmers seated himself in a brocaded chair.

"Of course I am glad to see you," interrupted Rosemary, seeking to divert him from the pages on which she'd been trying to arrive at the total of her debts. "To what do I owe the unexpected pleasure of your presence here at this time of day?"

So able a politician as Lord Chalmers was not likely to be put off by so feeble a ploy. He pondered his wife's guilty manner, and the haste with which she'd tucked those papers away. Only one explanation presented itself, and Lord Chalmers didn't like that explanation above half. "I wished to speak privately with you," he said, as he wondered how a man so greatly in the public eye as himself might best deal with an errant wife. "I take it that we *are* private, Rosemary?"

Rosemary was very strongly tempted to hurl herself upon her husband's manly chest, there to weep out her woes. She dared not, lest she sink ever lower in his estimation. If it was possible to sink lower, she amended, recalling the unfavorable and unalterable opinion which he'd already formed. "Of course we're private!" she retorted, in an unfriendly manner. "Gracious, Chalmers, are you gone horn-mad? Perhaps you would wish to look under the *longue*!"

Only with difficulty did Lord Chalmers refrain from doing precisely that, so taken was he with a sudden conviction that his young wife had embarked upon a course that would result in horns being planted on his brow. However, he did not wish Rosemary to learn how deeply this conviction wounded him— which, since Lord Chalmers already considered his wife a heartless baggage, cannot be blamed in him. "I merely wish," he said repressively, "to ascertain the whereabouts of your sisters."

Once more, as she plucked at the trimmings of her gown, Rosemary felt that her husband was a great deal more interested in her sisters than herself. "Lily and Fennel have gone riding in the park. I don't know where Angelica has gone, she's probably poking around some stuffy old museum. I can't think what she finds to interest her in such dreary places, but there's no denying Angelica has an inquiring nature."

So Rosemary had rid herself of her chaperones? Chalmers wondered to what end. He expressed an opinion that Rosemary should keep a closer watch on her siblings. London was rife with traps for the unwary, he explained; while dwelling beneath his roof, the Millikins were his responsibility.

"You mean they're mine," retorted Rosemary, thinking that it took scant effort on her part to deepen her husband's displeasure. Even without lifting a finger she sank further in his esteem. "As you say. You have *not* said what brought you home so early today."

No, and he did not intend to; Lord Kingscote's infatuation with Lily paled into insignificance in comparison with Lord Chalmers's suspicion that his wife was ear-deep in intrigue.

Since Lord Chalmers had chosen his wife carefully, on the basis of breeding and birth and conduct, as much for her adherence to the dictates of propriety as for her decorativeness, he considered this development extremely unfair.

Perhaps Rosemary didn't realize the vile scandal attendant upon her ruinous course. Tactfully, Lord Chalmers explained that ladies who failed to conduct themselves with discretion were apt to find their names bandied about in the most vulgar fashion, a situation which he would find extremely distasteful.

As a result of these gentle hints, Rosemary stared at her husband in blank bewilderment. He was extremely handsome in his plain blue coat with brass buttons and horizontally striped waistcoat, his snug-fitting inexpressibles and superbly fashioned cravat; and if he cared a fig for her he wouldn't load her with reproaches at every opportunity. What had inspired his current snit, she could not imagine, nor did it especially signify. "I hope that I am always discreet," she replied.

"As do I!" said Lord Chalmers, then paused. He was not an unfair man, and there was always the possibility that he had leapt to the wrong conclusion, though what other conclusion might exist he could not say. For this lack of comprehension, there is some excuse: Lord Chalmers was by lack of time and inclination not a patron of pretty ladybirds, and consequently unaware of the expensive nature of feminine fripperies. He thought he kept his wife in very easy circumstances, and failed to understand why she was forever short of funds; he was impatient of her failure to keep to a budget, and considered it his duty to curb her spendthrift ways, an effort in which he believed he had met with some success.

Lord Chalmers was not, however, thinking of Rosemary's wastrel habits just then. "It seems we cannot converse easily these days. I suppose it is my fault for leaving you so much to your own devices, and I am sorry for it. I did warn you that my time is not my own—but you are very young."

This attempt at reconciliation, though generously offered, was not well received; to Rosemary's ears it seemed as if her husband had for their marriage sounded a death-knell. "You refine too much on it," she responded frigidly. "I assure you that I rub along very well without your escort. Nor," she added resentfully, "am I a child, and for you to act as if I am annoys me excessively."

Obviously it did. With an oath, Lord Chalmers rose from his chair, crossed the room, grasped his wife's wrist and pulled her to her feet. She scowled up at him, belligerently. He had meant to sternly scold her for her conduct, since it did not suit his notions of wifely behavior that Rosemary should in his presence exhibit such churlish constraint. Now, glimpsing a hint of tears behind her hostile gaze, he found that he could not. "Rosemary," he said helplessly. "I wish that you might trust me."

But Rosemary was too wise to tumble for this gambit; she was not to be lulled into a candid confession which would likely land her in the divorce court. Still, her husband's sympathetic manner was not without effect, and she had to exert tremendous power of will to keep from weeping all over his horizontally striped waistcoat. "Do not think of it!" she gasped. "I cannot! Anyway, 'tis the most trivial of affairs!"

Lord Chalmers was, due to his long experience of politics, also well equipped to recognize dissemblement. "You seem to be," he observed, "sadly out of curl."

This remark, which Rosemary interpreted as an adverse comment upon her looks, put her further out of humor. "A passing indisposition, merely. I did not sleep well last night."

Had Lord Chalmers been of a different disposition, he might have expressed a willingness to help his wife achieve an excellent night's rest, to which his wife might have responded that she would like nothing better in the world; but he did not, and neither did she, and therefore nothing was resolved. "You are," he said, "overtaxing your strength with all these routs and *soirées*. I must request that you refrain from exhausting yourself."

Rosemary, contemplating one of the brass buttons that adorned her husband's coat, concluded that he didn't want her to have friends. Doubtless he would prefer to see her locked away somewhere where she could spend none of his money and behave in no way that was indiscreet—which would have suited Rosemary very well, if only her spouse was locked away with her. Reflecting that few of her acquaintances would care to claim a bosom-bow who was in residence at a debtor's prison, Rosemary became aware that her husband awaited a response. What had they been talking about? "Lily must have her chance," she said.

"Lily already has half the gentlemen in London dangling after her!" Lord Chalmers retorted. "If not more! Leave Angelica to look after the chit; she'll do it very well."

Rosemary could hardly explain that Angelica was too busy attempting to extricate her from difficulties to properly attend to Lily. "You approve of Angelica?"

"Why should I not?" inquired Lord Chalmers, with some surprise. "I like Angelica very well."

Perhaps Lord Chalmers had married the wrong sister. This realization, that an ugly duckling stood higher in her husband's estimation than she did herself, was an additional blow to Rosemary's pride. With all her might she strove to control her trembling lips.

It occurred to Lord Chalmers that the last discussion he'd held with his wife had not concluded amicably. In fact, as he recalled, it had concluded with himself in a temper and Rosemary in tears. Perhaps she was still sulking about that? He would not have thought her of so unyielding a disposition. There was one way to find out. "Are you still angry that I took you to task for squandering your pin money? Very well, give me an accounting and I'll settle your debts, but this is the last time, Rosemary! You must learn to practice economy."

Were Chalmers to settle her accounts, thought Rosemary, it would be permanently. He was a cheeseparer and a nipfarthing; he expected her to live in the very best possible style on a mere pittance; he was cruel to the greatest degree. Yet Rosemary loved her husband, despite his innumerable shortcomings; and she meant to delay as long as possible the inevitable moment when he cast her off without a farthing.

"Pooh!" she said, somewhat unsteadily. "You've no need to trouble yourself, I'm not in the basket yet. Now, if you will excuse me, this is not a subject on which I am particularly anxious, and there are matters to which I must attend."

Lord Chalmers grasped his wife's shoulders. "No," said he.

"No?" Rosemary stared at her husband with fascination. "Why not, pray?"

"Because," replied Chalmers, in husky tones, "I have not yet finished speaking with you."

"Oh," said Rosemary.

Alas, at this most promising of moments, the baron recalled that for a gentleman of mature years and serious inclination to be stricken all aheap by the mere proximity of his wife was the height of absurdity; and the baroness, similarly stricken, recalled her conviction that her husband had a high-flyer tucked away; and both resolved that the other should not learn that he or she had nearly succumbed to the fancies of a disordered brain. The baron abruptly released his wife; the baroness returned in good haste to her *chaise longue*. "Where are you engaged this evening?" inquired Chalmers, for want of anything better to say. "Perhaps I shall accompany you."

Rosemary, deep in contemplation of her husband's high-flyer, greeted this offer with no appreciable delight. "But your time is not your own!" she reminded him, rather pettishly.

Lord Chalmers was also deep in contemplation, concerning the identity of the gentleman who dared send his wife *billets-doux*. "I begin to think that in pursuing affairs of state, I have in other matters been somewhat remiss. Do you wear the sapphires this evening? They suit you admirably. If they are still at the jeweler's, I will fetch them home for you."

"Gracious, Chalmers!" Rosemary responded airily, as her heart sank. "I can only conclude you don't trust me to execute the simplest errand myself! And tonight I wear pink, so you see that the sapphires will not do." Frantically she wondered how she was to reclaim that accursed necklace.

Lord Chalmers, meanwhile, wondered what he was to do with a wife who so patently prescribed to wrong-headedness. One course of action recommended itself to him, but the baron decided regretfully that it was beneath his dignity to turn his wife over his knee.

Unaware that her husband contemplated taking gross liberties with her person, Rosemary eyed him warily. Were Chalmers to suddenly start living in her pocket, he was bound to quickly discover that those pockets were to let, which thoroughly ruined her pleasure in the rare prospect of having her husband at her side. "You accompany me then? I am engaged for the theater."

"Oh, yes," responded Lord Chalmers, in a manner that was distinctly ominous, due to his intention to keep a very sharp eye on the young hopefuls who habitually flocked around his wife. "I have neglected you shockingly, and I mean to do so no more." Perhaps this noble admission might kindle some slight degree of warmth in its object's breast.

It did not. "As you wish," said Rosemary, with a fine indifference attained only through monumental effort.

Lord Chalmers did not trust himself to answer. Wishing even more fervently that he was of a disposition that would allow him to apply a hairbrush to his lady's *derrière*, he stalked out of her boudoir. Rosemary listened to his footsteps fade down the hallway. Tears streamed down her cheeks.

Nine

Since Lady Chalmers was not one to suffer in stoic silence, Angelica was presented with an accounting of her sister's sorrows, complete in every minuscule detail. Rosemary related her most recent interview with Chalmers, including his offer to discharge her debts, and took great umbrage at Angelica's untactful suggestion that her husband's offer seemed the most practical solution to the current difficulties. Did Angelica *wish* Rosemary to be cast off? Rosemary inquired. Perhaps Angelica was not the font of impartial wisdom that the family thought her; maybe Angelica wished Rosemary's marriage to fail so that she could snare Chalmers herself! Rosemary wouldn't stand for it, even if Chalmers *did* like Angelica best. And she didn't care a fig for Angelica's suggestion that there might be a law against such a thing. Rosemary didn't see why there should be such a law, but even if there was, a man so influential as Chalmers could easily have it set aside. Moreover, were Angelica so devoted to her family as she professed to be, she would somehow contrive to reclaim the Chalmers sapphires. Since Angelica had failed to thus contrive, Rosemary surmised that Angelica wanted her to be miserable. If so, Angelica had her wish; Rosemary considered the sorrows of Cleopatra, as viewed the previous evening in company with her ill-tempered husband, far inferior to her own.

This diatribe was conducted, to the accompaniment of sobs and sniffles, over Lady Chalmers's breakfast toast. Nor was it the only diversion to accompany that meal. While Rosemary bewailed her lot, complained that she was the most unfortunate of beings, and in general acted the wet-goose, Fennel enlivened the little party with an account of the latest goings-on of his hero—who had departed England in a blaze of notoriety, scarcely avoiding the bailiffs who seized everything in sight; and was Angelica aware that at eight-and-twenty Lord Byron already had gray hairs?—and Lily dropped hints so arch and vague that they entirely missed their target. *Who* was running counter to conventional behavior, as Lily intimated? Wearily Angelica wondered, and cravenly decided that she would rather not know.

She had no time just then to worry about the further misadventures of her addle-pated family. Callously abandoning them, she donned a pelisse, crammed a bonnet on her head, and hurriedly summoned a hackney-coach. Sir Randall had sent her directly home from the cemetery, saying that he would deal with Durward. There had been no further word, though Angelica had half-expected to receive a strong intimation that her services were no longer desired. Durward had no authority to dismiss her, but his master did. Perplexed and anxious about her employer, Angelica pondered the puzzle of

Sir Randall's son, a man of such infinite littleness of soul as to set spies on his own father. Despicable, in short! Without setting eyes on him, Angelica had conceived for Sir Randall's offspring a large dislike.

Her head throbbed, her mouth was dry, she felt distinctly queasy from the swaying of the coach. Angelica swallowed, painfully. If Sir Randall's unhappy situation and Rosemary's predicament were not bad enough, Lily and Fennel had had their heads together over the breakfast table. Secrets! thought Angelica, with distaste. Angelica hadn't time to fret over that matter either, though she strongly suspected that she should; her destination had been reached. She climbed down from the coach, paid off the driver, and walked slowly to Sir Randall's front door.

Not Williams opened that portal, but Durward. Angelica surveyed his pinched and smirking countenance, and suffered a sharp apprehensiveness. She was right to do so. "Master Simon wishes a word with you, miss!" said Durward, with triumph that he made no effort to conceal. "If you will accompany me?"

Angelica had no choice but to follow, and little more hope that she was not to be summarily dismissed. So be it, then! Angelica had a few words of her own to import to Durward's master. Grimly she stalked into the study. Behind her, Durward closed the door.

A gentleman was there before her, apparently deep in contemplation of the overflowing bookshelves. He was tall and muscular, clad fashionably if carelessly in a dark-brown frockcoat, sage-green kerseymere waistcoat, buff unmentionables and gleaming Hessian boots. Angelica was in no mood to appreciate broad shoulders, a narrow waist, or a well-shaped calf. Deliberately, she cleared her throat. The gentleman turned around.

His hair was auburn, worn long; luxurious side-whiskers extended downward toward his chin. Eyes of an unusual clear shade of green gazed rather derisively out of a face that was a fascinating combination of crags and hollows and planes. He looked every bit his age, which was forty; and there was no doubt that he had lived each year of his adult life to the fullest, for on his harsh features dissipation had left its unmistakable stamp. In summation, Angelica beheld a sardonically elegant, diabolically seductive rake-hell. She blinked, as if to clear her vision. "You don't look at all like your father," she said.

"And you," responded the gentleman, "don't look like Haymarket-ware! Come, tell me what rig you're running. I can't allow it, more's the pity, even though you're a taking little thing. Still, I'll wager that a small gift—shall we say fifty pounds?—will make you heart-whole again." He extended a folded banknote. In so doing he noted that the object of his strictures had dropped her head into her hands.

Simon Brisbane, as Angelica had deduced, enjoyed a remarkable career with the gentle sex. Behind that staggering success lay a single simple secret: Simon liked women. All women. Even a bit of fluff so misguided as to try and set herself up as his elderly father's companion. In fact, so fond was Simon of the frail and the fair that he disliked to see even its humblest member weep. Therefore he crossed the room, put an arm around the frail one's shaking shoulders, and drew her comfortably against his chest. She must not take it so to heart, he soothed, that he had queered her game; he apologized for bringing her to a standstill; he promised that she would come about again. Sir Randall was beyond the age of fancying pretty lady-birds, moreover; May and December would not suit.

Angelica's reactions to these kind assurances, to say nothing of her reaction to being clasped against an unfraternal masculine chest for the first time in her life, were very complex. Above all, she found her position very comfortable— so much so that she made no immediate effort to inform the gentleman who so tenderly cradled her that she had been stricken by laughter, not tears.

"There!" said Simon, who was not so enamored of the ladies as to harbor improper intentions toward every specimen who came his way, and who therefore was quite composed enough to realize that this lady's shoulders no longer shook. "I did not mean to be harsh, but thought it best we lay our cards on the table. Though I admit to a certain puzzlement as to why you should think my father was hankering after a fancy-piece!" As he spoke, he set the fancy-piece away from him, the better to study her face.

It was a very pretty face, he decided, with those rosy cheeks and bright blue eyes. But the eyes were dry and the mouth quivering—he frowned and warned her very strongly against trying to play off tricks.

"Oh, no!" wailed Angelica, at the end of her self-control. "You are mistaken, sir: I have no wish to set up as your father's, er—"

"Light o' love!" supplied Simon, and grasped her arm. "My good girl, you're all about in the head if you think he'll marry you. Even my father isn't so eccentric as to marry Haymarket-ware—at least I don't think he is, though he did bring you home."

"He *didn't* bring me home!" Having laughed herself into stitches, Angelica clutched her aching sides. "I was recommended for the post—it was all above-board."

"You were *recommended*?" echoed Simon, and grasped her other arm. "Good God! By whom?" In the grip of yet another fit of mirth, Angelica was unable to reply.

This was not the first occasion on which a female had been rendered speechless in the presence of Simon Brisbane; indeed, such occasions had come about so frequently over the past many years that Simon had evolved a remedy. A simple solution, this consisted of embracing the afflicted lady so ardently that she either recovered her senses or lost them altogether, both of which eventualities led to the same final resolution, to wit yet another notch on Simon's gun-belt.

To give credit where it is due, Simon did not keep track of the ladies who favored him—and lest too much credit is given him, it must be added that keeping track of his conquests would have left Simon no time for further such pursuits. He was an incurable and impenitent rake; he enjoyed his life immensely; and there was not a one of Simon's conquests that did not similarly enjoy him.

As did Angelica, subjected to an ardent embrace, the likes of which she had never dreamed. "Gracious!" she uttered, when allowed to draw breath. The gentleman paid little heed to this observation. He kissed her once again.

"Simon!" came an indignant voice from the doorway. "Unhand Miss Smith this instant! Is no female safe from your degradations? My dear, do sit down!"

Angelica was pleased to do so, in the chair pushed forward by Sir Randall; her knees were feeling weak. "You must not blame him!" she said to Sir Randall, who was glowering in a malevolent manner upon his offspring. "He has taken the oddest notion that I am, er, Haymarket-ware—due to Durward, I conjecture! I cannot begin to imagine what that odious little monster of ill-nature has said!" Here Simon quirked an interrogative brow. "Yes, I mean Durward! How would *you* like to have the creature's Friday-face forever peering over your shoulder, and know that he will be forever pitching tales about everything you do and say? I'll wager you wouldn't put up with it for a minute!"

"Miss Smith!" Sir Randall patted her hand and looked very, very anxious. "You are overwrought!"

Had she not a right to be overwrought? Had she not been verbally then physically assaulted by a hardened rakeshame? In justice, Angelica admitted to herself that she had minded neither all that much; both had been most enlightening experiences of a nature not likely to again be encountered by an ugly duckling. It then occurred to Angelica that by speaking so frankly to Durward's employer she was hardly advancing her own case. "Sir!" she added pacifically.

Simon leaned against the desk and folded his arms across his chest. "You'd win your wager; I *wouldn't* put up with it. Furthermore, Durward is a gabble-grinder, and I don't like him much myself; but my father forces me to these distasteful expedients and shifts." Sir Randall muttered; Angelica patted his hand; Simon watched sardonically. "I'll even grant you that Durward is a curst poor judge of character. He said you were a straw damsel bent on worming your way into my father's affections with the intention of feathering your nest."

"Balderdash!" uttered Sir Randall, as he approached the

brandy decanter that stood on a bookshelf. "The man's a dashed loose-screw."

"Perhaps." Simon raised the gold-handled quizzing-glass that hung on a ribbon round his neck and subjected the alleged straw damsel to a thorough scrutiny. The pelisse of deep blue velvet was shabby, the matching bonnet definitely askew; both were outdated, though of excellent material and cut. A gentlewoman, fallen on hard times? It was very curious.

Angelica, who was very well acquainted with her mirrored image, knew exactly how she must look: a lady no longer in her first youth, plainly dressed and probably untidy, due to the haste with which she'd left Chalmers House and the thoroughness with which she'd been embraced. Her fingers itched to straighten her bonnet, twitch out her skirts, smooth back her hair. Naturally she did none of these things. Alas, she could not similarly restrain the blood that stained her cheeks.

Simon let fall the quizzing-glass, intrigued. Not without basis was he known in certain circles as a nonesuch. Whether the female who currently regarded him in so thoughtful a manner was a privy to said circles, the *entrée* to which was determined not by birth but by recklessness of temperament and disregard of consequence, was a matter of great interest to Simon. "I begin to think," he remarked, "that Durward erred, perhaps due to a lack of familiarity with females of an adventurous nature."

"A familiarity," said Sir Randall irritably, from his position at the bookshelf, where he was making astounding inroads into the brandy, "which you do not similarly lack. I must warn you that my son is a great favorite with the females, Miss Smith. Doubtless he'll be throwing the hatchet at *you* next!"

"Unfair, Papa!" Simon removed himself from the desk and tweaked the decanter out of his father's hand. "I had no intention of making your little friend an object of my gallantries—but only because you would not like it, mind!"

Here Sir Randall's little friend giggled outright and expressed herself totally impervious to flattery. "Surely not?"

Simon inquired of her, with interest. "Women adore to hear their praises sung, in my experience. But you are a queer sort of female, aren't you? A well brought-up lady should have at least exhibited horror at the suggestion that she might be mistaken for a fancy-piece, and at the most have cut up very stiff!" Having delivered this provocation, he waited curiously to see what she would say.

It was not at all what he had expected. "How absurd! Of course you would think the worst of me, because you are used to associate with females of that sort." Sir Randall made a choking noise and Angelica eyed him in bewilderment. "Have I said something I should not? But it was you who brought up straw damsels and Haymarket-ware, sir. It is improper of me to mention such things, but I merely meant to demonstrate that I understand perfectly how it is that you thought I was, er, less than I should be." She paused, to find both Sir Randall and his son staring at her. "Am I mistaken, sir? Are you *not* a rakeshame?"

Simon inclined his head. "Guilty, ma'am, as judged."

"Piffle!" retorted Angelica. "I don't see why you should feel the least bit guilty about it. I think it must be very pleasant to do precisely what one wants."

"It is." Simon had not achieved his legendary career by ignoring such tantalizing remarks. "I should be pleased to show you!"

"Oh, is *this* how the game is played?" inquired Angelica, bright-eyed. "How fascinating. Clearly one must be always on one's toes. But there is no point in trying to put me to the blush, and I wish you would not."

"No?" said Simon, very thoughtfully. "I believe I must beg to differ—"

"Simon!" said Sir Randall, horrified at this suggestion that his shameless son meant to get up a flirtation beneath his very nose. "Remember to whom you speak!"

"I would find it a great deal easier to do so," retorted Simon, no whit discomposed, "if I *knew* to whom I spoke! Explanations would seem to be in order, Miss—er?"

"Mil—" began Angelica. "Smith!" cried Sir Randall. "Oho!" murmured Simon, ironically. "How could so memorable a name have slipped my mind? I understand you have been engaged to assist my father in compiling his memoirs, Miss Smith."

Angelica glanced at Sir Randall, who obviously wished himself elsewhere, a sentiment with which she sympathized wholeheartedly. Since her tongue had already displayed an appalling tendency toward indiscretion in Simon Brisbane's presence, she would confine herself to monosyllables. "Yes."

Simon was long familiar with his effect on females; again his lips twitched. "How came that about, Miss Smith? What prompted my father to suddenly turn bookish?"

Once more Angelica eyed Sir Randall, who was half way toward the door. "You must ask your father that, sir."

"Simon!" he responded. "After all, you are become quite one of the family. And how would you have me address you?"

Definitely a profligate, mused Angelica, who despite her ugly-duckling status was not immune to his devastating charm, and who was not about to let that charm turn her head. "You may address me," she replied serenely, "as Miss Smith."

"Hornet!" remarked the gentleman, appreciatively. Sir Randall, who had achieved the window, announced that there was an altercation underway in the garden between the llama and the shawl-goat, and fled. "Tell me, Miss Smith, if you please: how comes it about that a gently bred female like yourself is reduced to earning your own keep?"

It did not occur to Angelica that she might render up the truth. Following her sister Lily's example of indulging in air-dreams, she spun a fine tale of squandered family fortunes and starving siblings, with herself the sole means of keeping the wolf from the door. Simon made no comment. Impressed with her own inventiveness, Angelica added a consumptive parent sewing seams by candlelight so that her ragged youngsters might have bread on the table at least once a week.

Angelica may have been impressed with her powers of invention, but her audience was not. "Doing it rather too brown!" he observed, when she fell silent. "Do you think me want-witted? I cannot lay claim to many virtues, but a flat I am not!"

84

Mention of virtue caused Angelica to contemplate vice, and Simon Brisbane's acquaintance therewith, which she concluded, and rightly so, was vast. If only she were a swan—appalled, Angelica banished the thought. "Cat got your tongue, Miss Smith?" inquired Simon. "I give you leave to speak."

Visited by a strong suspicion that the gentleman was aware of, and amused by, the shocking tenor of her thoughts, Angelica did precisely that. "This is a serious business!" she said sternly. "It is not kind of you to try and distract me. Oh, I know you do not mean it; it must be habit with you to try and beguile every lady who crosses your path—but it is your father you should be concerned with, your father and that odious little Durward! It is not my place to say so, but I expect you mean to dismiss me anyway and so I *will* say it: it is no wonder, the way Sir Randall is treated, that he should try and slip the leash!" Simon regarded the decanter that he still held and then picked up a glass. "You will be astonished at my temerity in daring to address you *so*," added Angelica. "I am myself! But I cannot bear that anyone should disturb your father's peace of mind, because I am very fond of Sir Randall."

"Yes, I see you are." Simon thrust the brandy snifter beneath Angelica's nose. "Don't fly into alt, my silly girl; I'm not accusing you of making a dead-set at my father."

Unaccustomed to being addressed as a silly girl, and certainly unaccustomed to being treated by a rake to the possessive pronoun, Angelica blinked and stared. "I don't take spirits, sir."

"Simon," he repeated, retreating not one inch. "You will in this instance make an exception—to oblige me, Miss Smith."

Prey to a suspicion that ladies generally did oblige Simon Brisbane, and a further suspicion that if she did not oblige him he would force the brandy down her throat, Angelica drank. She choked and coughed, wiped the moisture from her cheeks, then stared up at him. He returned her regard. Angelica dared another sip from the snifter she now held. On second tasting, the liquor wasn't half-bad. "Nor," said Simon, "do I intend to dismiss you. My father has taken a rare liking to you. I am not a cruel man, Miss Smith."

"No. I do understand," Angelica said somberly, "why you are under the necessity of having Sir Randall, er, chaperoned. He is a little imprudent, but surely his little eccentricities—"

"My father is *damned* imprudent, Miss Smith!" interrupted Simon. "And you are little better, my girl! I am willing to concede that Durward erred in claiming you are the slyest thing in nature—but an assignation in a *cemetery*? Don't poker up! I know my father inveigled you into accompanying him there. Perhaps I should explain his fascination with the place. Old habits die hard, and that cemetery is the site of—"

"I beg you will say no more!" Angelica recalled Mallet and Bimble, and her conviction that Sir Randall was prone to undertake his own resurrection work. "Who would have thought—I still find it hard to credit—but you must not fear that I will plunge you into scandal! I assure you my lips are silent as the—er. The secret is safe with me."

What secret was this? wondered Simon. Had his enterprising parent gotten into some mischief of which even Durward was unaware? Clearly Miss Smith would bear cultivating.

No one knew better how to coax a reluctant bloom to blossom than Simon Brisbane. He flicked Miss Smith's cheek with a careless finger. "Tell me, shall I apologize to you?"

Startled, Angelica touched her cheek. "For what?"

"That will teach me to overrate myself," Simon murmured. Still she looked uncomprehending. "For kissing you, little hornet!"

"Oh, *that*!" Angelica laughed and rose. "I don't regard it, I assure you!"

So much for pursuits floricultural, Simon thought ruefully. There was no doubt that Miss Smith had meant exactly what she'd said.

Ten

Even as these various dramatic events took place, April yielded the stage to May. The weather improved, if only marginally: the perpetual snow and fogs that had led Lord Byron to complain that Lord Castlereagh had taken over the foreign affairs of the Kingdom of Heaven gave way to rain. A week after the poet's hasty departure from England, to which he was never to return, Princess Charlotte, in a shimmering silver wedding dress and a wreath of diamond roses selected from the stock of Messrs. Rundell and Bridge, married her obscure German prince. This grand occasion took place at Carlton House, and a mob of hundreds clapped and cheered in the streets outside while the bride and groom knelt on crimson velvet cushions beneath candlesticks six feet tall.

For many inhabitants of London, even a royal wedding was not sufficient cause to disrupt daily routine. One such individual was Valerian Millikin, whose daily routine was a great deal more sacred to him than any religious ceremony, even a ceremony complete with six-foot high candlesticks. In point of fact, so absorbed was Valerian in his various endeavors that he had never heard of Prince Leopold of Saxe-Coburg-Saalfeld.

Even so, Valerian's routine had already been mightily disarranged on this particular day. His duties as a member of the honorary medical staff of St. Bartholomew's Hospital—founded in 1123 by a Roman monk, Rahere—were not arduous, and required his attention only twice a week. On one day he went his complete round of the hospital; on the other, which this day was, he saw out-patients and dealt with emergencies. Few emergencies had awaited him, and Valerian had returned to his lodgings in a cheerful frame of mind, only to find dishevelled and gasping on his doorstep a grave emergency indeed.

If illness had prompted this startling degeneration of the only sister whom Valerian held in affection, it was no physically debilitating malady: the first words to pass Angelica's lips expressed a very poor view of Valerian's dislike of bestirring himself. Though a less devious individual might have been rendered indignant by so censorious a judgment, Valerian's curiosity was pricked. Lest bystanders interpret this windblown harridan as indicative of the quality of his healing gifts, or of his personal preferences, Valerian ushered her into a grisly chamber of horrors known as his specimen room.

During that brief journey, Angelica's exhortations did not cease. Rosemary's problems grew daily more complex, she confided. Now it appeared very much as if Chalmers had begun to scent a rat, and even more like Rosemary would at any moment succumb to a fever of the brain. Meanwhile the others—

Here Valerian interrupted with a blunt inquiry as to why Angelica should think he wished to be regaled with the latest fits and starts enacted by what's-her-name. Surely Angelica must know him better than that? At the notion she might not, Angelica laughed outright. Valerian frowned and sniffed and demanded to be told why his eldest sister had brandy on her breath.

Angelica explained. She was not in her altitudes, she quickly pointed out, nor even a trifle foxed; her excessive good spirits were the result of laughing rather a lot. Angelica had not found much to laugh about of late—a gentle hint that was an exercise in futility. Ah, well, Marigold's offspring were not Valerian's concern. Thought of offspring recalled to Angelica the source of her recent amusement, and she recounted her meeting with Simon Brisbane.

As has already been established, Valerian was an unnatural sort of brother, and thus evinced no dismay that
88

Angelica had made the acquaintance of a hardened rakeshame. On the intelligence that the rakeshame had ardently embraced her, he raised a brow; on the further intelligence that Angelica had refused an apology for that grave misconduct, which she appeared to view as an excellent good joke, he lowered it again. Obviously Angelica was immune to the blandishments of Simon Brisbane.

That point settled to his satisfaction—Valerian was fond of Angelica and would not have happily watched her led astray—he set himself to ease her worries. Some solution to the problems of what's-her-name would present itself, he promised; meantime she could but patiently persevere. But he was not unsympathetic, and it was unfair of Angelica to accuse him of being a lazy fribble who'd left her in the lurch. In proof of his good heart, Valerian prescribed for his long-suffering sister syrup of poppies and a hot brick.

After Angelica's departure, accomplished in what is best described as a huff, Valerian was not left long to enjoy his solitude. Angelica was not the sole member of the family to recall the existence of her elder sibling; Valerian was privileged to receive in his specimen room no less distinguished a visitor than his aristocratic brother-in-law.

Lord Chalmers did not immediately announce the purpose of this unprecedented call, but politely introduced himself and embarked upon a conversation that might have been expressly meant to set Valerian at ease. That there was no need for such effort, Valerian did not explain; nor did he reveal the amusement that Lord Chalmers's petty condescension aroused in him. Valerian Millikin awarded awed deference to no man—or, for that matter, deity.

Be that as it may, and was, the gentlemen conversed. They discussed the Foundling Hospital, the conditions in which had so greatly improved since the institution's inception in 1739 that now only one in six children died; the difficulties faced by young apprentices, such as being forced into crime or being framed by thief-takers for crimes of which they were innocent; the unhappy fact that many of London's prostitutes were girls even younger than the age of consent, which was twelve, and the difficulty of securing a conviction for rape. At this point, Valerian grew weary of the exchange. "You have not sought me out to talk of this! Just why *did* you come?"

Lord Chalmers, who had expected to find Valerian as mutton-headed as all the Millikins except Angelica, and who was not wholly convinced that Valerian was not similarly want-witted, made a slight gesture of concession. "It is a slightly difficult situation—but you *are* the head of the family."

Devoutly, Valerian hoped he wasn't to be subjected to yet another tedious account of what's-her-name and the Chalmers sapphires. "Head of the family?" he echoed, with a crack of laughter. "Don't let my stepmother hear you say that or there'll be the devil to pay! Moreover, *I* don't want the tending of a pack of silly widgeons—no offense, you understand, to what's-her-name!"

To say that Lord Chalmers was visibly taken aback by this blunt rejoinder would be to understate the baron's sangfroid; but he definitely exhibited a slight degree of stupefaction. "What's-her-name?"

"Your wife." Valerian was not impressed with his brother-in-law's powers of intellect. "She's your problem, not mine. It's been years since I laid eyes on the chit, and don't think I regret the fact! I'm a busy man, and I've no time for hare-brained females, excepting Angelica, and she's not generally hare-brained. Although I suspect if she spends much time with Marigold's gooseish brats, she soon enough will be!"

The entire Millikin family, present company included, was very much of an oddity. "You misunderstand," said Lord Chalmers, with admirable composure. "Naturally I would not apply to you concerning my wife. Nor do I seek to involve you in the, er, problems of the family."

"Excellent!" responded Valerian. "Because I don't mind admitting that I'd as lief not be!"

"One of the matters I wished to discuss with you," Lord Chalmers persevered, "concerns Angelica. It has been brought to my attention that she has been absenting herself from my house, without escort or explanation, almost every afternoon."

Definitely stiff-rumped! decided Valerian. He couldn't

blame what's-her-name for not wanting to confide her financial difficulties to this cold fish. But that was what's-her-name's affair, and none of his. Thought of affairs recalled to Valerian that Angelica had made mention of a lady-bird. Chalmers didn't *look* the sort of man to have a high-flyer tucked away, Valerian mused, peering intently at him.

"You are shocked." Lord Chalmers misinterpreted that basilisk stare. "Believe me, I intend no slur on Angelica's character! I am convinced that there must be some innocent explanation of these disappearances."

Obviously Lord Chalmers was determined to discover what that explanation might be; very well, Valerian would provide him one. "Oh, yes! Just moments past, Angelica left me." No more than man or God did he revere veracity.

Lord Chalmers struggled toward comprehension, a progress that had suddenly grown prodigiously laborious. "Angelica comes *here*?"

"Didn't I just say so?" inquired Valerian.

Lord Chalmers thought he had, but could not be sure. "Why the need for secrecy? You are Angelica's brother, surely she may visit you openly?" Valerian's derisive expression caused him to reconsider. "You mean—your stepmother?"

"The incomparable Marigold!" Valerian supplied helpfully.

Though Lord Chalmers suspected there was a great deal about this matter that he had failed to grasp—why should Angelica and Valerian conspire to keep their stepmother ignorant of their association? Was the bird-witted Marigold prone to vengeful wrath? And why should Marigold care whether they associated or not?—he let the subject drop. Angelica was a creature of great good sense, and could be trusted to conduct herself in accordance with the dictates of propriety. "There is another matter on which I wish your viewpoint."

"If it's only my viewpoint you want, you're welcome to it!" Vastly relieved that no more strenuous effort would be required of him, Valerian flung himself carelessly into a chair. "You may unburden yourself!"

Lord Chalmers did not do so immediately, but paced

around the room, the walls of which were lined with shelves. On those shelves, on tables and in cabinets, were countless specimens, dry and in spirits and stuffed, a brief sampling of which included individual peculiarities of plants and animals, monsters and mummies; skulls of the five great divisions of the human race; examples of the development of the brain and spinal marrow from the knotted cord of crustacea upwards through fishes, reptiles and birds to the brain and spinal cord of mammalia; teeth, from the beaks of birds to the tusks of boars; instances of the effects of disease on brains, hearts, lungs, stomachs, intestines, spleens and kidneys. Although Lord Chalmers's demeanor was that of a man keenly interested in the wonders so lavishly displayed, this guise was misleading; the lord's concentration was turned inward. He was pondering the antics of the various young ladies in residence beneath his roof.

At least Angelica's conduct was explained, if not entirely to his satisfaction. He supposed he should be grateful for the resolution of one problem out of three. With Rosemary's megrims he did not intend to acquaint Valerian; since the eldest of the Millikins was not on terms of even nodding acquaintance with his younger sisters, Valerian could hardly offer an explanation of why Rosemary grew daily more distant and distrait. That left only Lily.

It was not Lily's conduct that posed Lord Chalmers a dilemma; Lily had done nothing untoward, although her habit of daily waxing more loquacious about a different one of her admirers—most often Messrs. Meadowcraft or Gildensleeve, Steptoe or Pettijohn—was a trifle exasperating. Lord Chalmers's dilemma as to Lily focused not on the young lady herself, but on the most determined of her suitors, whom she appeared to regard in an avuncular light, and who was also Chalmers's friend. Naturally he was disposed in Lord Kingscote's favor. All the same, he did not wish to be unfair. Nor did he want to prejudice Valerian in one direction or the other. Wondering how best to broach so delicate a matter to so plain-spoken and disinterested a mediator, the baron paced the floor.

Valerian watched, content to let the silence deepen; despite Chalmers's assurances, Valerian suspected that whatever confidences were granted him would not be free of ulterior motive. Since Valerian had no intention of exerting himself on anyone's behalf, regardless of whatever strong motivation toward such exertion was presented him, he was not at all distressed.

He watched and pondered the situation between Lord Chalmers and his wife, as explained by Angelica. Rosemary appeared to have taken to life among the aristocracy like a swimming-bird to water, playing ducks and drakes with her husband's fortune as if to the manner born. Chalmers, conscious of his rank, yet the perfect gentleman in all he said and did, would not relish his wife's irresponsibility. A tantalizing situation! Valerian wondered what would come of it.

That he wondered must not be interpreted as evidence of fraternal concern. Valerian was not even momentarily tempted to apprise Chalmers that his family sapphires were in hock. If Rosemary could not bring herself to confess the whole to her husband, which was clearly her only reasonable course of action, Lord Chalmers's enlightenment was not Valerian's responsibility. Enlightenment was bound to dawn on Chalmers, eventually. Meanwhile the situation daily grew more entertaining.

Nor, as he had bluntly informed her, did Valerian intend to offer Angelica any assistance in her attempts to row Rosemary out of the River Tick. Valerian was above all dispassionate, an impartial observer who derived vast amusement from the antics of his fellow-men; he had no compunction about manipulating them into position, but beyond that it was his rule to never interfere. Though Valerian set events in action, he didn't make the error of anticipating the outcome. Valerian's pleasure derived from the development of a situation, and he observed the behavior of his subjects as sharply as he attended his laboratory animals—but Valerian subscribed to the scientific theory, and as any scientist knows, tampering with the process negates the validity of the experiment.

Unaware that his host compared him to a laboratory rat in a particularly tricky maze, Lord Chalmers spoke. "I have hesitated to speak of this," he said, rather unnecessarily from Valerian's point of view, "but in all conscience I must. It concerns your sister Lily." He went on to explain that the young lady had the opportunity to form an extremely eligible connection, to settle in matrimony with a gentleman of superior breeding and wealth, about whom not one adverse comment could be made, unless it was that he was old enough to be her father. "He has not made an offer yet," concluded Lord Chalmers, "but I'm sure he will. He is most attentive, escorting her everywhere she may wish."

Valerian had heard out this account with growing disappointment; it smacked of the mundane. "That's all well and good, but why drag *me* into it?"

Lord Chalmers had developed no great liking for his eldest brother-in-law during this first of their encounters; in truth, Chalmers privately hoped that this first encounter would be the last. Still, Valerian *was* head of the family, and as such the final authority on the disposition of his younger siblings. This, the baron explained. Since Valerian appeared most unappreciative of the honor thus bestowed on him, Chalmers additionally explained that he could not honorably urge a damsel in residence beneath his roof to encourage his friend. On the other hand, if his friend was doomed to disappointment, Lord Chalmers was by honor bound to try and check the growing strength of his attachment. It was, the baron confessed, a very pretty puzzle, to the solving of which he could not see his way clear.

Tactfully, Valerian refrained from commenting that he failed to see why the baron was involved with the puzzle in the first place. "You've overlooked one vital point: what does the chit think?"

"Lily?" It had occurred to Lord Chalmers neither that Lily might have a viewpoint in the matter nor, if she did, that her opinion might signify. "She seems to like him well enough."

"Very near perfection, is she?" inquired Valerian. "To attract so very superior a gentleman, the chit must be. As I recall, they *all* were. Except Angelica, that is."

For this slur upon the only sensible member of the Millikin family, Lord Chalmers liked his eldest brother-in-law even
94

less. "I have always found Angelica a very superior young lady," he said stiffly.

"Oh, Angelica *is* perfection!" Valerian responded immediately. "I've thought so for years. All the same, it won't do for *you* to think so, because you're married to what's-her-name. You're not hankering after Angelica, I hope? I wouldn't like to have a divorce in the family. Which, now that I consider it, is probably the only point on which that ninny-hammer Marigold and I would agree."

Bewildered by this abrupt attack, Lord Chalmers protested that he was satisfied with his current wife, and that no thought of divorce had ever entered his mind. "Content, are you?" queried Valerian, looking inquisitive. Hastily, Lord Chalmers turned the conversation into less personal channels: "We were speaking of Lily."

"So we were." Contemplatively, Valerian crossed his long legs at the knee. "I don't know what you expect me to do about it, Chalmers—in fact, if you expect me to do anything, you're all about in the head!—but I can tell you now the chit will have nothing to say to him."

Lord Chalmers did not credit that even Lily would be that bacon-brained. His concern was not with Lily's acceptance of Lord Kingscote's suit; if that suit were proffered, he could not imagine Lily would turn it down. What *did* concern him, he explained in clear and simple language, was that Lily and Lord Kingscote might not be well-matched.

"Don't worry your head about it!" Valerian rose. "From what I hear of the chit, she'd never do anything so sensible as to accept someone so eligible. Her last infatuation was with a penniless poet who wrote sonnets to her earlobes, you know." It was evident from Lord Chalmers's expression that he had *not* known. "There, that's settled! Anytime I can be of service, don't hesitate to call on me!" Valerian whisked himself out the door, allegedly to deal with an urgent case of measles that awaited in his anteroom, actually to relate this encounter with his starched-up brother-in-law to his elderly housekeeper, with such irreverent gusto that they both succumbed to whoops. In a far from cheerful mood, Lord Chalmers found his own way out into the street.

Eleven

Although Lord Chalmers had not included Fennel among the Millikins in residence beneath the venerable roof of Chalmers House who had given their host cause for worry, he might well have done so; Fennel's sojourn in London had not been devoid of excursions and alarms, although Fennel did not view his progress in that light. Fennel considered that he was having a great deal of a lark, and found it all jolly good fun.

These matters he was explaining to Lily. As fog had not, the threat of rain did not keep the Millikins confined within doors; no impending downpour, no bleak and brooding clouds, no oppressive atmosphere could quench the exuberance of the younger members of that family. Since Lily's suitors were much less intrepid, Fennel and Lily—en route to Astley's Royal Amphitheater, which Lily had liked so well on her first visit that she had persuaded Fennel to take her back again— were *tête-à-tête*.

Fennel had no objection to squiring Lily to Astley's; the entertainment there, based on superb equestrian feats, was just the sort that appealed most to him. Fennel failed to understand what attracted his sisters to Almack's and the theaters; the former he adjudged very shabby, and the quality of the refreshments—stale bread and lemonade—as very much below par; the latter he deemed an even greater bore. Not for Fennel were the crowded interiors of the King's Theater in the Haymarket, Covent Garden, Drury Lane; he had as little liking for the bejeweled members of the *ton* who glittered in their boxes as for the actors who minced across the stage. Moreover, even if the decorations of the theaters were splendid, as he'd been assured they were, the wretched places were forever burning down.

Nor was Fennel appreciative of the routs and *soirées* so highly favored by his sisters; he intensely disliked standing for hours crushed against a wall or flattened on a staircase, copiously perspiring, listening to his fellow sufferers bemoan the dreadful squeeze. The gentlemen's clubs, Brook's and White's, to which Lord Chalmers had taken him, won from Fennel no plaudits: Fennel thought it ridiculous that grown men should have nothing better to do with their time than to quiz one another and slander the majority of their acquaintance, befuddle their senses with liquor and spend ruinous hours at the card tables. Cockfighting and bullbaiting did not interest Fennel, who had seen his fill of such gory sport in the country. Boxing he approved, and the occasional horse race; but one could not spend all one's time watching two bruisers pound one another to a pulp, or waiting to see which bit of blood finished first.

No sympathy need be squandered on Fennel, however, despite his disfavor with the fashionable diversions so dear to the *beau monde*; Fennel had managed to amuse himself tolerably well, as he was telling Lily.

"Thought she was a trifle bosky!" he explained, as with an appreciative eye he observed how Lord Chalmers's coachman tooled the ribbons of his lordship's calash with praiseworthy ease, his lordship's bays being less optimistic about the oppressive weather than were the calash's occupants. "She was talking like a nodcock, catechizing and sermonizing for quite an hour, saying I'd led Phoebe to make a byword of herself, which is a great piece of nonsense because *I* ain't the one who threw out lures!"

"Gracious!" gasped Lily, blue eyes alight. "Fennel, describe her to me."

"Oh, a dragon!" Fennel obliged. "Breathing fire and brimstone, I swear it!"

"No, no!" Lily giggled. "Not Phoebe's mama, Phoebe!"

Fennel squinted with concentration, trying to envision the features which he'd once thought so remarkable, and which, in point of fact, he'd seen but recently. Try as he might, those features would not come clear. "Dashed if I can!" he confessed cheerfully. "She's just another girl, puss. Can't hold a candle to you or Rosemary."

That the unknown Phoebe could shine with a brilliance equal to that of the dazzling Millikins—always excepting Angelica—had not crossed Lily's mind. Now that it did so, she giggled again at the absurdity. "You must remember *some*thing about her, Fennel! What was the color of her hair? Her eyes? Was she short or tall, plump or slender?"

"Short," responded Fennel, "and plump. Dark hair and brown eyes. Rosy cheeks and cherry lips, a fine vulgar miss. To tell truth, I don't know what I ever saw in her!"

Lily could have ventured a guess, having long acquaintance with calf-love. A gentleman's first attack of that malady, she thought, was apt to be severe; but Fennel seemed to have recovered as abruptly as he'd succumbed. "A brief madness," she said wisely. "The family are prone to such. Except Angelica, of course! What else did Phoebe's mama say to you?"

"Oh, all sorts of skimble-skamble stuff." Fennel grinned. "The entire afflicting interview was occupied with my shabby behavior; she said I'd played fast and loose with Phoebe, offered her false coin, and then when Phoebe's affections had become fixed that I began to declare off altogether, leaving the chit to wear the willow for me!"

"Goodness!" uttered Lily, round-eyed. "Maybe she was smoking you, Fennel."

"Trying to hoodwink me, you mean! Saying I'd made a dead-set at Phoebe and trifled with her affections and cast her off like a Paphian girl!" Fennel frowned. "I ain't sure she's *not* a Paphian girl, think on it! It's certain she ain't a well brought-up young woman. Anyway, *she* set her cap at *me*!"

"Fennel!" Lily's exquisite countenance was positively animated. "You didn't— *she* didn't—you know what I mean!"

"I do?" Fennel's expression indicated the opposite. "Oh, *that*! Of course I didn't! I didn't even *say* anything improper, or I *think* I didn't, though it's curst hard to remember. At least I'm *sure* I didn't offer the wench my heart and hand, like her mama claims I did."

"She does?" To Lily, her brother's account had begun to sound ominous. "Fennel, what did you say?"

"Said it was all a fudge! I never liked the chit *that* well. And for the old dragon to claim Phoebe wishes to put a period to her life on my account is so much twaddle, because Phoebe was sitting there the whole time, and she didn't look the least bit plunged into grief. You know what, puss? It's my notion the old dragon is playing a deep game."

Lily ruminated upon this viewpoint. "Why should she?"

Fennel's grin widened. "For high stakes, and that's the cream of the jest! The dragon's taken it into her head that the family's well-heeled!"

Though this remark might have stricken one member of the family with dread, that member the perspicacious Angelica, Lily found the suggestion that the Millikins might have a shilling with which to bless themselves delightfully absurd. Fennel regarded his chortling sister tolerantly. "Stands to reason, I collect!" he remarked. "Rosemary's married to Chalmers, who's rich as Croesus, even if he is reluctant to part with his blunt; and the *on-dit* around town is that you're plump in the pocket. So the dragon conjectured I was likewise blessed."

"Me?" Lily gasped ungrammatically, the rules of English usage being among the numerous things beyond the grasp of the Millikin intellect. "That's ridiculous!"

"*I* know that, but the dragon don't." Fennel laughed aloud at memory of the interview. "I tried to tell her how it is with us, but she accused me of spinning her a Canterbury story. As if I *could*! And then she said I was a scoundrel of the first water, and *I* said she should take a damper because she was coming it too strong! Thought she'd swoon from the shock, but she didn't! Instead she said she understood perfectly well how it was, that I had a decided partiality for Phoebe and was only pretending to be tiring of her company because I was afraid my family wouldn't approve."

"Mercy, Fennel!" Lily no longer looked amused. "Why shouldn't the family approve?"

"Dashed if I know!" Fennel pondered the matter. "Maybe because Phoebe ain't quite the thing. You know what Rosemary is! Deuced high in the instep! And I don't know why she should be, because she only married into the nobs. For that matter, the way she's going on I don't see she has any reason to rip up at us!"

"Poor soul!" murmured the kind-hearted Lily. Since Fennel did not know to whom she referred, he made no comment. Wearing her vaguest look, Lily studied him. "You could always elope! I have always thought elopements the most romantic of all things! Rosemary couldn't kick up too much of a dust once the knot was tied—and you wouldn't care even if she did, because you'd already have your Phoebe. It is the perfect solution, Fennel! I marvel that you didn't think of it!"

"You needn't!" retorted Fennel. "I don't want to elope!"

"Well, I do consider that poor-spirited! There would be a little talk, I expect, but it is very cow-hearted of you to stick at a little scandal when by it you could be happy as a grig!"

"But I don't want to be married!" Fennel protested, with praiseworthy patience. "Don't see how you could take so maggoty a notion into your head! Or I do see, because it is very like you, but you can forget it! I'll be hanged if I marry Phoebe!"

"Now that," Lily responded sternly, "is shabby! I don't think Rosemary would approve your setting up the girl under your protection any more than your marriage. Moreover, you have no money, so you could not provide for her. I think you should reconsider, Fennel!"

Fennel did so, and thought his only prudent course of action might be to remove himself from London immediately. But Fennel no more possessed the virtue of prudence than did any of his siblings, so he dismissed that milk-livered notion immediately and embarked upon the difficult task of persuading his indignant sister that he had no aspiration to frolic among the muslin company. Lily cast him a reproachful glance. "You needn't try and bamboozle me."

"As if I would! Listen, puss: even if I wanted to elope, which I don't, I couldn't; the dragon wouldn't stand for it. I'm telling you the truth, on the square!" Again, that irrepressible grin. "I haven't told you the best part! The dragon says that unless I wish to come under the gravest censure, I must do what is highly fit and proper, and marry Phoebe. And if I *don't* come up to scratch, she vows she will bring a breach of promise suit!"

Lily, whose miffs were of as short duration as her powers of concentration, had regained her habitually happy frame of mind. Still, she was not convinced that the dragon's oath was as amusing as Fennel found it. "What," she inquired with interest, "is a breach of promise suit?"

"I ain't exactly sure, but I think it's something to do with making a promise and then shabbing off. Nothing to worry about, I assure you! I'm *sure* I didn't pop the question! Can't be sued for declarations I didn't make, eh?"

Lily puzzled over the matter, and supposed that he could not. All in all, she thought that Fennel had not played his cards excellently well.

"Fits of folly!" he agreed cheerfully, when taxed with this judgment. "No harm done! Now tell me what you've been up to."

Lily was happy to do so, and regaled her brother with merry accounts of her gay life, as well as titillating tidbits of gossip, chief among which was a very mysterious affair between Lord Buckingham and Sir Thomas Hardy and Lady Hardy, which had led to a duel between the two men. From this Lily progressed to family affairs, speculation upon the strained relationship between Lord and Lady Chalmers, further speculation upon the inexplicable behavior exhibited by Angelica, and a possible explanation thereof.

"Lawks!" said Fennel, when gifted with Lily's theory that their eldest sister was embarked upon a clandestine romance. "*Angelica?*"

"Yes." Lily looked concerned. "At first I thought it was a very good thing because poor Angelica so seldom has any *fun*. But it has been going on for weeks now, and I fear the matter has grown serious. I can only think the gentleman is *most* unsuitable, Fennel, else she would not behave so furtively! He could be a fortune hunter, or worse!"

Here Fennel displayed a flash of the shrewdness with

which the Millikins were very occasionally blessed. He pointed out that fortune hunters seldom dangled after ladies who hadn't a shilling with which to grace themselves.

"Yes, but if people think *we* are well-heeled—your Phoebe's mama thought so, remember, and so do Meadowcraft and Gildensleeve, Steptoe and Pettijòhn—they will think Angelica is also!" Lily grasped her brother's arm. "We must prevent Angelica from falling prey to some rogue, Fennel! I have thought and thought, and there is only one solution: we must marry her off quickly to someone who *is* eligible."

So taken by surprise was Fennel at the hitherto unconceived notion that the ugly duckling of the family should marry anyone, that he didn't even protest that Lily was putting sad creases in his sleeve. "You are certainly concerned about this, puss."

"Concerned? Of course I am! First I thought that I might marry her off to Meadowcraft or Gildensleeve, Steptoe or Pettijohn, but upon reflection I decided that not one of them would do. Meadowcraft and I have had much conversation about Angelica, and he admires her greatly, but his mind is of a mean and little structure and I suspect he praises Angelica only to please me. Gildensleeve and I have had a great deal of joking about many things, and he is most amusing, but his accounts are in the most dreadful tangle. Steptoe and I are wondrous great together and we talk serious matters over by the half-hour—rather he talks and I listen, because I do not understand such stuff—but he is a vain, silly fellow and thinks too highly of himself. Pettijohn says everything kind and civil to me, but he won't do, either, because his cousins assure me he is most often sulky as a bear."

Distracted from the main topic of conversation by this spate of words, Fennel made free to inquire which among her suitors Lily favored. In his opinion, neither Meadowcraft nor Gildensleeve, Steptoe nor Pettijohn, was up to snuff.

"No," sighed Lily. "Beside, I have decided it must be a peer. I suppose I will have to settle for Lord Kingscote."

"Kingscote?" echoed Fennel. "He's old enough to be your father, puss!"

Lily looked startled. "Not for me, silly! For Angelica! Lord Kingscote is wealthy and well-connected and *clever*! And he assures me that he admires Angelica's mind."

In Fennel's admittedly limited experience, gentlemen did not marry ladies out of admiration for their mental faculties, but he hesitated to point this out to Lily, whose heart was so obviously set on a match between Angelica and Lord Kingscote. He did point out, gently, that he had not noticed Lord Kingscote exhibiting any marked preference for Angelica.

"I don't know how he can," retorted Lily, "when she's never around! I vow I am almost out of patience with her. No matter how I scheme to bring them together, Angelica always slips away, and I am left to entertain Lord Kingscote. It is no great trouble, you understand, because he is a very amiable gentleman—but sometimes I despair of ever bringing the thing off."

Another flash of intuition struck Fennel, an unprecedented event in that the Millikins were seldom clever twice in one week, let alone in one day: he thought that it was not with the purpose of becoming acquainted with the elusive Angelica that Lord Kingscote made Lily such flattering overtures. Delicately, he inquired whether Lily had informed the gentleman of his proposed fate.

Lily giggled. "Of course not! 'Twould be most ill-advised. Like leading a horse to water after the barn door has been closed —or do I have that right? Lord Kingscote may have a suspicion, because I make it a point to speak kindly of Angelica and he is a *very* knowing one. So you see it's all right, because if he *minded*, he wouldn't keep coming back again!"

Fennel had been mulling over the addition of Lord Kingscote to the family. It was not a bad notion, he decided; Lord Kingscote might be in his dotage, but from all one heard he was quite extraordinarily wealthy, and seemed quite civil. Though Fennel was not mercenary, he was worldly enough to realize that wealthy bridegrooms were highly desirable additions to a family whose pockets were perennially to let. Kingscote and Angelica? It suited Fennel very well, providing the gentleman didn't mind. However, he suspected that the gentleman might.

Accordingly, Fennel dropped a subtle hint. "Kingscote's a peer! Tell you what, Lily, you ought to marry him yourself!"

"Marry Kingscote? *Me*?" Lilly looked confounded. "Fennel, you've taken leave of your wits!"

Maybe, and maybe not; a conviction had taken root in the virgin soil of Fennel's brain, and he was not to be easily dissuaded from what he now realized would be an admirable solution to a great many difficulties. Precisely how to bring about so happy a state of affairs, Fennel did not yet know, but he was sure he *could* bring it about, did he but set his mind to it, which he intended to do. In the interim, Lily must not get the wind up. To this end, Fennel pinched his sister's cheek. "Doubtless you're right!" he conceded gracefully. "You ain't in Kingscote's style."

That Lily might not be in the style of any gentleman who came within her orbit had not previously occurred to her. She sampled the notion, and found it distasteful. "Poppycock!" said Lily.

Twelve

Since Angelica was not among the rapidly increasing number of people who were aware of the schemes Lily harbored for her eldest sister and the wealthy and well-connected and clever, if decrepit, Lord Kingscote, she felt no compunction about absenting herself from Chalmers House, as usual, the following afternoon. When this absence was discovered, Lily came very close to throwing the first temper-storm of her life, and expressed to Fennel a strong desire to lock Angelica in her room. Then, with a pungent remark about barred barn doors and thirsty horses, she set herself, in the absence of her sister, to console Lord Kingscote, and to prove additionally to her own satisfaction that she was very much in the style most liked by *all* the gentlemen, even one of such advanced years. Lord Kingscote, who at even the stupendous age of eight-and-thirty retained possession of all his faculties, and who was therefore well aware of what fate Lily planned for him and consequently better entertained by her efforts than ever he had been before, professed himself sadly cast down by what strongly appeared to be a singular string of ill-luck, and then bore Lily off for a ride in his dashing *vis-à-vis*, a treat both he and Lily enjoyed very well.

Angelica, meantime, had made her way to Sir Randall's house, had been directed by Williams to the garden, had discovered there not only Sir Randall but his scapegrace son. Both men turned toward her and smiled. Simon Brisbane, Angelica discovered, was no less damnably attractive on second meeting than he had been on first. Sedately she entered the garden, settled herself as requested by her employer on the marble bench, whereupon Sir Randall proffered paper, pen and ink, and announced an intention to embark upon the writing of his memoirs.

In this activity, they were engaged for some time. Sir Randall dictated; Angelica wrote down his words as rapidly as she could; Simon observed the proceedings silently. Angelica was very much aware of the harsh features that were turned toward her, the keen green eyes that were most often fixed on her face. Several times she had to interrupt her employer and ask that he go back a space because she'd lost the thread of his reminiscence.

Sir Randall exhibited no impatience that his amanuensis should display a loss of the ability to concentrate; in point of fact, he did not appear the least bit surprised that her mind should wander in that way. After all, was it not Angelica's responsibility to keep a firm rein on her bird-witted siblings, as well as to redeem the Chalmers sapphires? Nor had Simon adverse comment to make, though his harsh features bore an expression of distinct amusement. Fortunately, Angelica, her head bent over her paper and pen, did not observe those twinkling eyes, else she would have deduced, and correctly, that Simon knew she was far from oblivious to his presence.

That presence was very fine, clad in the attire requisite for riding in Hyde Park: blue coat with brass buttons, snowy linen and intricately pleated cravat, leather breeches and top-boots; and it displayed to excellent advantage a manly physique. Broad shoulders and narrow waist and—Well! Angelica decided to ask Valerian about this giddiness that afflicted her on sight of Simon Brisbane. Perhaps there was some simple medical explanation, some disease that included among its symptoms palpitations and an oppression that settled on the breast. That Angelica was an innocent in matters of the heart need hardly be explained; nor that the member of the Milli-kin family whom Lord Chalmers trusted to be always prudent, and the other members of the family trusted to be immune to fits of folly, was unwittingly embarked upon a most serious madness. The cool and sensible Angelica had fallen under the spell of a magnificent profligate, in which development can be found a most salutary moral: even ladies of great good common sense may conjure up visions of cloud-cuckoo-land.

Among the people ignorant of this departure from good sense was not Simon Brisbane. Wise in the ways of women, as well he should have been—let there be no doubt of the matter: Simon was a remorseless rakehell; his far from blame-less reputation had been very fairly earned—his lively sense of humor was still tickled by the unpredictable Miss Smith. Were she the designing woman Durward proclaimed her, he reflected, she had but recently embarked upon her infamous career. That Miss Smith was fascinated by a man so visibly used up by dissipation as himself strongly indicated to Simon that the lady had never before made the acquaintance of a reprobate. Since London teemed with such, and since it was a strange adventuress who had never encountered her male counterpart, Miss Smith was either new to London, or no adventuress. With the view of learning which explanation was correct, Simon interrupted Sir Randall's soliloquy, pointed out that Miss Smith's fingers must be quite cramped, and suggested tea.

"My dear Miss Smith!" cried Sir Randall. "You should have told me I was overtaxing your strength. Here, let me relieve you of this, and that—there! Now are you quite comfortable."

Angelica was anything but comfortable; outdoor gardens on cool if sunny days were not her idea of settings most conducive to the penning of memoirs, especially when such activity was conducted under the clear green gaze of a hardened rakeshame. "Perfectly comfortable, thank you!" she responded, in a tone she fancied was brisk and businesslike, and which might have been precisely that, had not her throat gone dry. She glanced at Simon. "Your father's memoirs promise to be most interesting, don't you agree?"

Simon quirked an auburn brow. "Dull stuff!" said he. "If you wish to make your fortune, Papa, you must be a great deal more libellous. Look at Caro Lamb, and that book of hers. You have read *Glenarvon*, Miss Smith? Then I take leave to explain to you that 'Glenarvon' is meant to be Byron. 'Buchanan' is Sir Godfrey Webster; 'Lady Mandeville' is Lady Oxford; 'Lady Augusta' is both Lady Jersey and Lady Collier—but you look doubtful! I assure you it is true; Caro told me so herself."

"Caro Lamb?" Angelica echoed, curious. "I have heard the strangest tales—that she dressed up like a page and hid herself in Byron's rooms."

"Where he eventually appeared with another lady-friend in tow," said Simon. "There was quite a rowdy-do."

"Here's Williams with the tea!" interrupted Sir Randall, before his aggravating offspring could issue further provocation, as it was clear from the offspring's expression that he meant to do.

As a diversion, the tea worked very well. Angelica grasped her cup and occupied herself with peering into its depths, contemplating the lifestyle of a rakeshame, which she vaguely fancied must involve all sort of depraved activities. A lady of gentle birth should not know of such things, alas, and would not dare speak of them—which was rather a pity because

Angelica was developing a keen interest in the subject, indeed was wondering precisely what was involved in an orgy. Meanwhile, Sir Randall balanced a teacup and a biscuit in one hand while with the other he scratched the ears of the shaggy buffalo, and Simon engaged in a tussle with one of the panthers for possession of a sandwich. Simon, too, was deep in contemplation, not of his various depraved pursuits but of the puzzling Miss Smith. His frequent requests of his parent to explain the lady resulted only in blunt suggestions that Simon address his questions to the lady herself. Accordingly, Simon put to her an inquiry concerning the condition of her consumptive parent.

Angelica was not easily roused from her mental foraging among the fleshpots. "My what?"

"Your consumptive parent," repeated Simon, with a Mephistophelean smile. "The one who works her fingers to the bone sewing by candlelight so that her ragged youngsters might have bread on the table once a week. Surely you haven't forgotten her, Miss Smith!"

"How could I?" replied Angelica, who had certainly forgotten that Banbury story, and therefore disliked this demonstration of Simon's excellent memory. "She does as well as can be expected, sir—Simon!"

"You do not like to think of so sad a matter; *I* see!" Simon's saturnine expression indicated that he saw all too clearly. Angelica transferred her gaze once more to her teacup.

"Consumption!" echoed Sir Randall. "My dear Miss Smith!"

"I hope you are paying her a generous wage," Simon persevered. "It is Miss Smith's *role* to keep the wolf from the door, she tells me."

The so-called Miss Smith, cheeks aflame, was at that moment tempted to gift Simon Brisbane with her blunt opinion of his aggravating character. That she did not do so was due to Sir Randall, in whom mention of consumption had sparked reminiscences of the London hospitals. He discussed the protocol of such establishments, where patients were accommodated in lines of parallel beds on each side of the ward, and those patients who were ambulant were required to assist in the work; he commented acerbically upon the offensive odor attendant upon closed windows and bedding that was not frequently enough washed and aired; he put forth the novel viewpoint that patients might recover quicker if their entertainment was not confined to religion, if they were allowed to play at cards and dice and other games, even to curse and swear. These latter activities put him in mind of the female hospital staff, who to a fondness for crude language added a weakness for drink, and who often turned up for work intoxicated, if they turned up for work at all. Then he paused and scowled at his son. "But *you* have no interest in such things."

"How can you say so?" Simon had given up his struggle with the panther and was now popping sandwiches into its grinning jaws. "I fail to understand what in my behavior has led you to believe that I hold the gentle sex in disinterest."

Sir Randall snorted but let this provocation lie. "You can't deny that you're lazy."

"I do deny it." Simon shoved the hopeful panther away and propped a gleaming boot on the marble bench that Angelica shared with the goat. "You have no notion of the exigencies involved in the life of a man of fashion. I must deal with my tailor and my hatter and my boot-maker; I must spend hours in the intricate and painstaking process of creasing down my cravat. Then I must saunter down Bond Street, exhibit myself in all the fashionable spots at the appropriate hour—to say nothing of my practice with the *épée* and my bouts with Gentleman Jackson, my clubs and my bits of blood."

And his high-flyers, silently added Angelica, whose errant thoughts had a shocking tendency to dwell on that forbidden subject. Suddenly, brilliantly, she realized that Simon Brisbane had no notion that she was a lady of gentle birth— if anything, he must think her the opposite. Since he didn't know she was a lady, he could hardly be surprised if she failed to comport herself with decorum and dignity. Therefore she demanded of him an explanation of orgies.

"Miss Smith!" Engaged in stroking the nose of the llama,

which had in an excess of affection deposited its head on his shoulder, Sir Randall looked absurd. He also looked appalled. "What did you say?"

"I suppose I am being vulgarly inquisitive," sighed Angelica, "but I am cursed with an inquiring mind. Since I am very likely to never be freed from the shackles that hamper single ladies, I shall never know what it is like to be, er, unfettered, unless I ask." She gazed beseechingly upon Simon. "Moreover, I am most unlikely to ever have a better opportunity, because it is most unlikely that I shall ever encounter another rakeshame."

"Oh, not so unlikely as all that!" Simon sat down beside Angelica, and the goat, on the marble bench. "We aren't quite so rare. Very well, Miss Smith, I will instruct you with the greatest pleasure. Just what is it you wish to know?"

"Simon!" said Sir Randall, rather awfully. With the llama in tow, he took up a position very near the bench. Simon regarded this chaperone, grinned, and brazenly promised to refrain from making a violent attack on Miss Smith's virtue.

"Palaverer!" Miss Smith responded appreciatively. "I should imagine you're beyond such stuff. A gentleman who has for years been philandering with pretty wenches would hardly conduct himself so indelicately." The expression on Simon's face gave her pause. "*Would* he, sir?"

"He might," Simon retorted, "were the temptation sufficiently great! I freely confess I do not know what to make of you, Miss Smith. One moment you are all propriety, and the next a rag-mannered baggage. I expect that now you will ask me to recount the various escapades and scandals in which I have been involved."

"Oh!" breathed Angelica. "Would you? I vow my heart is quite wrung with envy—not that I could similarly serve as an object lesson in triumphant depravity, of course, but I can see that *you* like it excessively!"

"Good God!" Simon was simultaneously horrified and amused. "What will you say next, you little wretch? And why *can't* you?"

"Why can't I what?" Angelica ignored her employer, who was making grotesquely cautionary gestures at her from behind Simon's back. "Oh! You are in a very teasing mood, I think; I am not at all the sort of female to indulge in *affaires de coeur*. Gracious, *you* must know that! I'll wager that among all the ladies to whom you've paid your court, there was not one who bore the least resemblance to me."

Simon reviewed that long list of bits o' muslin and fair barques of frailty, and was forced to admit that Miss Smith was correct. Obviously his education was shockingly incomplete. He offered to remedy the situation immediately.

"You'll catch cold at that!" chuckled Miss Smith. "I've told you that there's no need to try and turn me up sweet, though it is very kind of you to make the effort! I have been impertinent, and I did not mean to be—I beg your forgiveness. Nor did I mean to sound as if I disapprove of you, because I can understand perfectly how a gentleman might prefer to remain unattached, to flit from flower to flower."

For temerity, Simon accorded Miss Smith full marks; no one had ever before dared compare him to a lustful bumblebee. Never had Simon met a female who made so little effort to administer to his vanity. Because he had not, he began to wonder at the degree of truth in the romantical effusions whispered into his receptive ears by bits o' muslin and fair barques of frailty. Clearly he was not so wise in the ways of women as he had previously thought himself. There was a large gap in his education, a gap which must be bridged before he could again enjoy the honors of his position as a hardened rakeshame.

With an eye to bridging that gap in his education, Simon reached across the goat and touched Miss Smith's hand. The task he had set himself was not an easy one. Miss Smith might be equally fascinated by his dissipations and himself, but she had no understanding of the basis of that fascination, interpreting it as a very natural interest in one of the greatest curiosities that had ever come her way. Simon could not force realization on her, lest with that enlightenment she take fright, thus ruining the pleasure derived by both of them from this bizarre acquaintance. How was he to number among his amorous vagaries a lady who had no notion but to hold him at a distance? It was a pretty puzzle! Moreover, the lady was

111

regarding him quizzically, perhaps because he still retained possession of her hand. "Your fingers are cold!" he said, rather foolishly.

Sir Randall saw his opening and immediately jumped in, with several erudite remarks concerning the body-heat of vegetables, while Simon pondered how best to persuade Miss Smith that she was his favorite of the moment, and Angelica thought wistfully of the countless fair unfortunates privileged to participate with Simon Brisbane in the exhibition of his natural inconstancy. Precisely what that exhibition might involve Angelica could not guess; but even the most innocent of ladies had only to glance at Simon to know that, whatever the practicalities of the matter, he sowed his wild oats with praiseworthy panache.

The shadows had lengthened considerably when Sir Randall ceased to speak; He had progressed from vegetables to folk remedies, sovereign among which were the application of goose dung to alleviate baldness; the placing of a live eel in liquor to ward off drunkenness; the use of grated human skull, mixed with food, to cure fits. He might have continued much longer in this vein had not Simon pointed out the lateness of the hour and the delicate condition of Miss Smith's consumptive parent.

"My dear Miss Smith, you are a perfect angel," said Sir Randall, "to allow me to ramble on this way!" "I," Simon interrupted firmly, "will escort Miss Smith to the gate." Angelica disentangled herself from the goat and placed her hand on Simon's extended arm.

"On one point, at least, my father was correct, Miss Smith," he offered genially. "You are truly not mortal but divine."

Angelica surveyed her escort, rather ironically. "And you, sir, are the most complete hand! Are you seeking to revenge yourself on me for my impertinence? I wouldn't blame you for it! It was abominable in me to be quizzing you that way. You must think me dead to shame."

"Not at all," Simon responded politely. He might easily have explained to Miss Smith why she acted like the greenest of girls in his presence, but he had no wish to sound the

112

veriest coxcomb. "And, as you have pointed out, *I* should know."

If Simon had intended with this gentle reminder of her effronteries to abash his companion, his efforts were for naught. "I don't know why you should wish to put me to the blush," Angelica responded, "but apparently you do. Or are you trying to get up a flirtation? Matters have come to a sad pass when gay and profligate men have no more amusing way to pass their time than trifling with fubsy-faced old maids."

"Fubsy-faced? You?" Simon paused in mid-stride to grasp Miss Smith's delicate chin and tilt up her face. "You actually believe that you're an antidote, eh? And I conjecture you would not credit me if I said you weren't? I thought not. Tiresome creature! But to answer your question, you blush very prettily." Almost absentmindedly, he stroked her cheek. "As for the other—I promise you will have no doubt whatsoever about the matter when I *do* trifle with you!"

"Odious man!" retorted Angelica, blushing once again. "As if you *would*! But here is the gate."

"So it is, fair one." So saying, Simon opened the gardengate, having taken the first step toward closing the large gap in his education. Definitely Simon Brisbane meant to trifle with the mysterious Miss Smith, mightily. Savoring already the sweet thrill of victory, he leaned against the gate and watched his next-scheduled conquest walk down the street.

In this manner, Simon Brisbane fell into an error common among gentlemen of his ilk; to wit, counting chicks still hidden in their shells. Simon's favorite of the present moment was, as has already been stated, without experience in matters of the heart; she truly had no notion of the cause for her giddiness and palpitations, the oppression that had settled on her breast. Yet, even had she understood her symptoms, the outcome would have been the same. Miss Angelica Millikin would have allowed herself to be nibbled to death by ducks before she confessed her nonsensical *tendre* for a hardened rakeshame.

Thirteen

Lord Chalmers paced the floor of his elegant drawing room, then paused before the marble-fronted fireplace to gaze irritably upon his audience of one. Reproachfully, she returned his accusatory stare. "I do think you might have warned me," Lily complained. "I was gone quite giddy with surprise."

Lord Chalmers strove for forbearance, and did not entirely succeed. Had he not enough to deal with? Had not the government at last been forced to reduce expenditures, to jettison the income and malt taxes? Just that morning Castlereagh had spoken sadly of an ignorant impatience of taxation, a sentiment with which Lord Chalmers agreed. Alas, the people were ignorant of the fact that a government deprived of a portion of its income lost an equal portion of its strength. The services had been again drastically cut, the Regent forced to abandon his dream of gracing his metropolis with a new palace, the northward march of Regent Street halted at Piccadilly Circus. Economy was the order of the day. There was even a proposal afoot to send the Elgin Marbles back to Greece. As if that were not enough to drive a man halfway to distraction, what must Lily do but make a scene.

Still, she had a point: he *should* have intimated to her that she was to receive a most advantageous offer. It was not often Lord Chalmers found himself in the wrong, and he did not care for it. "You should not have been surprised," he responded sharply. "You made no effort that I could see to check the growing strength of the attachment; you appeared
114

flattered by the attention. Consider, Lily! Gervaise has been dancing attendance on you for weeks. He wished to give you time to fix your affections before making you a declaration. All of this he explained when he asked my leave, as your guardian, to press his suit. He has all along conducted himself very commendably."

Lily did not look the least bit gratified by Lord Kingscote's adherence to propriety. "Oh, yes!" she said gloomily. "A perfect gentleman."

Lord Chalmers was beginning to feel greatly imposed upon, a sentiment which he was not reluctant to express. "I have always deprecated this tendency to kick up a dust over trifles!" he uttered, most unfairly; Lily was conducting herself not like a hysterical harridan, but like a damsel plunged into grief. Why she should fall into a lethargy at the prospect of a highly eligible alliance he could not imagine, and it put him even further out of frame. "You might exhibit a little more enthusiasm that Gervaise has made you an offer! *I* hold it to be a piece of astonishingly good fortune."

"You," responded Lily, through the delicate handkerchief that she'd pressed to her nose, "aren't being pestered to settle in matrimony with someone who is *old*. It utterly sinks my spirits, and so I shall tell Fennel, because it is all his fault!"

Nor could Lord Chalmers imagine what Fennel had to do with Lord Kingscote's proposal, which he considered a stroke of luck quite undeserved by the young lady to whom it had been addressed, and which she seemed to regard as a very unpleasant and unexpected event. He recalled Valerian's prediction that his pea-goose of a sister would do nothing so sensible as make an unexceptionable match. That Valerian had been proven most prescient did not elevate him in Lord Chalmers's estimation. Lord Chalmers had decided that the whole Millikin family was unendowed with brains.

Since common sense had no effect on Lily, he would subject her to a little scold. "If you did not seriously entertain Lord Kingscote's addresses," he said severely, "you have behaved in a way that is open to very unfavorable interpretations, Lily. *I* know you would not be so shameless as to play fast and loose with a gentleman, but the world would not take so generous a view. You must marry Gervaise, or people will say you are a hardened flirt."

Lily lowered her handkerchief, unmoved. "As if I should care for that! I *am* a flirt! It is not kind of you to accuse me of encouraging Lord Kingscote's pretentions when I didn't *know* he was trying to fix his interest with me!"

Perhaps she was just being missish? Lord Chalmers was beginning to find this interview a dead bore. "You do not mean to tell me that you hold Gervaise in low esteem?"

"Oh, no!" Lily widened her tearful blue eyes. "I have a great regard for Lord Kingscote. But I do not *love* him, and the idea of marrying anyone that I cannot love is very repugnant to my feelings."

"Love!" Lord Chalmers's derision derived from thought of his errant wife. "Young ladies of your station do not marry for love, Lily. They marry for advantage, wealth, position—all of which Gervaise will provide you. To make precisely such a match was the purpose of your Season, and for you to cut up stiff over achieving just that purpose is the height of ingratitude."

"But—" protested Lily.

"Cut line!" abjured the baron, who had little liking for feminine chatter at the best of times, and who, gifted with Lily's gooseish opinions, had reached the end of a scant patience already severely strained by a failure to discover what inspired Rosemary to act as if she were afraid of him—though were his suspicions proved correct, Rosemary had every reason to be frightened out of what few wits she possessed. "You are of no age to make such decisions for yourself, Lily, and must abide by the judgments of older and wiser heads. In this instance, mine! Make no mistake about it: you *will* marry Gervaise!" On this Parthian shot, he exited the room.

Only moments later, Fennel entered, to find his sister collapsed on a needlepointed sofa, a handkerchief obscuring her face. "Just met Chalmers in the hallway!" he remarked, as he disposed himself on a window seat. "Have he and Rosemary been at dagger-drawing again? He looked like a thundercloud."

"Not Rosemary." Feebly, Lily allowed the handkerchief to drop. "Me. I must tell you, Fennel, it is all your fault."

Fennel pondered that remark. Had Lord Chalmers been aware of the current state of Fennel's affairs, he might well have flown into the boughs; Fennel felt strongly inclined to fly into the boughs himself. However, the baron was *not* aware, although Fennel had little hope for the long duration of that blissful innocence. All the same— "That won't fadge! I didn't put Chalmers so devilish out of humor. Stands to reason: I wasn't even here. You know what, Lily; you did it yourself! And you shouldn't have! Putting Chalmers in a tweak ain't going to help Rosemary."

Lily regarded her brother with a distinct lack of affection and asked to be informed what Rosemary had to do with anything. "Thought you had a good memory, puss!" said Fennel. "Rosemary's in the suds! Popped the Chalmers sapphires!"

Briefly, in contemplation of her own dilemma, Lily had forgotten the necklace. The reminder did not cheer her; a damsel who took her self-imposed tasks seriously, she realized that it must be very selfish of her, when Rosemary stood in such grave need of financial assistance, to whistle the Kingscote fortune down the wind. She sighed deeply.

Fennel might not have been the most perspicacious of souls, but it had become evident to him that Lily was behaving queerly. Stretched out on the sofa, one hand pressed to her brow, the other hand trailing the handkerchief on the floor, she gave every appearance of a lady teetering on the brink of a decline. "In the mops?" he inquired sympathetically. "Tell me about it!"

Lily greeted this suggestion with a visible shudder. "Lord Kingscote!" Her voice was hollow. "I am very angry with you, Fennel, because if you had not said I wasn't in his style I would not have set out to prove you wrong, and now I wouldn't be in the basket! But you did, and *I* did, and now he has—and Chalmers says I should be quite content to have landed a fish who's so plump in the pocket, and that I should take care he doesn't wriggle off my hook!"

So fascinated was Fennel by these disclosures that he

moved from the window seat to sprawl on the sofa at Lily's feet. "Threw the handkerchief in your direction, did he? I thought he might! Now don't go glowering at me, puss; Kingscote's been dangling at your shoe-strings this age. You'd have known it wasn't Angelica he was taken with if you wasn't such a pea-goose!"

Admittedly she must be a pea-goose, confessed Lily; she hadn't had the ghost of a notion that Lord Kingscote fancied herself. "Poor Angelica!" she sniffled. "If all the eligible gentlemen make *me* offers, I don't know how I am to contrive to get her off the shelf! None of this would have happened, Fennel, if you had not driven me to persuade Kingscote I was the very woman calculated to suit his taste. You might have had a thought for Angelica, who's at her last prayers!"

Fennel was not thrilled to be cast as the villain of this piece. "Don't go into alt over Angelica again!" he begged. "I have other things on my mind!"

"Oh, yes! Macaws and drinking cups fashioned from skulls and silver funerary urns!" Lily elevated herself on one elbow, the better to glare. "You are very *selfish*, Fennel!"

Drinking cups fashioned from skulls? Funerary urns? What the deuce would Byron have done, wondered Fennel, if plagued with Phoebe Holloway's dragon of a mama? This was obviously not a propitious moment in which to inform Lily that his own affairs had progressed from bad to worse. Reflecting that she was spouting a great deal of gammon, he rubbed her pretty little feet. "Take a damper! It ain't at all like you to go cutting up so stiff, especially over a gentleman popping the question. Kingscote ain't the first to make you flattering overtures."

"No." Lily sank back once more and spoke in dying tones. "But he may well be the last! Chalmers has ordered that I must marry Kingscote. I suppose if I refuse I will be kept on bread and water in my room. Rosemary is right about Chalmers; he *is* cruelly unfeeling! He actually dared accuse me of blowing first hot, then cold."

"If that don't beat all!" In Fennel's opinion, Lord Chalmers had made a rare mull of the thing. Charitably, he decided that his brother-in-law's cow-handed dealings with
118

Lily were due to a lack of understanding of the feminine mind. Fennel, blessed with a bevy of sisters, suffered no such lack. If applied to for guidance, which he wished that he had been, Fennel would have been happy to inform the lord that the way to insure that a young lady followed a certain course of action was to bid her do the opposite. "No wonder you're in a pucker! Still, you was telling me just the other day that you and Kingscote rub on very well."

"I do not love him," Lily said simply.

With that viewpoint, Fennel had empathy. To a man, or woman, the Millikins believed the world well lost for romance. "Poor puss! Then of course you shan't marry him. Did you tell Chalmers?"

"I did. And Chalmers told me I should console myself for a lack of affection with Kingscote's position and wealth." Looking highly indignant, Lily again sat up. *"Then* he gave me a rake-down! Oh, Fennel, I *do* pity Rosemary!"

Fennel could only contend with the problems of one sister at a time. "Maybe Chalmers was roasting you?" he suggested hopefully.

"Hah!" retorted Lily.

"Then tell Kingscote! He can't still want to marry you if you don't want to marry him, surely?"

"Fennel!" Lily looked reproachful. "As if I could be so cruel. Think of how the poor man must feel were I to say such a thing—his heart broken, his hopes dashed! No, no, do not ask me to wound him."

It occurred to Fennel that there were inherent in this situation complexities which he had failed to grasp. "Seems to me you're mighty concerned over the feelings of a man you don't like above half!"

"I didn't say I didn't like him; I said I didn't *love* him. You are not paying attention, Fennel, or you would not say such things. How could I possibly love a man who in his make-up hasn't a speck of romance?"

"No romance?" Fennel echoed blankly. "When he just made you a proposal—offered you his heart and hand? You know what it is, Lily: you've got bats in your attic! I never heard such fustian."

Lily regarded her brother soulfully. "That's just it, Fennel: he *didn't*! Offer me his heart and hand! He didn't even profess to be my very ardent admirer! It was all very proper and above-board, and the dullest stuff. To marry such a man, who clearly hasn't a grain of proper feeling—it is much too dreadful to contemplate!"

It was not only Lord Chalmers who failed to appreciate the feminine mystique. Fennel concluded that Lord Kingscote was similarly unblessed with sisters, else he would have known better than to make so romantically inclined a young lady as Lily a declaration that was devoid of flowery passages, passionate professions of devotion that must extend beyond the grave and avowals of a similar nature, transports that could not help but cast a fanciful maiden into a state of blissful idiocy. In defense of such omission, Fennel pointed out that Lord Kingscote had long been a confirmed bachelor, and therefore probably lacked practice in such endeavors.

"Then he should have practiced!" retorted Lily. "Indeed he *would* have practiced, had he any real fondness for me. Not that it signifies! Because I mean to marry for love, and I cannot love a man who is *old*!"

Fennel saw no profit in argument. Though he thought marriage with Lord Kingscote would suit Lily very well, there was no purpose to be served in setting up her back. "What did you say to him?"

"Oh! I expressed myself with the greatest of delicacy. It is unfair of you, Fennel, to infer that I did not! In such situations, I *always* say what is polite."

Fennel was possessed of an uncharacteristic desire to tear at his hair, his own little problems having already strained his good humor. "But *what* did you say? Don't look daggers at me, puss! I ain't accusing you of behaving shabby!"

"I said I must count myself honored, that I was very much obliged, but that I must have time to think. *You* know the sort of thing, Fennel!"

Certainly Fennel did; he had for years listened to rehearsals of similar speeches. "What did *he* say?"

"He begged I give him leave to hope, so I did." Lily scowled at her handkerchief, which she was in the process of ripping to shreds. "Not that *that* signifies, either, because he may hope till doomsday and it shan't do him the least good! I shall not let myself be bullied, and so I intend to tell Chalmers and Kingscote and anyone else who may ask, and I don't care a groat if it *does* mean I shall be locked in my room!"

Horrified by this intimation that Lily was about to throw the first temper-tantrum of her life, Fennel hastily sought to pour oil on troubled waters. "You wouldn't like it! Trust me, puss! You'd get curst bored with your own company. Better you keep Kingscote dangling until we figure a way out of this coil!"

"If there *is* a way out," Lily said sadly. A brief silence descended while the Millikins engaged in ponderous thought. Then Lily sat bolt upright. "Fennel, I have the very thing! Chalmers will not be driven to relent by tears and threats of suicide; Rosemary's already tried that. Moreover, I perfectly see that to put a period to my existence would be to sink myself quite below reproach! So I shall delude Lord Kingscote into thinking I *will* marry him—and then I'll elope!"

"Hold fast!" pleaded poor Fennel, clutching his aching brow. "I thought you didn't *want* to marry Kingscote! And if you *do* want to marry him, what have you been nattering on about this half-hour? Anyway, thought you meant to have the knot tied at St. George's, Hanover Square, with half the city in attendance! Not that *I* should like it, but you must suit yourself! And I daresay Kingscote don't care!"

Restored to happy spirits by the evolution of an escape from the worst of all her scrapes, the number of which was remarkable in a lady of tender years, Lily was kindly disposed toward even her thick-headed brother. "Gudgeon! Not Kingscote."

"Then *who*?" inquired Fennel, not unreasonably.

"I have not decided, exactly." Lily looked pensive. "I must think! Is it not the perfect solution, Fennel? Angelica is not the only one who can be clever! Because when I am discovered to be gone, she can then console Kingscote."

In such event, thought Fennel, Lord Kingscote would not be in need of consolation so much as vengeance upon the young lady by whom he had been so thoroughly diddled. To say so would achieve as little as a discussion of the drawbacks of the scheme. Far better, he realized, in one of his sporadic bursts of intuition, to delude Lily into a belief that he would stand her ally, so that she might continue to confide in him. "That's hit the nail square on the head!" he therefore applauded. "Take your time in making your decision, Puss! Remember you mean to make a love-match."

"Oh, I shan't rush my fences!" With energy astonishing in a young lady but so recently teetering on the brink of a decline, Lily scrambled to her feet. "You know perfectly well, Fennel, that if I set my mind to it I can fall in love with anyone!" Having reassured her anxious brother on this head, Lily retired in good order to her bedchamber, there to decide who among her chief admirers was to be befallen by so singular a mark of favor as a flight to Gretna Green in company with herself. Meantime Fennel stretched out upon the needlepointed sofa and pondered the most diplomatic means of intimating to Lord Kingscote that his courtship was in dire need of a liberal spicing of romance.

Fourteen

Lady Chalmers, all unaware, had followed her eldest sister's example of discretion, and procured for her own use the services of a hackney-coach, a vehicle that offended both her notion of the dignity of her station and her innate fastidiousness. However, there was no alternative. Lady Chalmers had no wish that her husband should learn of her destination, as he was bound to do had she proceeded there in her own dashing cabriolet, which among its other elegancies bore the Chalmers crest. Already Lord Chalmers was suspicious of his wife, as witnessed by his newfound tendency to stick as close to her as a court-plaster, to live practically in her pocket, to exhibit what in a less inimical man might have been called a dog-in-the-manger attitude.

Rosemary made no such mistake. It was no sudden fondness for her, she thought, that caused her spouse to cling to her like a leech; and her own suspicions were borne out by his habit of pinching at her under the guise of what he fondly called "having a comfortable prose." Since this activity most often consisted of animadversions by the baron on such subjects as the Regent—whose debts and extravagant domestic expenditures had the previous year been brought to light and denounced in parliamant, where this year it had been announced that he meant to erect in Rome a monument designed by Canova in honor of exiled Stuarts, an ambition which had led Brougham to suggest that his Regent might profit from that family's sorry example of being ousted from the throne; who was hated by the working people for a way of life that included chandeliers, in the music room of the Brighton Pavilion, costing in excess of £4,000, and dinner parties where guests chose among one hundred and sixteen dishes—Rosemary could only conclude that her husband had the wind up in regard to her debts, and meant her to be miserable. It was a conclusion further borne out by Chalmers's predisposition to make subtly accusatory remarks, the gist of which Rosemary failed to grasp, and the delivery of which was ominous. Her husband must dislike her very much, she thought, to expend such strenuous efforts toward cutting up her peace.

Lord Chalmers had succeeded very well in that ignoble intent: Rosemary was very miserable indeed. Her health had suffered to such extent that she had resorted to daily dosages of Godbold's Vegetable Balsam, for asthma and consumption, and Velno's Vegetable Syrup, for all else; her rest was every night disturbed by alternate nightmares of being dragged away to debtors' prison, of being publicly denounced by Chalmers on the floor of the divorce court. Rosemary had a horror of scandal quite commensurate with her exalted rank. She also had a horror of separation from the husband whom, despite his inhumanity, she adored; and a more immediate horror yet of finding bailiffs in the house. Since the bills that she received daily had by now reached staggering proportions, this was not an unlikely contingency. How she had managed to run so deeply into debt, Rosemary did not know. As Fennel had so succinctly stated it, she was in a cleft stick.

Nor, in this ticklish situation, were the various members of the Millikin family in residence beneath Lord Chalmers's venerable roof proving to be of any practical assistance. If anything, they might have deliberately combined their efforts to make matters worse. True, Angelica had given Rosemary some money with which to stave off her disgrace— but such money as Angelica provided was only a drop in the well of Rosemary's obligations, and had acted upon her creditors like the smell of blood on ravenous hounds. At any moment, the slavering pack would close in for the kill. How Angelica had come by that money, Rosemary did not know, or care. She was not feeling kindly toward her eldest sister who, according to Lily, had so far abandoned her responsibilities as to engage in a clandestine romance, conduct which Rosemary felt was most prodigiously unfair.

Then there was Lily, who stood little higher in Rosemary's affections, due to that young lady's fits and starts, which had so exacerbated Lord Chalmers that he had read his wife a dreadful scold. Secretly Rosemary sympathized with Lily; Rosemary knew well the less pleasant aspects of a loveless marriage, being engaged in such a match, at least on her husband's part. Too, Rosemary was a little piqued that Lily stood fair to make even a better match than she had done herself: Chalmers was a mere baron, Kingscote a duke. At least Lily was no longer going about muttering of thwarted romance and promising to sink into a decline. Rosemary supposed her sister had realized she would be obliged to knuckle down.

Nothing, but nothing, was as Rosemary had expected it to

be when she so blithely embarked upon a marriage of convenience; absolutely everything had from that day forward gone wrong. Latest among Rosemary's adversities had been an epistle from the pawnshop where she'd left the Chalmers sapphires, intimating politely that were not the interest due on that item paid promptly, it would be forfeit—an intimation, however politely phrased, that had inflicted its recipient with a spasm from which she had been revived only with vinaigrette and hartshorn wielded by her husband, who had then demanded an explanation of this latest queer start. Rosemary had rendered an explanation, as best she could on the spur of the moment. Even to her own ears it had sounded weak. Apparently it had sounded similarly to her unfond spouse, who had delivered himself of a few pungent and unappreciative remarks concerning vaporish females before taking himself off to Westminster. Or so he claimed. Rosemary believed his destination was more probably a lady-bird of sympathetic and scheming nature, who would immediately seek to further widen the abysmal gap between Lord Chalmers and his wife.

Yet, in justice, her husband had scant time for such recreations between his duties with the government and his assiduous attentions to Rosemary. It was such a puzzle! Rosemary, hitherto convinced that Lord Chalmers had a fancy-piece tucked away somewhere, had begun to wonder if perhaps he disliked females in general, and not just herself. But that was a profitless line of speculation; she approached her destination, a destination recommended by no less than Madame Eugénie. Perhaps it had not been the wisest action to confess the extent of her pecuniary embarrassments to the modiste, but Rosemary had not known where else to turn. Madame Eugénie might have in the past exhibited an aggravating determination to be paid, but there was no denying she was shrewd. Nor had Rosemary's faith in the Frenchwoman been misplaced: Madame Eugénie had uttered some unflattering comments on ladies who sought to satisfy extravagant tastes on extremely slim purses, but she had come across handsomely. In accordance with the modiste's advice, Rosemary was en route to confer with a certain Mr. Thwaite in Newgate Street.

As in this manner Rosemary pondered her predicament, the hackney-coach proceeded along the Strand, a broad thoroughfare lined with pleasantly proportioned buildings and superior shops, which connected the fashionable West End with the mercantile City. Progress was not rapid, due to the throng of drays and carts, saddle-horses, carriages and chaises; the shopkeepers who now and then ran out onto the pavement to personally usher into their establishments their more important customers. At last the coach won clear of the crush at the Temple Bar, crept beneath the shadow of Newgate Prison, drew to a halt before one of the houses in Newgate Street.

In some wonder Rosemary looked about her. The City, with its warehouses and tenements, was not an area familiar to most members of the *ton*, the main exception being young bloods who considered it rare sport to mingle with the lower orders in the City's countless public-houses. The vista before her further outraged Rosemary's fastidiousness. The street was ankle-deep in dust, thick with vendors and merchants and ladies of dubious character. The gutters overflowed with accumulated refuse. The dustman's clapper pealed, as did the muffin-man's bell; strident cries of sweet lavender, chairs to mend, cherry-ripe, cockles and mussels, smote Rosemary's ear. Slops flung from an upper story window caused her to leap quickly aside, only to collide with an old-clothes man, hunched into a long greasy caftan and wearing a tower of hats, who was pushing a barrow-load of unsavory rags. She gasped and escaped into the building that housed Mr. Thwaite.

The interior of that building was little more appetizing than the street outside, the stairway littered with a mountain of rubbish. She extracted her vinaigrette from her reticule and inhaled deeply of the pungent scent. For the first time, she doubted the quality of Madame Eugénie's wisdom.

But having been driven by desperation to come so far, Rosemary could not now turn back. As the modiste had shrewdly pointed out, Lady Chalmers would not wish to patronize a moneylender frequented by persons of rank, lest she suffer the embarrassment of there encountering some

126

acquaintance. Certainly no one of her acquaintance would frequent such a hovel as this, thought Rosemary. She had reached the top of the staircase. Screwing up her flagging courage, Rosemary tapped at a certain door.

It opened but a crack, through which peered a suspicious eye. That eye traveled over Rosemary, taking in every detail of her toilette—a stone-colored habit trimmed with swansdown, black beaver hat, large sealskin muff, black kid half-boots. The door swung open.

"Mr. Thwaite?" inquired Rosemary of the individual thus revealed, a person of slight stature and homely features which were further disfigured by a squint. "I wish, if you have a moment, to speak with you."

Mr. Thwaite, for it was he, stepped back a pace or two and made a sweeping bow. Rosemary entered the chamber, which was shabby and sparsely furnished and none too clean. Mr. Thwaite wiped off a hard wooden chair with his coatsleeve, indicated that his visitor should be seated, and took up his own position behind a battered desk.

Rosemary sat down, and readily; she was heartily regretting the decision that had brought her to Newgate Street. If Chalmers learned of *this*, he wouldn't merely divorce her, he'd murder her outright. Since she *was* here, regretful or no, she might as well get on with the business. How best to broach so delicate a subject? "You *are* Mr. Thwaite?" she inquired doubtfully.

That individual propped his elbows on his desk, touched his fingertips together, and smiled. "That I am, missy! Open your budget, I'm here to please. For I'll tell you as shouldn't that you ain't the first to run aground and be fretting your guts to fiddlestrings because your pockets are all to let. Fine feathers make fine birds, I always say, and so they may, but it ain't quite so easy as winking to catch the eye of a well-breeched swell, even if you are square-rigged! Which brings us to a little matter of securities and credentials, if you follow me."

That Rosemary did not follow is not surprising; Rosemary was unfamiliar with the protocol observed by moneylenders, practices that had earned the practitioners of that benevolent

127

profession many sobriquets, mildest among which were "damned bloodsuckers" and "curst cent-percents"—practices at which Mr. Thwaite so excelled that his address was claimed by various young bucks of his acquaintance to be the legendary Queer Street. "I beg your pardon?" said Rosemary.

Mr. Thwaite frowned. He had on first inspection cast his visitor as demure immorality in beaver and sealskin, such worthies being prone to deck themselves out in the most extravagant rigs, for which they generally lacked the means to pay the reckoning, a habit that had greatly enriched Mr. Thwaite's own pocketbook; but it was being borne in on him that his visitor was in a most nervous and prostrated state. Bits o' muslin, in Mr. Thwaite's experience, were not prone to nervous states of mind.

"Seems to me we're not getting any forwarder!" he observed shrewdly. "Let's start at the beginning. You *are* a trifle scorched? Under the hatches? Badly dipped? Set yourself up in the very latest mode and now find yourself a little short of the Ready-and-Rhino?" Rosemary, interpreting these colorful queries to mean she was in the unhappy position of being unable to discharge her debts, nodded. Mr. Thwaite frowned yet once again. "Who set you on to me?"

Here, at least, was a clear enough question. "Madame Eugénie."

"Aha!" Mr. Thwaite regarded his fingertips. Not a fair Cyprian, but a delicately nurtured gentry-mort. He should have known it right off; this was not the first flat to be dispatched to his tender mercies by the enterprising modiste, who received a share of the profits made therefrom. "Then all's bowman, missy! You should have said so at the onset, but no harm done. Now let's get down to the nitty-gritty: you needn't fear *I'm* a gabble-grinder; you can get on to puckering because I'll keep dubber mum'd!" This generous invitation drew from the lady only a wide-eyed stare. "But I shouldn't be talking flash to you, because it's plain as a pikestaff you don't understand a word of it," added Mr. Thwaite. He explained that his visitor might speak frankly, because they were quite private; he was a positive marvel of discretion, and would never repeat to any living soul a single word she said.

In so kindly a manner was this invitation delivered, such kindliness being no small part of Mr. Thwaite's stock-in-trade that Rosemary without hesitation told him the whole. As her story progressed, Mr. Thwaite's eyebrows rose. The tale itself was not unfamiliar; he'd heard many such; the lasses, ladies and lady-birds alike, had a proclivity to get themselves under a cloud, bless their little hearts. What caused the elevation of Mr. Thwaite's eyebrows was the growing certainty that before him sat the plumpest pigeon ever to tumble into his cooking-pot.

"And so you see," concluded Rosemary, "I have been guilty of shockingly irregular conduct. I have been so worried I couldn't think *what* to do!"

"Now don't go nabbing the bib, because it'll cut no ice with me!" Mr. Thwaite said sharply. Rosemary looked blank. He condescended to explain that she should not cry, though he refrained from further explaining that he was long-inured to weeping females, of whom he had enjoyed large acquaintanceship during his long and prosperous career. "No need to be fretting yourself to flinders when I'll help you raise the wind!"

"Oh, *will* you?" cried Rosemary, excessively relieved. "I dared not hope—because if Chalmers should find out—"

"Who's this Chalmers?" interrupted the quick-witted Mr. Thwaite.

It never occurred to Rosemary that the most prudent course of action might be to withhold that particular information. Indeed, Rosemary was glad to inform Mr. Thwaite of her status, a piece of data that generally met with a gratifying obsequiousness from shopkeepers and merchants and people similarly in a position to profit from the patronage of a lady who had married such stupendous wealth. Rosemary thought the common Mr. Thwaite very fortunate to receive the business of so exalted a lady as herself, which is an excellent example of the Millikin processes of reasoning, or the lack thereof. "My husband, Baron Chalmers," she said.

To the obsequious attentions lavished on Lady Chalmers by shopkeepers and the like—until, that is, said shopkeepers discovered her ladyship's unfortunate habit of leaving debts unpaid—Mr. Thwaite was no exception. The moneylender made it his business to be cognizant of the Upper Ten Thousand, and therefore was aware that Lady Chalmers's husband was rich as Croesus.

With an airy gesture of one hand Mr. Thwaite dismissed such inconsequential matters as securities and credentials; with the other he unlocked a certain desk drawer; in the most amiable manner he put forth an opinion that it was a pity a lady could not determine whether a gentleman was of choleric temper and clutchfisted tendencies before she was hitched, by when it was a great deal too late. This piece of presumption Rosemary swallowed with good grace, partially because she did not understand precisely what was being said to her, and partially because Mr. Thwaite had with a flourish bestowed upon her a large bundle of bank notes. Her ladyship must not fear he would press her for payment, promised Mr. Thwaite; none knew better than himself that needs must when the devil drove. There was one other little matter, pure formality; he was sure her ladyship would understand he couldn't dispense with such petty details even in so exceptional a case. If Lady Chalmers would just sign this silly little piece of paper, there, and there? Her ladyship was exceedingly obliging, to be sure!

Solicitously, Mr. Thwaite escorted Lady Chalmers down the cluttered stairway, out into the street. He made short work of the old-clothes man who lurked near the doorway with the sinister intention of tossing her ladyship into his barrow and trundling her away; he settled her ladyship carefully in the waiting hackney-coach and watched her depart. No sooner had her ladyship passed out of hearing-range than Mr. Thwaite burst into a most immoderate fit of loud laughter. Chuckling still, Mr. Thwaite repaired to a nearby boozing-ken, where he treated his cronies to mugs of flesh-and-blood, and the information that he was about to step much higher up into the world.

Fifteen

Had Angelica known of her sister's private stock of Godbold's Vegetable Balsam and Velno's Vegetable Syrup, she might well have had recourse to those remedies. Angelica's state of health deteriorated daily, a fact that of course had nothing to do with her daily encounters with a certain hardened rakeshame.

"Palpitations!" she said, as she paced the floor of her eldest brother's specimen room. "An oppression of the chest! And I warn you, Valerian, that if you prescribe me a hot brick, I am very likely to throw it at your head!"

Valerian cast a professional eye over his sister, who had paused in her perambulations to gaze gloomily into a display case. "You're looking knocked into horsenails, Sis. Leave what's-her-name and the others to deal with their problems and go home. You need a rest."

"I am to have a rest in the country?" Angelica turned away from the display case, in which were very advantageously arranged a remarkable variety of spinal cords, and moved to inspect a fine array of teeth. "A quiet country holiday? In company with Marigold and Hysop, Hyacinth and Violet, Amaryllis and Camilla, every one of whom is every bit as aggravating as Rosemary? Thank you, Valerian, but no! Apropos of which I have had another letter from Marigold. She claims it is taking me too long to fire off Lily, and accuses me of being dilatory in my attentions to my family. And she hints that she might come to town herself to take over our affairs."

"Egad!" responded Valerian with prompt horror. "Put her off, Sis!"

"I have tried," Angelica said, to the fine display of teeth. "The truth of the matter is that Marigold has grown weary of coping single-handed with the children. In Fennel's absence, Hysop has taken to putting toads in *her* bed." She sighed. "Clearly, if Rosemary doesn't win free of this muddle of hers, Marigold will hold me to blame."

The most practical of Valerian's sisters—or the sister who had once been the most practical, turned to him with an appealing expression that Valerian did not approve. "No!" he said with brutal candor. "It won't do you the least good to make sheep's eyes at me; I refused to be plagued by Marigold and her curst brats. If you take my advance, you'll wash your hands of them. You're looking—"

"Knocked into horsenails!" Angelica concluded wryly. "So you've already said; and so I was informed over the breakfast cups. Lily announced I was looking worn to the bone; Rosemary said immediately that it wasn't *her* fault if I am fagged to death, and that she is scandalized by my conduct. I couldn't imagine what Rosemary meant, since it is very much her fault if I am a little peaked—not that I begrudge the child my efforts—and so I set myself to find out. Valerian. those two ninnyhammers have convinced themselves that I am embarked upon an *affaire!*"

That Angelica should engage in such uncharacteristic behavior was not among the contingencies foreseen by Valerian. He gave it his judicious consideration. "I shouldn't think *affaires* would suit you."

"Oh, no! Not the ugly duckling!" Angelica responded rather irritably. "Sometimes I wish very strongly that I had been born beautiful, because then I should very likely bid the whole family to the devil and enter into a carefree life of dissipation, pleasing no one but myself!"

Angelica's behavior grew momentarily more erratic. Valerian was not surprised that his sister should voice so startling a suggestion; it was but another of her mysterious symptoms —mysterious to Angelica, that is; Valerian was perfectly aware of the nature of her malady, although he had never experienced it himself. That he allowed his sister to remain in ignorance was due less to compassion than to curiosity. Valerian was interested to see which way she would jump. Anyway, for what ailed Angelica, there was no cure.

"Did you tell what's-her-name about Sir Randall?" he inquired. "We agreed that the fewer people who know the truth, the better. For you to be working for Sir Randall is hardly ladylike—in fact, it looks damned odd. Perhaps I shouldn't have—"

"Piffle!" Angelica leaned in an exhausted and most perilous manner against a case crammed full of skulls. "I told Rosemary nothing; there was no opportunity. She was kicking up a dreadful dust, accusing me of making a cake of myself. Oh, I would like to *shake* her!"

Here, Valerian interrupted, with an opinion that what's-her-name was queer in the attic, and a request that Angelica have a care for his specimen case. Obligingly, Angelica undraped herself from the case and took another turn around the room. "I haven't told you the best joke of all! Rosemary hopes I have not conducted myself in a manner that would leave me open to reproach; as the sister of a baroness I must at all times comport myself with decorous dignity. Though Rosemary does not like to speak of it, she fears I may have been a little indiscreet—but she is willing to make allowances, because I do not know how to go on in society!" Valerian choked; Angelica grimaced. "I don't know where the girl comes by her ideas. Or I *do* know, because Lily is forever spinning fairytales. And when I think that Fennel dared say—in the kindliest of manners!—that if I am offered a slip on the shoulder he hopes I'll remember my obligations to the family—it is no wonder I'm distraught!"

"Were you?" interrupted Valerian. "Offered a slip on the shoulder? Because if you were, you should have told me about it, so that I could defend your honor."

At this noble offer, Angelica stared. "Defend my honor? *You*? Valerian, I never heard of such a thing!"

Unabashed by this blunt rejoinder, Valerian grinned. "I'm the head of the family; Chalmers said so himself. Answer my questions. *Has* he offered you a slip on the shoulder?"

"Chalmers? You must be mad!" Angelica then realized whom her perspicacious brother thought capable of such infamy. "How can you say such a thing? Or even think it? Of course he has not, nor will he. In point of fact, he promised Sir Randall he would *not* make a violent attack on my virtue, so you see this is a fuss over trifles. I am not at all the sort of female whom Simon Brisbane would invite to toss her bonnet over the windmill."

By this latter confession, Angelica looked so cast down that Valerian nearly laughed aloud. "Don't let him, there's a good girl! I doubt I'd care for pistols at daybreak. Sis, do stop that pacing before you break something! Come here and sit down."

Angelica obeyed. "Naturally I am subject to liverish depressions," she said gloomily. "With Rosemary accusing me not only of entering into a ruinous entanglement but of enjoying it excessively—Valerian, she actually informed me that I should not have sullied my reputation because *Marigold* would be broken-hearted at the disgrace!"

This, too, was a novel notion. Valerian sampled it. "No, that won't fadge," he said, the digestive process complete. "Mind you, Marigold would be cross as cats, but she's not the sort to go off in an apoplexy."

"What is this? When did Chalmers say you were head of the family? Valerian, did he come *here*?"

"Haven't I said so? You're asking a lot of deuced silly questions, Sis. Chalmers seemed to think I might have some influence with the other one—not what's-her-name but the pea-goose! You know who I mean."

"Lily. I assume you disabused Chalmers of the notion that you would provide him assistance?"

"Oh, yes!" Valerian was unmoved by his sister's heavy irony. To move Valerian Millikin to compunction was beyond the capacities of a mere mortal, and very possibly beyond the capabilities of even the Almighty. "I made that very clear. I also told him that the chit would have nothing to do with anyone eligible."

Without hesitation, Angelica took the wind out of her brother's sails. "You're out! Lily is going to make the most eligible of matches." She related the saga of Lord Kingscote's courtship, Lily's brief sulks and sudden capitulation, the plans for the upcoming nuptials. "*She* informed me over the breakfast cups this morning that I have cut up all her hopes. Lily has been contriving to throw Lord Kingscote at my head, being convinced that since we both are *clever* we would deal delightfully! But she has given in with good enough grace, so her future is assured."

Definitely, thought Valerian, his favorite sister was growing hare-brained. Though he barely remembered Lily, he doubted very strongly that a pea-goose of a damsel would suddenly transform herself into a pattern-card of respectability. Valerian did not air his suspicion that another of their sisters was engaged in grave duplicity, lest Angelica further exhaust herself trying to persuade the pea-goose to desist from her vagaries.

He glanced at Angelica, who was looking somber. "Chalmers also said you were an excellent creature, which was very pretty in him. Are you certain you're not nourishing a *tendre,* Sis?"

A *tendre* for Lord Chalmers, who had never in all his life indulged in a single depraved pursuit? As is frequently the case with ladies, Angelica's acquaintance with a gentleman admittedly steeped in vice had inspired in her a conviction that virtue was a dead bore. "How absurd you are! Rosemary herself is quite *éprise* in that direction, I believe. What Chalmers may feel is difficult to guess; he doesn't wear his heart upon his sleeve. Valerian, it is the queerest thing: Rosemary told me this morning—while taking me to task for neglecting my duties!—that she has come by the means to reclaim the Chalmers sapphires. I don't know what to think! Except that I'm very doubtful Chalmers gave her the money. He is acting in the oddest way—were it anyone but Chalmers, I would say he is exhibiting the unmistakable signs of an enraged spouse!"

Valerian had grown weary of the problems of what's-her-name and husband; he was much more interested in why Angelica looked so pulled-about. Therefore, he aired his opinion that Lord Chalmers was wonderfully stiff-rumped, and inquired how Angelica fared with Sir Randall and Simon Brisbane.

"Oh, very well!" Angelica laughed. "Simon keeps us *au courant* with the latest stories fabricated in the bay-window at White's and whispered in the clubrooms of St. James's and Pall Mall."

"Certainly Simon should be *au courant*," said Valerian. "I believe he is the subject of a great many of those *on-dits*."

Had Valerian meant to remind his sister of the infamous character of the gentleman who kept her so well entertained, he would have failed. "People will always talk about Simon," Angelica responded, somewhat wistfully. "He *is* a hardened rakeshame."

"A regular dash." Valerian took up a position near Angelica's chair. "You don't *mind* that he's a rakehell, Sis?"

"Mind? Why should I?" Angelica looked perplexed. "Under more ordinary circumstances I would feel differently, I suppose—had we met in society I could hardly converse so freely with him, lest people think *I* was wishful of becoming a lesson in depravity. But these circumstances are not ordinary; to Simon I must seem a female of dubious origin; and since he doesn't know I'm gently bred none of us need consider delicate principles and tender sensibilities. I tell you, Valerian, it is marvelous to be so free of restraint!"

Definitely Angelica was growing hare-brained. Valerian put forth a warning that, lest she wish to see him carve out Simon Brisbane's liver and fry it for daylight, she had best insure that Simon did not equate freedom with liberty.

"Valerian!" Astonished by the notion that she should tarry among the flesh-pots in company with a hardened rakeshame, which is not to say the notion had not previously occurred to her, though she had failed to take it seriously, Angelica gaped at her brother. Then the humor of the situation struck her, for Valerian's suddenly protective attitude was as absurd as the notion that Simon should give her brother cause to rush to her defense. She giggled.

"You misunderstand, Valerian, truly! Simon is careful to give no offense; as opposed to paying me attentions that are
136

too pointed, he pays me no attention that is not merely courteous!" She put herself to rights, preparatory to departure. "Why, he is even so kind as to answer all my questions—or most of them. It occurs to me he still has not explained to me just what is an orgy."

"A *what*?" echoed Valerian, in such shocked tones that Angelica paused half way through the act of rising from her chair.

"An orgy," she repeated. "Are you gone deaf? Why are you staring at me? Oh! Do *you* know what an orgy is, Valerian? Because if you do I wish very much that you would tell me."

"You asked Simon Brisbane to explain to you an *orgy*?" Valerian said again. "How *could* you be so hare-brained? And don't be saying it doesn't signify a straw what you ask him because he doesn't know who you are—that's so much moonshine! You've taken some deuced queer notions into your head lately, Sis, and I don't mind telling you I don't care for it."

"*Don't* you, then?" Angelica had heard out her brother's admonitions with a growing sense of injustice which was not at all lessened by a faint fear that what he said was true. "It was not bad enough that Rosemary accused me of low conduct, now you must accuse me of worse! It is very poorly done of both of you, because I haven't misbehaved—at least not enough to warrant comment! And even if I *had*, I don't know anyone who is more entitled!"

Bizarre behavior indeed was this, from his cool and sensible sister; Valerian made an attempt at conciliation. "I didn't—"

"You did so! Don't try and bamboozle me! Oh, there is no point in trying to talk to you!" Angelica stalked across the room and through the door. With such force did she slam that portal that the glass rattled in Valerian's display cases. Anxiously he insured that no damage had been done. It had been very bad of Angelica, he thought, to act in so thankless a manner. He had only meant to put her on guard against imparting an impression that she was susceptible to weaknesses of the flesh.

Down the stairway tramped Angelica, through the hallway,

to the front door. This she yanked open. Before her, on the uppermost step of the flight that ascended from the street, were two figures whom Angelica had hoped to never see again. No less startled, the resurrectionists stared.

Angelica was first to recover from her surprise, and to realize that here was a perfect opportunity to at least partially quench her newfound thirst for violence: frankly, she demanded to know the object of their visit. This had to do, she speedily discovered, with a giant currently on exhibit in a raree-show, the skeleton of whom Mallet and Bimble believed would make an excellent subject for anatomical study.

"Monstrous!" uttered Angelica at this point. "Can you not wait until the poor man has expired before you make arrangements for his remains? Or is it that you think to hasten his demise? What an extraordinary affair! I've a good notion to turn you over to the authorities."

Lest she do so on the spot, Bimble spoke hastily. He expressed himself in the most subdued and penitent manner; he begged the lady to consider his unenviable position; he professed himself no more, or less, than any other man with his own way to make in the world. Perhaps the nature of his livelihood was a little gruesome, a bit beyond the pale—but it was a livelihood which must be undertaken by someone. As for the giant, they meant him no harm, were merely looking to the future.

"Talking don't pay toll!" interrupted Mallet, when Bimble showed indication of proceeding in a philosophical vein. "Now that you see how it is with us, ma'am, you won't be running rusty. We wouldn't be quick forgetting if you was to have us nicked—why, we might be so overset that we was to blab all we knew about yourself and a certain gentleman—and it would be terrible if a lady of your position was to be placed in such a fix!"

Unfortunately for the dire implications of this speech, Angelica didn't properly grasp the gist of it. "*What* fix?"

"Ah, now, don't be trying to persuade us you don't know the time of day!" responded Mallet. "*We* very well know chalk from cheese! Don't be thinking to run to your gentleman friend with this tale, either. He couldn't see us quietened before we laid an information against him, much as he might like to, because there's no denying he's devilish disagreeable when he takes one of his bad turns."

"Bad turns?" echoed Angelica, faintly.

"*You* know how it is," Mallet retorted, erroneously. "Don't pretend you don't! Still, it might stay our little secret, was you to persuade us not to give evidence."

Such was the effect of these disclosures on Angelica, in her current enfeebled state, that she felt as if she might swoon. Could she possibly have mistaken the resurrectionists' meaning? Surely Sir Randall had not—she must find out. To that end, Angelica regarded Mallet and Bimble sternly; requested in icy tones that they withdraw from her pathway; decreed in the most decidedly unequivocal terms that, did they not take summarily to their heels and thenceforth refrain from darkening her path, she would summon an officer of the peace.

"In a pig's whisker you'll call a horney!" said Mallet, as neither he nor his companion budged an inch. "Climb down off your high horse, missy, unless you want to see your gentleman friend hobbled and taken off to gaol. Which now that I think on it is where the gaffer belongs to be! He can't be up to his tricks in quod, or do harm to those as doesn't deserve it done to."

Sir Randall had committed some past offense so heinous that exposure would result in imprisonment? Even worse, Mallet intimated that Sir Randall might repeat that offense? Here was something more ominous than Angelica had feared —more ominous certainly than a simple preoccupation with the organic remains of souls called to their eternal rest. Angelica recalled her employer's operating room, and his zealous comments about dissection, and thought she knew what that offense might be. Poor Sir Randall, a once-eminent physician now deteriorated into the most loveable of madmen! And poor Simon! At last Angelica understood why he had set spies on his sire.

"What," she inquired in cowed tones, "do you want *me* to do?"

Mallet was pleased to see the young lady conduct herself

at last in a highly fit and proper way. In a handsome manner, and with an evil smile, he intimated that the resurrectionists would, if their palms were properly greased, keep quiet as oysters about Sir Randall Brisbane.

Sixteen

Miss Lily Millikin was deep in contemplation of a most important matter: who among her swains would be privileged to escort her to Gretna Green? Prolonged rumination had brought Lily only the realization that she could love neither Messr. Meadowcraft nor Gildensleeve, Steptoe nor Pettijohn. Quite naturally, Lily would not elope with a man she could not love—and she was finding it very difficult to fall in love on cue. Furthermore, if she was to betray her own high principles, especially the principle that the world was well lost for romance, that betrayal would not be accomplished for and with a penniless jackanapes. Lord Kingscote might not be the soul of romance, but he at least offered his bride-to-be position and advantage and wealth.

That Lily had no interest in such practical aspects of her upcoming nuptials, she did not feel free to inform the duke, nor that a display of ardor might have done much to reconcile her to an absence of romance. Had Kingscote given the slightest indication of passion held strongly in check, Lily might have looked on him with a much more kindly eye; had the duke allowed himself to be carried away by the violence of his feelings, she might have discovered in herself a positive enthusiasm for her hitherto unappreciated betrothal. But Lord Kingscote was very careful not to frighten his young *fiancée* with passion, violent or otherwise; and Lily, in whose shell-like earlobes heated effusions had been murmured since she was old enough to hear, keenly felt her prospective bride-groom's lack of appreciation. In short, her vanity was piqued.

But Lily was a kind-hearted girl, and therefore did not seek to repay Lord Kingscote in his own cold coin. As she had once told Fennel, Lily held the duke in great regard. Much time passed in his pleasant company had led her to believe that, despite his advanced years, they might have dealt very well together, had he only formed a true attachment for her. Unfortunately Lord Kingscote had not formed that attachment. Why he should wish to marry her, Lily could not guess; perhaps her remarks about decrepit peers had reminded him that he was embarking childless on his own old age. Angelica was much more in Kingscote's style, Lily thought somberly. Aloud she made a comment about the folly of clasping vipers to one's bosom, and the sharpness of adder's teeth.

These profound utterances met with little enthusiasm from the other occupants of the Chalmers drawing room. Fennel, who was striking Byronesque poses before a mirror, glanced at Lily in the glass and abjured her in a brotherly fashion to refrain from enacting them a Cheltenham tragedy; while Rosemary, already much too familiar with Lily's selfless motives for encouraging Kingscote to dangle at her shoe-strings, denied her younger sister even that much heed.

"After the opera!" she said dramatically. "A midnight flit to Calais—Brummel, of all people! They say he lost £5,000 in a gambling hell on Jermyn Street—and then that odious Meyler denounced him as a swindler to everyone who entered White's. Who would credit it? Of course poor Brummel had no choice but to flee. Had there been a scandal, he would have been asked to resign from his clubs—but heavens! The Beau!"

Fennel saw nothing so remarkable in that yet another dandy had run under the hatches, even the most illustrious dandy of them all. He gave his narrow white cravat one last twitch, coaxed down a curl upon his noble brow, and turned away from the mirror. Since Rosemary seemed so interested in the ruin of Brummel, Fennel informed her that Mr. Christie was to auction off the belongings of the gentleman of fashion most recently departed to the Continent. One would be able to avail oneself, Fennel had been told, of Sèvres vases and snuff boxes and chocolate cups, and a letterscale on a black plinth with Cupid weighing an ormolu heart.

"Fiddle!" responded Rosemary. She was not feeling kindly disposed toward her brother, who had given her a dreadful start earlier that day by using a poker to break off the heads of several bottles of soda, *à la* his hero, a proceeding that had resulted in a din so awful Rosemary thought her creditors en masse battered at the front door. "First Byron and then Brummel—I declare I don't know what the world is coming to when gentlemen must flee the country in such a havey-cavey manner due to pecuniary embarrassments."

Fennel was fond of his sisters, even the starched-up Rosemary, but that Rosemary should get into her airs again was too much to be stomached by a young man who already, and for very good reason, felt a little out of sorts. "*That* won't wash!" said he. "You're badly dipped yourself! Don't pull a long face over me, because it won't do you any good; I know very well you're a trifle scorched—you told me so yourself!"

Lily, whose unhappy thoughts had progressed from her failure to kindle Lord Kingscote's ardor to a contemplation of how Lord Chalmers's affections might best be sparked, was here urged by her good heart to intervene. It was not kind of Fennel, she remarked, to point out again that Rosemary was first of all the Millikins to try and outrun the constable; nor was it admirable in Rosemary to play the hypocrite. If Mr. Brummel and Lord Byron had deep doings, as they so obviously had, it was not to be wondered at, since gentlemen of fashion were expected to fall into debt. However, ladies of quality were not expected to run similarly aground. Moreover, Lily did not see why Rosemary and Fennel should both glower at her in that unfriendly manner. And were those *sapphires* hung round her sister's neck?

"What else would they be, silly?" Smugly, Rosemary patted the gems. "The Chalmers sapphires, my dears! What do you think of them?"

"A trifle old-fashioned, ain't they?" inquired Fennel, while Lily expressed an opinion that a heavy necklace of large sapphires was not quite the accessory for mid-afternoon. "I
142

must say," added Fennel, before Lily's ill-advised opinion could earn them both a rake-down, "it was very clever of you to get them back, Rosemary! How *did* you?"

"Hush!" Rosemary cast a cautionary look at the door. "Do you mean to publish it to the world?"

Mention of publication recalled to Lily another little matter, one from which she had derived much amusement. Lily, quite worn-down by the difficulty of determining with whom she should elope, was very much in a mood for additional amusement. "Fennel, what about Phoebe?"

Fennel looked, in that moment, much less like an aspiring poet than like a hunted fawn. "Phoebe?" he echoed weakly. "Who's this Phoebe? What maggot have you taken in your head now, puss?"

"Why, Fennel! How can you accuse me of such a thing?" Lily clasped her little hands in genuine distress. "It's true that I may sometimes get the cart before the horse, but I don't generally make things up out of whole cloth, and I remember very clearly you told me about Phoebe yourself. You said she was a fine vulgar miss and that her mama was a dragon who—"

"Yes, yes!" Fennel interrupted, hastily. "Never mind that— I recollect it now! Nothing to worry your head about, puss!"

"I wasn't *worried*," responded Lily, oblivious to Rosemary's frowning countenance and Fennel's frantic glance. "Not about that, anyway! I merely wondered if you were able to convince the dragon that your pockets are to let—because the more I think about it the less I like this threat of a breach of promise suit!"

Nor was Rosemary elated by mention of such a thing. Even as her brother verged on departure, she grasped his ear, led him to the needlepoint-covered sofa, and ordered that he sit. Fennel's long experience with sisters had taught him the futility of argument. He sat. "Tell me of this breach of promise suit," Rosemary said grimly.

Fennel obeyed. "It was only a bit of frolic!" he protested. "Just a lark! If the dragon hadn't taken the notion we're well-heeled, no one would be a penny the worst of it! Phoebe wasn't adverse to a little flirtation, I'll have you know."

143

"Flirtation!" pronounced Rosemary, in such dire tones that Lily sped across the room. "How unspeakably odious! Now we *are* undone! Fennel, how *could* you have gone frolicking among the muslin company?"

"Take a damper!" responded Fennel, looking most uncomfortable. "It was no such thing. On the square, Rosemary! I ain't *that* full of frisk, even if the dragon does accuse me of being a gay deceiver and trying to hedge off." He dropped his gaze to the floor. "It's the very devil of a business! I don't know whether I'd do better to murder the dragon, or to blow my own brains out."

"How very like you to botch the thing!" Rosemary retorted unsympathetically. "And then to maunder on about doing away with yourself, as if it would answer the purpose. Well, I assure you it wouldn't! Oh, I could weep with pure vexation! Fennel, you are a cabbage-head."

Lily, who had hovered undecided by the couch, waiting to see which of her siblings was in most need of her sympathetic ministrations, was horrified to hear Fennel express an opinion, that if Rosemary did not cease moralizing over him, he would forthwith blow out *her* brains. "No, no!" gasped Lily, and threw herself upon her brother. "Fennel, you must not! I'm sure it would be a thing no one could blame in you, because it is most aggravating to be forever nattered away at—and I know all about that because I have been badgered incessantly about Kingscote! As if I *could* find it amusing to keep him dangling, like Chalmers accused me of doing. You were correct, Rosemary: he *is* an unfeeling brute!"

Rosemary's spouse had given her no cause to take exception to this accusation, his latest excursion into the realm of insensitivity having 'been a graphic description of angry workmen currently engaged in destroying threshing-machines and attacking mills and pulling down houses, bands of whom were marching about the countryside waving flags marked "Bread or blood." Still, she felt no obligation to enter upon a denunciation of her nipfarthing spouse. " 'Hedging off', Fennel?" she said with determination. "I think you had better tell me the whole!"

This Fennel did, once he had disentangled himself from

Lily and assured her that he would wreak no physical violence upon Rosemary, an assurance that did not inspire Lily to relinquish her vise-like grip on his arm. He told Rosemary of his initial encounter with the merry Phoebe Holloway outside the Pantheon Bazaar, of their subsequent trysts, of his last meeting with Phoebe's mama, who clung with the tenacity of a bulldog to her intention of involving him in a breach of promise suit. "At first I thought *she* was queer in the attic!" Fennel offered in conclusion. "Thought I couldn't be sued for promises I didn't make. Now I'm not so sure! The dragon made some very nasty suggestions about the indignity of being brought to court, and what the family might have to say to it."

What sentiment might be expressed by the family, were Fennel to be prosecuted for failure to keep his promises, whether those promises had been made or not, was quickly aired by Rosemary. "This is all Angelica's fault! As if it were not bad enough that she should indulge in a sordid little intrigue, she must allow you to do likewise!"

"Flim-flam!" interjected Fennel. "It was no such thing."

"Oh? Then why is this odious female threatening a public washing of dirty linen?" Rosemary paced the floor. "She could hardly do so were there no dirty linen to wash! One thing is certain, you cannot apply to Chalmers for assistance. It's been all I can contrive to get myself clear."

Fennel, in the unenviable position of having given Rosemary his head for washing, as well as his dirty linen to Mrs. Holloway, seized on this red herring gratefully. "How *did* you get clear? If I could similarly come up with sufficient of the ready, the dragon could be bought off. She said she doesn't *wish* to make trouble, but that it ain't right Phoebe should go without some compensation for her loss. Which seems fair enough, though I don't think I'm any great loss!"

Nor did Rosemary, and so she said, which resulted in a set-to with Lily, who considered that her brother had quite enough misfortune with which to contend without Rosemary's addition of insult to injury. As a result of this spirited defense, Fennel turned to her. "You're a dashed good girl, puss! Kingscote's a lucky fellow. Come to think of it, so are you—not a fellow, that is, but lucky! Eh?"

Due to Fennel's various misfortunes, Lily did not reward this delicate attempt to learn the condition of her emotions with the truth. Though Fennel was responsible for Lily's efforts to show Lord Kingscote how well she suited him, and for Lord Kingscote's subsequent offer of matrimony, that was all spilt milk under the bridge, and Lily had no desire to add her own unhappiness to her brother's budget of woes. "Oh, yes, very fortunate! So fortunate that I sometimes do not quite believe in it! Just think, I might have been left on the shelf. Now let us talk about you and Phoebe."

Fennel was immeasurably relieved to hear that Lily had grown resigned to her eminently eligible catch. If Phoebe's mama carried out even half her threats, Fennel would have no time to instruct Lord Kingscote in the proper way to court a damsel prone to romantical high-flights. Seeing that his attention had strayed, the damsel nipped him smartly with her fingernails. "To say the truth," muttered Fennel, "I'd as lief *not* talk about the silly wench!"

"I'll warrant you wouldn't!" snapped Rosemary, from a gilt chair near the fireplace, where she had arranged herself with regal dignity that was marred only by the circumstance that in the process she'd somehow smudged her cheek. "But if we're to wrap this disgraceful peccadillo up in clean linen, you must!"

"It *wasn't* a peccadillo!" insisted Fennel. "We didn't—"

"I beg you, say no more!" cried Rosemary. "Pray remember that you are in a lady's drawing room, Fennel! Other females of your acquaintance may not be so nice in their notions, but *I* have no interest in low vulgar talk."

Fennel had opened his mouth to deliver a scathing, and justly merited, denunciation of Rosemary's posturing but Lily pinched his arm. "You may tell *me* all about it later!" she promised. "Just now, I think we should decide what you are to do."

"What *can* I do?" moaned Fennel, as Rosemary contemplated whether it was worth her effort to scold Lily for being an incurable busybody. "The dragon gave me the choice
146

of buying Phoebe off or marrying her—that is, if I don't wish to be dragged into court. And I don't wish, more's the pity, because I don't see what else is to be done!"

"*Marry* her?" screeched Rosemary, so wild with horror at the suggestion that Lily was spared her tongue-lashing, which would doubtless have accomplished as little as its innumerable predecessors. "Fennel, you cannot!"

"It's sure as check that I don't want to," Fennel admitted handsomely. "I don't like the chit above half! But how the deuce am I to buy her off without any money? Don't worry, I shan't apply to Chalmers! He's such a curst high stickler he'd haul me over the coals and then tell me I must pull my own fat out of the fire! But if Chalmers won't fork over the rhino for me, who else—" His blue eye lit on Lily. "Kingscote!"

That Fennel suffered a certain dilatoriness of memory, Lily already knew; but she bitterly regretted that the dilatoriness should exhibit itself just then. Since Rosemary was as high a stickler as her starched-up spouse, and consequently couldn't be trusted to look with approbation upon a huggermugger elopement with a gentlemen as yet undetermined, Lily could hardly in Rosemary's hearing remind Fennel that she had no intention of marrying Kingscote. Too, though Lily might be embarked upon a course that made of the duke a dupe, such was her feeling for her *fiancé* that she could not relish the thought that anyone else should make him look a fool, as appeared to be Fennel's intent. Therefore, Lily stated an opinion that to seek assistance of Lord Kingscote in this matter would be a trifle indelicate.

"Lily is correct!" said Rosemary, with surprised approval, when Fennel exhibited a tendency toward argument. "Now do hush, the pair of you, for I've hit upon the perfect thing. Even Angelica would say so, did she but know if it, which I am determined she will not, because I cannot but consider she is entirely to blame! None of this would have happened had she not kept Fennel on so loose a rein. What Marigold would say I dare not even think!"

Fennel blanched at the intimation that his mother might be informed of his predicament, which would doubtless inspire her to convulsion fits. "No need to tell Marigold!" he gasped. "Or Angelica. By the bye, where *is* she?"

Lily smiled to see her brother gazing around the room in an apprehensive manner, as if Angelica might suddenly spring from behind a chair. "Don't fret! Angelica has gone to her room with a hot brick. Fennel, we must decide what is to be done about Phoebe. Despite what Rosemary has said, I think we should tell Angelica. She always knows what to do!"

"Oh, yes!" cried Rosemary. "She knows very well, it seems—well enough to engage in clandestine meetings with an ineligible *parti* when she should have been helping me! That shows very clearly where we stand in Angelica's priorities. There is no use in acquainting Angelica with our little puzzles—better we solve them ourselves!"

Cautiously, Fennel eyed Rosemary. In his past association with this particular sister, he had never known her to solve anything—the Chalmers sapphires were an excellent case in point. Fennel's apprehensive eye alit on those gems. Into that eye came a gleam. "By Jove, I've got it! You can pop the sapphires again, Rosemary!"

"No, I cannot!" snapped his unobliging sister. "Not after working myself into a fever of the brain to figure out how to redeem them. But don't despair, Fennel; I have an even better notion! There is a Mr. Thwaite in Newgate Street who will help you—he is the most obliging man!"

Again came one of Fennel's sporadic bursts of intuition: Rosemary had redeemed the Chalmers sapphires with the assistance of a moneylender. Fennel's intuition, alas, failed him at that point. He thought it was an excellent notion to buy off Phoebe's dragon of a mama with money procured from a curst cent-percent.

Seventeen

Angelica and Sir Randall were alone in the garden—alone, that is, except for the zebras and the panthers, the sheep and the ram, the buffalo and the llama and the East Indian shawl goat. In the absence of the irrepressible Simon, whose habit it was to entertain them both with such unsuitable topics as the preponderance of brothels around Piccadilly, examples being The Key in Chandos Street and the Archbishop's Nunnery situated across Westminster Bridge hard by the Archepiscopal Palace and highly favored by the swells, the conversation was desultory.

"Miss Smith," observed Sir Randall, in an irritable tone, "you are acting very out-of-sorts. Have you been teasing yourself with thoughts of your sisters' problems? I wish that you would not; it makes you very bad company! Anyway, it can not be so desperately bad as all that."

Sadly Angelica surveyed her employer, who was toying in an absent manner with a letter knife. She could hardly ask him if the shocking intimations made by Bimble and Mallet were fact; she could not trust that even Sir Randall would tell her the truth. In any event, it mattered little whether Bimble and Mallet were correct. Angelica knew enough of the world to realize that were information laid against Sir Randall his reputation would be ruined, even were the information a gross misrepresentation of reality. Angelica had no alternative but to apply to Simon, both for corroboration and financial assistance—but where was he? The resurrectionists had not impressed Angelica as being patient folk.

While his amanuensis thusly pondered, Sir Randall had launched into a soliloquy upon scarlet fever, progressing from the time of year most conducive to the sickness (late summer) through the symptoms (rigors and shivering and red scaly spots) to the efficacy of blisters and paregoric draughts. "Animal food must not be taken," he said, then paused. "Miss Smith, I do wish you would tell me what ails you!"

Tell Sir Randall that she feared him guilty of the worst of all crimes? Never! Nor would she reveal her speculation upon the missing Simon's whereabouts, lest Sir Randall misinterpret her anxiety. "It is nothing of importance. Do not press me further, I beg."

"Certainly not, if you do not wish it!" Sir Randall responded, rather stiffly. "Although it has me quite in a puzzle why you suddenly cannot bring yourself to trust me. I had thought we were friends. No, not another word, Miss Smith! I am very displeased with you and I wish you would go away."

"But, Sir Randall!" cried Angelica, very close to tears. "I didn't mean that I cannot trust you. Truly, I do!"

Sir Randall contemplated his paper knife, then with it gestured violently in the direction of his amanuensis. "Do I not pay your salary, Miss Smith? Have I given you leave to argue? We will continue our discussion some other time when you are less distracted and a great deal more composed. And now, good day!"

Angelica looked at the paper knife, and at her employer's annoyed expression, and abruptly admitted defeat. She walked slowly toward the house, there to retrieve her bonnet and pelisse from the study. Sir Randall, whose ill-humor was resultant upon yet another interrogation conducted by his son on the subject of Miss Smith, gazed upon her retreating, lachrymose figure and irritably informed the llama that Miss Smith stood in grave need of remedies much stronger than syrup of poppies and a hot brick.

Unbeknownst to Sir Randall, Miss Smith was fated to endure just such stronger measures, though whether the result was beneficial remains to be seen. Sir Randall's study was not empty. Standing near the bookshelves, in very near the same spot where she had originally glimpsed him, stood Simon Brisbane. "Oh!" gasped Angelica. "I have been wanting particularly to see you. You will know precisely what to do and I do not—indeed, my thoughts are not worth the purchase of a guinea, no matter how greatly I cudgel my brain!"

Was this an adventuress? Simon asked himself again. He had delayed his decision in hope she would betray herself, but thus far she had not. Clearly more direct action was required. How was he to persuade her that, as his favorite of the moment, she need not hold him at arm's length? With a twinkle in his green eyes, Simon suggested that his next-intended conquest take a seat. "Now tell me," he invited generously, "what has put you in a tweak!"

Ah, but he was a handsome devil, Angelica thought wistfully, with his athletic figure, his harsh and dissipated features, his diabolically irresistible charm. Then she took herself to task for this lack of concentration. Was she in her dotage that she should forget everything, even the possibility that Sir Randall might be dragged off to gaol, just because she received a smile from a hardened rakeshame?

Resolutely she averted her eyes from his face. "I think that the most dreadful moment came when Sir Randall brandished that paper knife in my direction and demanded that I go away. I had not believed it until then, had thought perhaps it was all no more than the result of an unlucky mischance." Again she looked at Simon, this time with disapproval. "I could wish that you had told me the whole previously! Heaven knows I could easily have made a fatal misstep. Oh, do not look so taken aback; I have already told you the secret is safe."

Simon, who had not the most distant guess why Miss Smith should be in the devil of a pucker, unless it was because Sir Randall had given her her *congée*, consequently interrupted her disclosures in a most uncomplimentary light. Clearly the tale-pitching Durward had been more astute than Simon had previously realized; it was Simon himself who had lacked perspicacity in doubting that Miss Smith could be a

151

straw damsel bent on worming her way into his father's heart. Had Miss Smith not been a designing female, as Durward had all along sworn she was, she would not now be mouthing dire comments about nonexistent secrets. It was not the first time she had done so, and that previous occasion had led Simon to inquire very particularly into his father's recent activities. As a result of that inquiry Sir Randall was acquitted of misdeeds, and Miss Smith convicted of nourishing some very evil design. "Precisely what is it you want, Miss Smith?" Simon asked, without the least change in manner. Simon treated all females alike, duchess or adventuress, which since ladies like to be treated as if they aren't, and lady-birds as if they are, suited them all fine.

Because his manner toward her had not changed, Angelica did not immediately perceive that she had been cast as the slyest thing in nature. "It is not what I *want*," she responded frankly, "but what I must have. The thing simply cannot be accomplished without money. Oh, it is very dreadful, but I do not know where else to turn. But you are a man of substance—"

Even as she spoke, Simon had walked toward her. Now he reached out and took her hand and drew her to her feet. "Exactly so!" he said, wryly. "In short, I could set you up in very easy circumstances, such as must seem most desirous to a female with a consumptive parent who sews by candlelight to keep the wolf from the door. Let us begin as we mean to go on, my darling—without secrets! You tell me what's in your mind, and I will oblige with anything you wish. I will even explain to you precisely what is an orgy."

Angelica did not grasp Simon's intent, thought in fact that his comments were deuced odd. "Naturally I should like to know," she said, gazing doubtfully up at him, "oh, all sorts of things! But is this the moment for such stuff? Shouldn't we deal with the matter of your father first—that is, if you do mean to oblige me?"

As Simon had previously suspected, he had made a grave omission in never dallying with a lady in the style of the mysterious Miss Smith. With an eye to making Miss Smith aware of that omission and his wish that it be speedily
152

rectified, he placed his hands on her shoulders. "I shall try and never disoblige you!" he promised recklessly.

Somehow, decided Angelica, this conversation had gotten out of hand, as conversations with Simon tended frequently to do. More than once an innocent discussion of, for example, the strategies employed by Napoleon had deteriorated into, say, an exposé of an elegant establishment in Berwick Street, wherein had been introduced various refinements witnessed by its owner while on tour of the more distinguished houses of pleasure existent in Paris. Because Simon was an abominably provoking creature who delighted in putting her to the blush, Angelica had learned to pay his more outrageous sallies very little heed. Currently he seemed in a very funning mood. Consequently Angelica requested that he cease trying to cut a wheedle because important matters were at stake.

And because Angelica had never displayed the strong sense of propriety cherished by any well-brought-up young woman as proof of her birthright, Simon had no reason to believe she was above his touch. His fingers tightened. "It makes me very melancholy to think that you would try and put the screws to me. It is very enterprising of you, but there is no need, my darling. Had I not liked you very well, I would not have made you the object of such persistent gallantry."

"Gallantry?" echoed Angelica, dumbfounded. "What *are* you talking about?"

Simon was a man of great patience. For what purpose she played off her tricks he couldn't assess, but he was willing to wait for enlightenment. Therefore he brushed back a curl that had fallen onto her cheek, and informed her that he didn't mind if for some incomprehensible reason she sought to pretend ignorance of the fact that he had no sooner set eyes on her than he immediately began to pay her court, to bestow upon her delicate attentions that betokened absolute enrapturement—but she must not think she could beat him at the post.

"Humbug!" responded Angelica, rather weakly. Though a great many of Simon's comments had been incomprehensible to her, she had gained the distinct impression that he was inviting her to persevere with him in loose morality. Since it was inconceivable that even so hardened a rakeshame as Simon Brisbane should escort any but a dazzling barque of frailty down the primrose path, and since Angelica did not fit that description in the least, she could only assume he spoke in jest. Ah, if only she were the sort of female who might carelessly engage in open intrigue, wish her exasperating family to the devil and embark upon a life of carefree dissipation without heed of consequence—but she was not, and thus would never know the bliss of misbehaving with a gentleman so lost to propriety as to encourage her in every sort of excess.

Meanwhile, and with considerable amusement, Simon looked down into Miss Smith's bemused face. Since Simon had in all his life encountered not a single lady who could resist his devastating charm, and since Miss Smith had hitherto given little indication of being the exception to this universal susceptibility, he may perhaps be forgiven for presuming that she would accept the highly flattering alliance that he verged on offering her. Before he made that offer, however, he must have Miss Smith's promise that toward Sir Randall she would harbor no more evil designs. With that intention, he gently hinted that once she came under his protection he would expect her to drop every other connection of every sort and kind.

Could the man seriously contemplate that Angelica would toss her hat over the windmill? It boggled her mind. With great effort, she regained the use of her tongue. "Now I think you *must* be trifling with me!"

Obviously he had failed to make clear his intention, which was most unlike him, but an error that could be immediately remedied. "No, my little hornet, I am not!" Simon drew her into his arms and embraced her with a rough ardor that various other Misses Millikin would have thoroughly approved. Then he put her away from him. "Now I have trifled with you. What say you to that?"

To Angelica's prior disabilities, her giddiness and palpitations and the oppressions on her chest, was now added a shortness of breath. Valerian had been correct in predicting that Simon Brisbane would interpret a freedom of speech as an invitation to take liberties, a piece of prescience that put

Angelica thoroughly out of charity, not with Simon, but with her brother. "So *that* is how one trifles? How very enlightening! To say the truth, I liked it excessively—but you should not have done it, all the same. You seem to think—but I am not—at the cost of appearing prudish, I must ask that you cease to pester me!"

"*Pester* you?" echoed Simon, in amazement. Simon was, after all, a gazetted rakehell, and not accustomed to hearing his polished advances spoken of in such crushing terms. "Come down off your high ropes, my girl! I have promised you may set yourself up in the latest mode, but this habit you have of trying to imitate your betters is damned tedious. Which brings to mind another matter—what the devil is your name? I can hardly address my *petite amie* as Miss Smith!"

Confronted with yet further proof of the very low opinion in which she was held by Simon Brisbane, Angelica did not long retain her powers of speech. "Your—?" she gasped, and sought to free herself from his grip. "Oh, no!"

"No?" This seduction was monstrous up-hill work. Inexorably, Simon drew his excessively silly bit of fluff close once more. "Why have you turned so suddenly missish? Next you will say that a liaison with myself is much too dreadful to contemplate, which is a great piece of nonsense. You will like it very well, my darling, I promise. As for what the wicked world will say of such an entanglement—why should you care?"

Angelica was, by these remarks, thoroughly appalled. It was no more than she deserved for encouraging Simon to speak frankly to her about the path he followed; he thought her no more than one of the wicked herself. She was not surprised at it, especially. Admittedly she had not expected to be offered a slip on the shoulder—but amazement had quickly taken a lesser place to a much more disgraceful emotion. Scandalous as it was in her, Angelica came within an ace of responding to Simon Brisbane's infamous proposal with a simple yes.

Passion did not get the better of reason, however, though the race was close. In the very nick of time, Angelica recalled Fennel's request that in exactly such a case as this she should remember the obligations owed her family; and Valerian's promise, again in precisely such a case, to challenge Simon to pistols at daybreak. "You go beyond the line of being pleasing, sir!" Angelica murmured into Simon's snowy cravat. "I am not—I have never—oh, this is all a hum!"

"Never!" echoed Simon, in tones of stark disbelief. "That, my girl, is doing it *much* too brown. I don't mind, you know—after all, I *have*, and frequently! It would be very shabby of me to mind if in the past you've been a little indiscreet. What a silly girl you are, my darling. As if—"

"Pray, stop!" wailed Angelica, and struggled so frantically that Simon quirked a quizzical brow. Angelica glared at him and spat: "Sir, I find your suggestions insufferable and yourself offensive and demand that you apologize immediately!"

Had he been mistaken in her? Could Miss Smith, as she seemed to wish him to think, view him with repugnance? She looked so very unhappy, with her heaving bosom and tousled hair and blue eyes filled with tears, that he sought to soothe her. "I do apologize, my darling," he said in kindly tones. "I would not cause you unhappiness for anything. If I have misread your character, let us consider it a temporary aberration on my part, deriving from concern for my father, and speak no more of it!"

But Angelica, in the perverse tradition of every female since Eve, was no sooner presented with a reasonable resolution to her dilemma than she decided it would not do. "Your father!" she echoed blankly.

Simon caught up her hands, which had flown to her hot cheeks. "Don't try and pull the wool over my eyes," he said, though sympathetically. "You must know I will not stand for it."

"Stand for what?" wondered Angelica, and then illumination burst upon her. Simon Brisbane thought her a designing hussy who had set her cap for Sir Randall, and it was with the purpose of thrusting a spoke in her wheel that Simon had paid her court. Thus was the mystery of why a hardened rakeshame should offer *carte blanche* to an ugly duckling solved: he had never dreamed she would agree. Angelica sent up thanksgiving that she had not betrayed the fact that, had not circumstance and birth and every shred of common sense prohibited, she would have liked more than anything to be Simon Brisbane's *petite amie.*

Naturally Angelica would endure a thousand agonies before she betrayed to Simon the fool he had made of her, or the pain that smote her with the realization that she had been his dupe. "Fiend seize you, release me, you brute!" she hissed. So startled was Simon by her vehemence that he complied. He was soon to be even more startled: Angelica boxed his ears.

Eighteen

It was a quiet afternoon in the fashionable part of town where stood the Chalmers town house; a lazy dreaming kind of day that inspired in adventurous souls a sudden yen for some disruption of their daily routine, and in the less bold a tendency to air-dream. Since the Millikins, for all their fits and starts and hankering after romance, were not especially bold, they had chosen to remain within doors. The one exception was Fennel, and he had not set forth wholly of his own accord.

Having dispatched her brother to the office of the benevolent Mr. Thwaite, Rosemary then turned her attention to those other of her siblings beneath the venerable Chalmers roof. Lily she found closeted with Angelica, applying cool cloths to their eldest sister's brow. In response to Rosemary's sharp inquiry, Lily recited a list of symptoms that ranged from giddiness and palpitations to an oppression on the chest; and Angelica herself

157

proffered a faint statement that she had come by her just deserts and was no more than consequently fatigued. Though Rosemary could not help but think Angelica had been well-served—had not Angelica selfishly abandoned her family to pursue an ineligible romance?—she could not stand idly by and watch her sister suffer. Therefore she sent a servant to fetch her own supply of Velno's Vegetable Syrup and Godbold's Vegetable Balsam. Alas for Rosemary's kindly intentions, greeted by Angelica with an incomprehensible remark about the inefficacy of syrup of poppies and hot bricks: the servant returned not bearing the prescribed remedies, but the intelligence that Lord Chalmers wished to speak immediately with his lady.

With a haste not at all commensurate with her exalted position—baronesses were definitely not expected to pick up their skirts and run hell-for-leather down the hallway—Rosemary sped toward her boudoir. Panting, dishevelled, she paused on the threshold. Surely Chalmers dared not rummage through her possessions!

Again, alas: Chalmers had done precisely that thing. He waved a sheaf of papers beneath his wife's delicate nose. "Come in," he commanded, "and close the door!"

Rosemary obeyed. With a fine display of nonchalance, she walked to her *chaise longue*. If she sat down a trifle abruptly, her husband was not to know it was due to a quaking in her lower extremities. "You wished," she said blandly, "to speak with me?"

"Not especially," her lord retorted irately, "but it seems I must. What the devil have you been about, Rosemary? Did I not warn you about running into debt? Yet you have openly defied me—have in fact made me a figure of ridicule."

"Oh, surely not!" protested Rosemary. "It is *I* who have run into a little scrape, not you! For my foolishness, you are hardly to blame."

By this generous admission of folly, Lord Chalmers's wrath was not assuaged. A most unbecoming jealousy had led him to ransack his wife's boudoir in search of the identity of the man who dared send her *billets-doux*, and with whom he feared she connived to plant the antlers on his brow. Instead he had discovered that he wronged his wife in suspecting her
158

of infidelity, which left him feeling very silly; and had paid her much too high a compliment in believing she had heeded his exhortations to refrain from running into further debt. In short, she had made a thorough laughingstock of him, which was a sore blow to his pride.

"Not to blame?" he echoed, looking like a thundercloud. "I would that were the case, madam. Could I but do so without coming under the gravest censure, I would wash my hands of you! But I am responsible for your conduct, as well as your debts. Good God, Rosemary, what possessed you? Next I suppose we would have been dunned in the streets!"

Though this was not Rosemary's first encounter with an enraged spouse, she had never before seen Lord Chalmers make quite so horrid a kickup. She was sorry to have enraged him, and at the same time resentful; she thought it would behoove her to proceed most diplomatically. Accordingly, she remained silent.

But her husband was spoiling for a battle, and his wife's silence further roused his spleen. "I am very much disgusted with you!" he announced, rather redundantly. "You have displayed a sad unsteadiness of character, a lack of stability—you have shown no more regard for the dignities I have bestowed upon you than—than the kitchen cat!"

"Have we one?" interrupted Rosemary. "A cat?"

"How the devil should *I* know?" snarled Lord Chalmers. "That's *your* province! Pray do not interrupt! As I was saying, er—ah! Had you wished to make us food for scandal, you could not have acted differently. I make you my compliments! All the same, I've no intention of allowing a disagreeable stigma to be attached to my name."

Despite her excellent intentions, diplomacy was not Rosemary's long suit; with these extreme incivilities Chalmers tried her patience too high. With immeasurable majesty Rosemary rose from her *longue*, placed her fists on her slender hips, announced that her husband's accusations were more than flesh and blood could bear. Lord Chalmers, who on second thought would realize he may have been a trifle high-handed in his dealings with his wife, had not yet achieved the coolness of temper conducive to hindsight. He fired up and repeated that

159

her behavior left much to be desired. "Your profligacies," he concluded, "make me uneasy to a very considerable degree. Understand me, Rosemary, this is absolutely the *last* time you may expect me to bear the expense of your extravagance. To that vow I shall hold fast! You must perforce learn to practice economy."

"Economy!" Rosemary's lovely eyes flashed. "If you had a grain of proper sentiment you wouldn't be talking such fustian to me. Yes, fustian!" she repeated, as Lord Chalmers, nettled, made as if to speak. "Hear me out, sir; you owe it to me after the horrid things *you* have said! It is cruelly unfeeling of you to scold me when the whole thing is your fault—you keep me without money for common necessaries and yet expect me to live in the very best possible style. I'm sure it is no wonder I am brought to a standstill!"

Lord Chalmers was again strongly tempted to turn his wife over his knee, and might very well have done so had it not occurred to him that he had already conducted himself with a great deal less than baronial dignity. He said, repressively: "You are severe."

"Oh, no!" responded Rosemary dramatically. "It is not *I* who am severe. Even so, it is useless to expect you to enter into my feelings on this subject—or any other! I'll warrant that in the entire history of our marriage you have not been conversant with my feelings on *any* subject. Well, I take leave to tell you, sir, that I don't care a button for your starving workmen and your political stratagems and your Hampden clubs!"

"So I perceive!" said Lord Chalmers frigidly.

"You perceive nothing!" snapped Rosemary, who was so sorely tried by all this fuss that she had not the least inhibition about displaying a definitely vulgar rage. "You are so enamored of your accursed affairs of government that you have no affection left to bestow upon *people.* I never expected that you should love me; that would have been a great deal too much to ask. I did think that you must *like* me a little to wish to marry me, but evidently I over-anticipated your capacity for warmth!"

Astounded, Lord Chalmers regarded his wife, who possessed the Millikin ability to look quite splendid in a rage. A brilliant
160

orator as regarded affairs of state, Lord Chalmers now found himself in the most uncomfortable position of not knowing what to say. Even had words come to him, however, it is doubtful whether Lord Chalmers would have been given the opportunity for speech; Rosemary, who had for months been painstakingly discreet about her sentiments, was now throwing caution, with great gusto, to the winds.

"Because if you *did* like me, even just a little," said she, "you would not be eternally ringing peals over me. It was used to make me very sad, I can tell you! You will say it was no more than I should expect. Certainly you never gave me reason to think you might come to care for me."

Not only astounded but more than a little embarrassed by these frank disclosures, Lord Chalmers sought to silence his wife. He shook her, ungently. "Rosemary, mind your tongue!"

Rosemary was not so easily dissuaded once embarked upon a bout of histrionics. "I will not!" she snapped. "It has never been the least use disputing with you, for you always have the best of it—and you shan't this time! You may cut me off without a farthing, or publicly denounce me; it makes no difference. I would rather you did either than remain married to a man who won't allow me sixpence to scratch with even though he's rich as Croesus!"

Always it came back to his fortune, Lord Chalmers thought acerbically. Once more he shook his wife, this time with such savage energy that her mouth dropped open and her hair tumbled forward on her brow. "Chalmers!" she gasped. "How dare you use me in this way?"

"It is all of a piece with the other, madam!" retorted Lord Chalmers, shaking her still. "Am I not a brute?"

Rosemary suspected, from the look on her husband's face, that her prudent course of action would be to disagree. Since the Millikins were not prudent folk, she said instead that her husband was indeed a brute, at which point he abandoned all remaining shreds of dignity and did indeed turn her over his knee.

It was perhaps an hour later when Fennel Millikin made his way down the upstairs corridor that opened into his sister Rosemary's boudoir. His steps were not quite steady, nor his sense of direction trustworthy; he blundered into any number of chambers, including the chamber where Lily administered to Angelica, before broaching the boudoir. "What the deuce ails Angelica?" he demanded of Rosemary, who was stretched out face-down on her *chaise longue*. "Lily says she's suffered a disappointment of the heart."

"The devil," responded Rosemary, sitting painfully upright, "fly away with Angelica! The worst has come to pass, Fennel: Chalmers Knows All!"

To this ominous utterance, Fennel responded with a frown. It was not possible that Lord Chalmers could be aware of *all* the ramifications of the awkward businesses in which the Millikins were involved; Fennel himself had just learned of some of those ramifications, which had been of a nature to send him posthaste into the nearest boozing-ken, there to revitalize his flagging spirits with a lethal potation known as Blue Ruin. "All what?" he said.

So profound a lack of comprehension was remarkable even in a Millikin, and Rosemary awarded her brother a sharp glance. He was looking mussed; his gaze was owlish, his smile both lopsided and foolish. "Fennel! Are you *foxed*?"

"Foxed? In mid-afternoon? Not a bit of it!" The room had begun to spin around him, and Fennel sat quickly down beside his sister. She winced. "Maybe a *trifle* bosky," he admitted, "but were you in my position so would you be!"

Had Rosemary taken a little nip to fortify herself against each of the troubles gathering around her head, she would have been drunk as a wheelbarrow for the past sennight. That she had refrained from so doing was out of consideration for her thankless spouse. Already exasperated by his wife's inability to remain within a budget, Chalmers was like to positively froth at the mouth were he to discover that she additionally indulged a fondness for strong liquor. "What position *are* you in, Fennel?" she asked cautiously. "Was not Mr. Thwaite able to see you comfortably bestowed?"

"Comfortably!" Fennel enacted brotherly contempt. "A curst bloodsucker! It beats me, Rosemary, how you thought to bring everything off safe by allowing the gull-gropers to get their talons fast in you."

162

Rosemary suffered a dire presentiment, which she sought to brush aside. "Talons? Fiddle! Perhaps you did not properly explain—"

"Hah!" sneered Fennel, with curling lip. "It was he who explained, and most thoroughly. You signed a piece of paper, didn't you? Chowderhead!"

"Nothing of the sort!" responded Rosemary, though with little hope that this might prove to be the case. "'Twas mere formality!"

"In a pig's eye!" Fennel retorted bluntly. "You've run from Queer Street into the River Tick, and there's no getting away from it. Your Mr. Thwaite is a dashed rum customer! And you've let him back you smack up against the wall. There's nothing for it now but to tell Chalmers what you've done, because if you don't, Thwaite will!"

"Oh, Fennel, I cannot!" Rosemary wrung her hands. "Chalmers is already out-of-reason cross with me—were he to learn I'd pawned the sapphires, he truly would cast me off!" Suddenly she leaped up from the *longue*. "I have it! I'll pawn the sapphires again and repay Mr. Thwaite!"

"No, you won't!" said Fennel, gloomily. In response to his sister's perplexity, he explained to her the facts of life as concerned the exorbitant rate of interest charged by money-lenders. "In short, you're hard up against it, Rosemary. But I'll tell you what you *can* do: give me the sapphires and I'll buy off the dragon. That way at least one of us needn't go on puzzling our heads!"

To this suggestion, Rosemary responded in decidedly unappreciative terms. Fennel might easily have taken offense, especially at the intimation that he harbored bats in his church-loft, had Rosemary not simultaneously hurled herself upon his lap and wept all over him. "There, there!" he soothed, and patted her shoulder. "We'll figure some way out of this fix."

"I hope we may!" sniffled Rosemary. "But I doubt it very much. Chalmers will divorce me and that vulgar girl will marry you and we shall *both* be miserable. Oh, if only I had never set eyes on those wretched sapphires!"

Fennel wasn't certain what such an omission would accomplish, but he offered once again to take the offending article off his sister's hands, or neck. Belligerently Rosemary refused. Fennel did not press the matter at that moment, though he did cast an extremely thoughtful glance at his sister's jewel-chest.

"If I am to be made miserable," Rosemary said at length and removed herself from Fennel's chest, leaving him further mussed as well as damp, "there is no reason why you should also suffer. Do you tell your dragon to call on me, Fennel, and I will explain to her how it is that our pockets are to let."

By this nacky notion Fennel was so impressed that he wondered why he hadn't thought of it himself. Then he misdoubted that Lord Chalmers would approve the invasion of his ancestral home by a female who was rather less than respectable. In point of fact, Fennel suspected that if Lord Chalmers learned of Phoebe's mama's visit, he would subject his wife to the very devil of a scold. "It doesn't signify," interrupted Rosemary, despondently. "We always *do* come to cuffs, even when I try to be conciliating."

"So he does. Still, I would not mind his cheeseparing ways if only he were kind." Rosemary realized that her brother was eyeing her askance. "You doubt me? I cannot blame you for it. But I would feel no differently about Chalmers even if he squandered every bit of his fortune on play. Sometimes I wish he would! At least then I shouldn't have to keep up appearances!"

"The deuce you say!" ejaculated Fennel.

"Oh, yes, I am quite *épris*!" Rosemary admitted hollowly. Then, ashamed of her cravenly admissions, she proclaimed herself exhausted by the events of the afternoon and requested that she be left in solitude. Fennel left her, having reaped much food for thought.

Solitude achieved, however, Rosemary did not immediately sink back down upon her *longue*, there to contemplate her prospective existence as the least gay of *divorcees*. Instead she seated herself at her pretty writing desk. That Rosemary's siblings could not but be caught up in the scandalous backlash of her divorce was a circumstance she sorely rued. She could not change the ways of the world, unhappily; but she could at least warn Marigold that disaster would soon strike.

Nineteen

Fennel was not the only Millikin to over-indulge in the grape on that most inauspicious of days; Lily, that very evening, discovered in herself a great fondness for champagne. Since this discovery smote her in the midst of a masquerade ball, which Fennel complained was crowded as the very devil before deserting his sisters to drink himself under the table with all possible dispatch, Lily was able to indulge her thirst without any difficulty. As did a great many other guests, she soon took note. These were not the sort of people with whom Lily would expect her sister Rosemary to associate; they were definitely not persons of the first quality. But Lord Chalmers had insisted on their attendance, had roused Angelica from her sickbed and rousted Fennel from the wine-cellar and borne them all before him victoriously.

Why he had done so was a puzzle to Lily, who harbored no illusion about her brother-in-law's philanthropy. Had Chalmers acted wholly out of a concern for the well-being of the Millikins in residence beneath his roof, Lily would eat her head-dress—and since Lily's head was dressed in the style of the late Queen of France, complete with towering powdered wig decked about with flowers and fruit and wildlife, this would have been no mean feat. All the same, Lily was pleased enough to attend this masquerade, even though the company *was* a little fast, and so she stated to her escort, who was clad in the garb of a buccaneer. Immediately he responded that she must trust him to keep her safe from harm.

"Very well!" Lily's flirtatious glance was rendered no less

effective by the mask she wore. "If you should not object, sir, I should be most pleased—because I feel a fit of folly coming on, and though I do not *wish* to make a byword of myself, no Millikin yet has chosen the road of decorum and dignity. Oh!" Her hands flew to her mouth. "Now I have told you who I am. How careless of me!"

"Don't tease yourself." Her escort signalled to a servant for additional champagne. "I had already guessed your identity."

"Oh?" Lily's pretty nose wrinkled as she breathed bubbles from her glass. "Do you know me, sir?"

"Everyone knows Miss Lily Millikin!" He made an elegant little bow. "Quite half London is mad for the Fair Incomparable. You have broken countless hearts, my cruel lovely!"

"Oh yes, I'm all the crack!" admitted Lily. Where once this nonsense would have gratified, it now turned flat. "It is a very sad fix to be in."

"A sad fix?" echoed the buccaneer, who seemed most extremely affected by these remarks. "That is an odd comment, surely, from an acknowledged beauty? Or is it something else that has put you in the pathetics?"

Lily emptied her glass in one unmaidenly gulp and with it gestured rather dramatically. In so doing she only narrowly avoided collision with several of her fellow guests. "Sir, you can have no idea! Were I to make you a candid confession you would understand the delicacy of my position, and why I wish I were well out of this whole business." She sniffled, enchantingly. "But this is a very loose way of talking, and you will not wish to hear any such things!"

"You err, Miss Millikin; your unhappiness has quite wrung my heart." The buccaneer took her arm. "Furthermore, I nourish a burning wish to know what has made you so unhappy. Come here, into this alcove. Now tell me all about it! Surely a young lady so first-rate that all the gentlemen sigh and die for her cannot have cause for complaint."

"Not *all*!" she said, bitterly.

The buccaneer saw her to a sofa, seated her with fine attention to the wide panniers of her skirt, then positioned himself at her side. "Miss Millikin, I find that difficult to credit."

"To own the truth, so do I." Lily heaved a great sigh. "It is very dull work for *me* to say I'm fine as fivepence, but it would be very silly of me to pretend that I am not! Yet it avails me absolutely nothing to be at the top of the tree, because the gentleman to whom I am betrothed is totally indifferent."

"The devil!" ejaculated the buccaneer.

"So you may say! I have tried and tried, but nothing I can do will throw him into transports, and as for the notion that he should be carried away by the violence of his feeling—well! It is too much to ask, I guess, that a man who has been everywhere and done everything should be less than *blasé*. Doubtless he has grown immensely unsusceptible to feminine attraction—in which case I don't perceive why he should wish to marry me!"

"My dear Miss Millikin!" said the buccaneer.

"I should not speak so frankly to you." Lily signalled a passing servant and procured more champagne. "It is not at all the thing. Even so, if I do not tell someone I must surely scream, and I cannot confide in my sisters, who have troubles of their own, or my brother, who is entirely at fault! I beg you will forgive my impropriety."

The buccaneer stated his opinion of propriety, with a harsh lack of the same. Lily regarded him with awe. "Upon my word, that was a most colorful turn of speech!"

"Yes but don't repeat it or you *will* be in the suds! What I meant to say, Miss Millikin, was that I should be honored if you would confide in me. Shall I promise you never to repeat a word?"

"Oh, I don't care about that!" Lily drank deeply from her glass. "I shan't be here anyway—although I shouldn't wish any scandal to attach itself to my *fiancé*. I like him very well, even if he does regard me with a want of affection. I do think it all *very* hard! We might have dealt delightfully, even if he is so much older than myself. Still, he is the very pink of perfection, and I am a mere dab of a girl even if I *am* a nonpareil! No doubt he has already come to repent of his choice. So I shall slip away and leave Angelica to take the field, as she should have done in the first place—providing, that is, that Angelica recovers from the sickness of the heart attendant upon her infatuation with an ineligible *parti*!"

Because the buccaneer wore a full face mask, his expression could not be glimpsed. Nonetheless, there was a tension in the way he held his body that hinted at strong emotion held in check. Also, in his voice was a touch of distress. "Angelica? Do you think you might start at the beginning, my dear?"

Lily was nothing loth. She poured the whole tale of her association with Lord Kingscote into the buccaneer's receptive ear; she explained how she had meant the duke for her elder sister, and how when the duke and her elder sister had not proved obliging she had become betrothed to him herself. "That came about when Fennel said I was not in Kingscote's style; of course I had to set proving I was the very woman calculated to suit his taste! Then he offered for me and I could not dash his hopes." The buccaneer inquired why she had entered into an engagement which she didn't seem to fancy overmuch. "I do not like to be unkind, you see, and I needed time to think. Now that I *have* thought and thought, there is only one solution. I must fly to Gretna Green."

"Elope?" The buccaneer sounded even more startled. "What is this? Have I misunderstood? *Do* you wish to marry your *fiancé*?"

"What *I* wish has little to do with it!" Lily responded sternly. "Though my understanding is not great, I perfectly comprehend that Lord Kingscote would not be happy with me, nor I with him. He has never even professed to be my very ardent admirer, no matter how strongly I intimate he should—and I can hardly ask him outright to do so, because he would probably think I wished him to administer to my vanity."

The buccaneer removed Lily's empty glass from her careless fingers and set it on the floor. "Is that *not* what you want, Miss Millikin?" he inquired quietly.

Lily's eyes, behind her mask, filled with tears. "No, it isn't! It is most unkind of you to hint that I wish my vanity puffed up, especially when all I care about is that *he* should care about me! And I think that he must not, because he has not offered me a single attention that is a little too pointed, or subjected me to any such gallantry." She turned her head away, so that the buccaneer found himself eye-to-eye with an improbably-colored stuffed bird, and added delicately: "I have had the opportunity to observe at close range a marriage between two people who do not *suit*. It is not what I wish for myself, or for Lord Kingscote. So you understand that you misjudge me. Not that I hold it against you, sir! You clearly do not know me well."

"Clearly I do not," said the gentleman, rather drily, and extended a handkerchief. "I fear, Miss Millikin, that I am grown a trifle obtuse, but on one point I am exceedingly confused. If I may be so bold as to inquire, what *are* your sentiments regarding Lord Kingscote?"

"Marriage to Lord Kingscote," said Lily from behind the handkerchief, "would suit me to a cow's thumb. That is, it would if he—"

"Nourished a wild and ungovernable passion for you," interrupted the gentleman, "and displayed it to you at every opportunity. My dear girl, have you not considered that a man of Lord Kingscote's er, age and experience might have wished to give you time to fix your affections, might have hesitated to exhibit ardor lest you grow frightened by his lack of restraint?"

From behind the handkerchief peered one skeptical blue eye. "Twaddle!" said Lily.

"You are," persisted the buccaneer, who seemed to nourish an odd ambition to convince Lily to look more kindly upon her *fiancé*, "very young and innocent."

To this viewpoint Lily responded with what sounded very much like a snort. "I am not so green as all *that*!" said she, and in proof presented an accounting of all the hopeful gentlemen who had made her declarations, culminating at length with the impecunious poet who'd written sonnets to her earlobes and with whom she had very nearly eloped.

"Ah!" said the buccaneer. "It is this poet with whom you mean to fly to Gretna Green?"

"Lud, no!" Such a hubble-bubble notion made Lily giggle most delightfully. "What nonsense you do talk, sir! I only mentioned him to make my point—though he did pop the question with a great deal of address!"

"Lord Kingscote did not exhibit a comparable finesse?"

"He said everything that was proper." Lily's amusement dissolved into an onslaught of hiccoughs. "Oh, let us speak no more of it! Lord Kingscote made a grave mistake when he cast the handkerchief in my direction, and I made a grave mistake when I picked it up. Now *I* must undo the error because he is too much the gentleman to cry off. He will be most annoyed with me at first, I daresay, but in time he will come to understand that I have acted for the best." Here the buccaneer muttered something beneath his breath. It sounded very much to Lily like he called her a pea-goose, but what reason could he have to say such a thing?

One reason occurred to her. Lily imagined Lord Kingscote's reaction were he to learn that she had unbosomed herself to a complete stranger. "I do most earnestly conjure you," she cried, "not to repeat what I have said. There is no hope now for *my* happiness, but at least Angelica and Kingscote may yet find solace in one another." This thought offered Lily herself so little consolation that she sniffled. "Oh, I wish I were dead!"

No gentleman presented with a Millikin damsel—including even Angelica—in so lachrymose a mood had ever yet refrained from the temptation of taking her into his arms. The buccaneer, beneath his mask, was not different from any other gentleman. He took Lily in his arms, which was no easy task in light of her powdered wig and wide panniers. Nor, once she was settled neatly against his chest, did the buccaneer cease this unseemliness. Lily hiccoughed once again, which quite naturally inspired him to kiss her very ardently.

"That was very nice!" wept Lily, once the buccaneer had disentangled his mask from the improbably painted stuffed bird that adorned her headdress. "I do not compliment you idly, because I have kissed a great many gentlemen, and so you understand I *know*! Why is your chest shaking in this odd manner, sir? Are you *laughing* at me?"

The buccaneer was doing exactly that. "Oh, Lily—if I may call you Lily, since our acquaintance has progressed so far so fast? Thank you!—you are so very droll! No no, don't pucker up on me! Instead tell me why a kiss that you adjudged very nice should cast you into woe. Ah! You were wishing that someone else was kissing you in my place! I play second fiddle to your *fiancé*."

"My *fiancé*," Lily responded sadly, "has never kissed me at all, which will give you a very good notion of how matters stand with us. But enough of my little problems! You have not given me your promise."

"To say nothing? I swear I shan't." Fervently, the dashing buccaneer grasped Lily's hand and raised it to his lips. "You have not said with whom you mean to elope. I am positively athirst with curiosity."

If Lily had read the signs correctly, and there was certainly no reason why she should not have, curiosity was not the emotion that stirred her buccaneer, who was currently raining kisses on her wrist. Not even briefly did Lily consider administering for this presumption a stinging rebuke, and not only because her companion's salutes were balm to her neglected soul. She was flattered by the buccaneer's attentions and by no means insensible to his air of breeding and his polished address. He was obviously a man of substance and sound mind; he was also obviously quite enamored of herself. That it was unusual for a gentleman to form a lasting passion in but a few scant moments did not occur to Lily, nor should it have: this was not the first gentleman to gaze upon Lily and abruptly discover that his heart had been wrenched from his breast and pinned by Cupid's arrow to his sleeve.

But Lily was not without foresight, despite the Millikin belief that contemplation of consequence was vulgarly low-bred. Politely she requested to be informed of her swain's identity.

Just as politely, he refused. He was not disfigured, he promised, nor was his countenance generally considered displeasing to the feminine eye; but there were reasons why his identity must remain undivulged. Those reasons would in time be made clear. And in case Lily was interested, he was a bachelor.

Whether Lily would have persisted in her quest for the buccaneer's identity remains unknown. Angelica passed by the alcove, looking very distrait. Lily rose so quickly that she

171

very nearly came a cropper via her wide skirts. Once equilibrium was restored, she moved to the entry arch. Close on her heels was the buccaneer.

And close on Angelica's heels was a tall gentleman with auburn hair and green eyes and a harsh face on which dissipation had left its stamp. He caught Angelica's arm and spun her around to face him, looking excessively angry. Not without reason was Angelica adjudged the most clever of all the Millikins: she kicked her captor in the shin. Wincing, the gentleman instinctively grasped his wounded limb. Angelica glanced around desperately. Lily gestured. Angelica sped into the alcove and ducked behind the sofa.

Once more Lily contemplated the auburn-haired man who now stood again upright. Looking absolutely murderous, he turned his head this way and that, searching the throng. Briefly his green eyes touched Lily, who was with her buccaneer very effectively blocking the alcove's entry arch. Then he turned on his heel and disappeared into the crowd. Lily released her pent-up breath.

"If I may venture a guess?" murmured the buccaneer. "Have I just witnessed an encounter between your sister and her ineligible *parti*?"

The case had grown more desperate than Lily had guessed; she had never dreamed that Angelica's ineligible *parti* might be a hardened rakeshame. The inexperienced Angelica would never deal effectively with such, as witnessed by that recent brief encounter, which smacked of a shocking degree of familiarity. One did not go about kicking gentlemen with whom one was not on the most intimate of terms, surely? Lily had never done such a thing. Furthermore she doubted that even Rosemary, as a married lady, dared take such liberties.

Angelica must be saved from folly; Lily must quit the field. She glanced shyly up at her companion, who was certainly more sympathetic than Messr. Meadowcraft or Gildensleeve, Steptoe or Pettijohn. "We have passed a charming evening, have we not?"

The buccaneer had during that evening gained a fair understanding of the workings of Lily's mind, had a good idea and an even greater hope of what she might next say. "The most charming evening I can ever recall. I fear, Lily, that it is midsummer moon with me."

Why, oh why, wondered Lily, could it have not been midsummer moon with Lord Kingscote? Now that she had made up her mind to leave the stage to Angelica, she wanted more than anything to remain before the footlights. But Angelica could not be abandoned. Nor could she be left much longer cowering behind the sofa.

Lily swallowed hard and plucked at the buccaneer's sleeve. He bent his head toward her, placed his hand over her own. Said Lily in a faint little whisper: "Sir, would you care to fly to Gretna Green with me?"

Twenty

On the morrow, Valerian Millikin returned from his duties at St. Bartholomew's Hospital to be greeted by his elderly housekeeper with the intelligence that a madman had taken possession of his specimen room. In that direction Valerian proceeded, his curiosity pricked. An auburn-haired gentleman —clad in a greatcoat with many capes, pantaloons, Hessian boots, a curly-brimmed beaver hat and an expression of profound displeasure—restlessly paced the floor. "Aha!" said Valerian.

Upon this friendly salutation, the caller elevated his glittering green gaze from an especially fine boar's tusk to glower at the doorway. "Dr. Millikin? Pardon my bursting in on you like this but it is a matter of some urgency. But I anticipate myself." He strode forward. "I am Simon Brisbane. You may not recall the occasion, but we met some years previously."

Valerian could be extremely civil when it pleased him to do so, as it did in this case. He begged that his guest be seated, he summoned his housekeeper and demanded refreshment, he entertained Simon with a great deal of lively conversation concerning his experience at St. Bart's. With total frankness, he expressed his unflattering opinion of the matron there, whose duty it was to order food for the patients, who each day received a pint of water gruel or milk porridge for breakfast, eight ounces of meat or six ounces of cheese for dinner, and for supper broth. Each patient was allowed twelve ounces of bread and two pints of beer daily.

"All that is very interesting," interrupted Simon, in a manner which under the circumstances was very tolerant. "However, I have not come here to be enlightened as to conditions at St. Bart's!"

"Exactly so." Valerian settled himself more comfortably and prepared to be amused. "You mentioned a matter of some urgency?"

"I did." Simon gazed into the teacup with which he had been presented by Valerian's housekeeper as if it contained some alien brew, which indeed it did, for Valerian and his housekeeper were partial to teas of herbal variety. As unobtrusively as possible, Simon set the teacup down on a display case situated very near his elbow, in which was arranged a fine selection of skulls. Then he turned on his host the full force of his green stare. "My father has told me it was you who drew his attention to Miss Smith."

"Miss Smith?" Valerian echoed blankly. "Oh, *that* Miss Smith! What of it, Brisbane? Don't you approve of the wench?"

"*Approve*? Of a straw damsel bent on worming her way into the affections of an elderly gentleman?" Simon's tone was scathing. "It would seem she duped you also. Since you are sincerely devoted to my father, I cannot credit that you were privy to Miss Smith's evil design."

"What design was that?" inquired Valerian, hoarse with suppressed mirth.

Simon frowned. "I'm not sure, precisely; she was marvelously inconsistent. Had she not kept hinting at secrets that do not exist, and then that her silence should be bought, I might acquit her of being a designing female. Still, there was a want of openness about her behavior, and she spun me the most appalling taradiddles about consumptive parents sewing seams by candlelight—I beg pardon, did you speak?"

Since it did not seem politic to repeat his muttered wish that Marigold would in truth succumb to a consumption, Valerian waved aside the interruption. "If you don't like the chit," he said, "why didn't you just send her packing?"

"I didn't say I didn't like her," responded Simon, with quirked brow. "And I *did* send her packing. You look confused. Suppose I tell you the whole of it."

"Yes, do!" Valerian was thoroughly delighted at the prospect of being regaled with the history of his sister's acquaintance with a hardened rakeshame, as presented from the rakeshame's point of view.

Simon thought it odd that his host should be so cheerfully eager to be regaled with the misdeeds of a young female acquaintance, but no odder than any other aspect of this affair. Sir Randall had carried on in a dreadful way when informed that his amanuensis had been dismissed, had accused his son of being so hot-at-hand as to make her take fright, had when presented with his son's opinion of the lady's intentions castigated his offspring as being still damp behind the ears. Were mishap to befall Miss Smith, Sir Randall had warned, the responsibility for that mishap would rest squarely on Simon's head. More than that Sir Randall would not say, except to admit in utter exasperation that Valerian Millikin had recommended Miss Smith, and then to request acerbically that his son repair to the nether regions in a hand-cart. After delivering himself of these denunciations, Sir Randall had taken himself into the garden, there to seek solace from his menagerie. When last glimpsed, Williams had been wending his way thither, bearing before him an epistle on a silver tray.

Very much belatedly, Simon wondered what that epistle might portend. Sir Randall carried on a voluminous correspondence, from which Durward's surveillance was exempted, much to Durward's chagrin. Could Miss Smith have known of that exemption, have chosen that way to communicate? If so, her effort was for naught. Sir Randall had given his solemn and most vituperative word that he had no intention of shackling himself to any female, legally or otherwise, no matter how many hatchets were cast at him. Simon's relief at this promise was short-lived, due to Sir Randall's additional remark that his son was a cabbage-head.

Had he misjudged Miss Smith? Was she *not* an adventuress? These questions had gained a paramount importance. So Simon explained.

"I seem to be laboring under some confusion of ideas," he admitted humbly. "If Miss Smith is a female of quality, as my father insists, I have behaved abominably—yet in my own defense I must add that she never *behaved* like quality! Good God, my reputation is far from blameless, and she certainly knew that. What did she *expect* me to think when she went about asking me questions about orgies and the like?" He paused. "I hesitate—you are after all acquainted with the lady—it is a delicate subject and I hesitate to be frank!"

"Don't!" said Valerian, encouragingly. "Hesitate, that is! *I* don't mind."

Apparently his host's acquaintance with Miss Smith was slight, decided Simon, as he related how the lady had tried to delude him into believing she was unaware that he paid her court. Valerian exhibited neither shock nor dismay, merely inquired why Simon had paid his court to her. "I wished to divert her attention from my father! Why else?" snapped Simon. Valerian looked very much as if he might try and teach his grandmother to suck eggs. At this notion, Simon grinned and said reluctantly: "Oh, very well! She amused me, and was quite unlike any other female I'd ever, er, known."

Nobly Valerian refrained from a digression into the fascinating topic of his guest's amorous vagaries. "*You* don't think she's an ugly duckling then?" he inquired. Simon looked puzzled. "Neither do I! Go on."

Obviously Simon would much rather not have done so.

"We had a slight disagreement," he admitted, even more reluctantly.

"Offered her a slip on the shoulder, did you? No, no, don't tell me about it! I'm not fond of the notion of pistols for two and breakfast for one, especially when you're doubtless the better shot. It's not my affair if you pretended to her hand, or whatever you *did* pretend to, so long as you didn't succeed." Valerian cast his astonished visitor an astute glance. "And if you'd succeeded, I think, you wouldn't be here, so *that's* all right!"

Valerian Millikin had a most original outlook. Since Simon was no more eager to engage in pistols at daybreak than Valerian had been, he did not argue that Miss Smith's rebuff made his own actions no less reprehensible. "It was all very stupid of me," he confessed. "However, you need not concern yourself with Miss Smith's honor; she provided a very adequate defense. First she said she'd *never*, and I expressed disbelief; then I told her I didn't mind if she *had* in the past been a trifle indiscreet and she accused me of pestering her." From Valerian's direction came a strangling noise. "Yes, it was unhandsomely done, but what else could I think? She'd just asked me for money! And then to see her again last night, rubbing shoulders with the *ton* at a masked ball—this whole business is too smoky by half. I wish you would tell me, Millikin, just who *is* she?"

Direct explanations, alas, were foreign to Valerian, who could not remember when he'd been better amused. "If it was a masked ball, how can you be sure it was her you saw? Maybe you mistook some other female—"

"Hardly." Only a coxcomb would have pointed out that one did not amass a legendary success in the petticoat-line by mixing up one's lovelies. "I am not likely to mistake the female who boxed my ears!"

"Boxed your ears?" echoed Valerian.

"Indeed!" Simon rose abruptly from his chair. "*Why* she did so I am not certain unless she is by nature a termagant! And I think she must be, because last night she kicked me in the shin."

"She *what*?" Valerian's voice had grown faint.

177

"I *had* meant to apologize," Simon said bitterly, to a lively looking hedgehog that was an excellent specimen of the taxidermist's art, "but she gave me no opportunity. Nor could I find her anywhere after, though I searched high and low. Now you understand why I am so anxious to locate Miss Smith. There needs to be between us a settling of accounts."

Valerian understood very well, perhaps even better than his guest: Simon Brisbane had been sent to the roundabout by a lady for probably the first time in memory. What would be the result of these various awkward misapprehensions Valerian could not begin to predict. To be sure, he could have straightened out this tangle, was in fact the most proper person to do so; but it was no part of Valerian's philosophy to involve himself in straightening out the tangles of people who were sublimely incapable of managing their own affairs.

Nonetheless, Angelica was the only of his siblings for whom Valerian felt a fondness. Though it meant breaking his own rule of uninvolvement, he was prompted to offer a word in her defense. "I can see you're a trifle put about by all that's chanced," he said sympathetically. "But I assure you there's not an ounce of vice in the chit!"

Of this assurance Simon stood in no need, and so he ruefully said. Fancy-pieces did not ordinarily cavil at profitable alliances; certainly they did not turn mad as fire; never did they admit to an excessive liking for improper advances and then turn around and bestow upon the purveyor of their pleasure a clout on the head. In this line, Simon could have said much more, because he had come to realize that he had gravely wronged Miss Smith, but his host had fallen into a fit of the whoops and between guffaws struggled for breath. Simon administered the only remedy he knew: he clapped Valerian hard on the back.

In so doing, Simon stood very close to his host, almost as close as he had stood recently to another individual with brown hair and blue eyes and unexceptionable features. Now that Simon considered the matter, there was a very distinct resemblance between Valerian Millikin and Miss Smith. He swore a mighty oath.

"On to us, are you?" Valerian wheezed for breath. "It took

you long enough! But don't think that because I'm related to Angelica I'll try and tell her to look on you more kindly."

Simon opened his mouth to retort that nothing would induce him to do such a thing, and then realized that such a statement might not be quite true. His sentiments toward the erstwhile Miss Smith were very complex and equally confused; he knew only that it grew increasingly imperative that he speak with her. He studied Valerian and arrived at another conclusion: Valerian Millikin was a very queer sort of relative.

"I'm not one to kick up a dust over trifles," said Valerian, who had with good accuracy followed Simon's thoughts. "And I told Angelica how it would be if she didn't check her curiosity—asking you to explain orgies, forsooth!" He frowned. "Come to think of it, I also told her I'd carve out your liver and fry it for daylight if you misbehaved."

The intensity of his host's gaze recalled to Simon the passion for dissection harbored by physicians. Diffidently he pointed out that, despite Miss Smith's tendency to manhandle him, she *had* professed to enjoy his addresses very well. Whether those addresses were to continue, Simon could not say; but he rather doubted Miss Smith would be grateful were Valerian to destroy the source.

"That's all well and good," objected Valerian who though he had no notion of carving out his caller's liver had not the least reluctance to giving him a good scare, "but I can't have you making any more improper suggestions to Angelica, because I don't know but what she might take you up on them." He studied Simon, whose expression had grown increasingly sardonic. "Brief fits of madness, you know! It's nothing to signify; the whole family's prone to them, except me."

That Valerian Millikin was thus immune to madness Simon took leave to doubt. "The family?" he asked craftily. "There are others beside you and Miss Smith?"

"I think," said Valerian, "that you might call her Angelica, not because you've trifled with her, but because Smith isn't her name." He ruminated. "It's not what I like but I suppose you must be told something of the situation, for Angelica's sake, because it's clear the pair of you aren't thinking exactly straight! Lord, yes, there are others—a passel of them, and I'll

179

warn you right now that you'll never persuade Angelica she's not responsible for Marigold's brood." Then he looked speculative. "Or *you* might; I couldn't! If you mean to have Angelica you should try; Marigold is a hell-cat and she don't like Angelica above half. But Angelica promised our father on his deathbed that she'd look after Marigold and the brats."

From this rather muddled explanation, Simon did manage to glean some facts. That Miss Smith—or Angelica—was sister to Valerian Millikin did not surprise him, due to the strong resemblance. Valerian's other statements, however, surprised Simon very much indeed. Why had Angelica, a lady of good birth, sought employment? Was she in truth the sole support of a consumptive parent and starving siblings? Why did Valerian not offer assistance? And why did he refer to the consumptive parent by her Christian name? Only one theory presented itself: Marigold was not mother to Valerian, nor by extension Angelica. "The brats?" he said.

Valerian shrugged. "Angelica chooses to claim them; *I* don't. Blood may be thicker than water, but it's not what I should wish to drink."

From these remarks, Simon derived certain other conclusions. "On the wrong side of the blanket, I conjecture?" he inquired delicately.

"Call it what you will!" Valerian replied with a fine and wholly unassumed indifference. "I've already said more than I should." Pointedly, he glanced at the wall clock.

It availed nothing; Simon was deep in thought. The tenor of those thoughts was remorseful; he had gravely misjudged Angelica and treated her even more shabbily; she had sought not to ensnare his father but to provide sustenance for her own father's impoverished by-blows. How good she was, how selfless and noble; never before had Simon been privileged to know so saintly a female—or if not precisely saintly, because he could not forget that she had appeared to enjoy his most outrageous sallies very well, at least generous. "My poor, poor darling!" he exclaimed.

Nor for a moment did Valerian think that it was to himself Simon spoke. He cleared his throat and stated politely that he had appointments to keep.

"As do I." Simon had taken good stock of his host. "Since

you will not acquaint me with your sister's whereabouts, I must needs apply to Bow Street."

With a thoughtful grimace, Valerian contemplated his guest. Then he smiled. "That's the dandy! Keep on in that high-handed manner and you'll deal very well with *all* the Millikins! And if you *don't* want to deal with them, tell Angelica so—though if I were you I'd figure out some means of disposing of them first, because she's as protective of them as a bitch with pups." This rather unflattering comparison brought another thought to mind. "Come to think of it—"

"Yes, yes!" Simon said hastily, lest Valerian embark upon a frank discussion of his sister's qualifications for motherhood. "First you must take me to her, must you not? May I recall to you that upon our last two meetings she has kicked me in the shins and boxed my ears?"

"Fudge! You of all people must know how to deal with a recalcitrant female." Valerian rang for his coat and hat, reflecting as he did so that he'd violated his policy of uninvolvement a great many times this day. Still, Simon Brisbane would run Angelica to earth with or without his assistance—and Valerian could not deprive himself of the fireworks that must ensue when the ugly duckling of the Millikin family was once more confronted by her hardened rakeshame. What would be the outcome of that meeting Valerian could not guess; Angelica was the best of his sisters but still an unpredictable female.

About one thing, however, Valerian's curiosity could not wait. "Tell me," he said as in a fraternal manner he accompanied Simon through the door, " *did* you ever explain to Angelica what is an orgy?"

Twenty-One

"Nothing, but nothing is how I thought it would be!" wailed Rosemary. "Lord Byron has been exposed as a thoroughly infamous scoundrel—he actually *admitted* that from childhood on he'd been engaged in some very nasty practices, *what* I am not certain but I believe they involved his page and a schoolmate at Harrow and countless other persons in Turkey —while Brummel was forced to flee to Calais. He left behind the secret of his perfect cravats in a note on his desk—starch, of all things! And when Mr. Christie auctioned off his belongings, there was found a snuffbox with a note in it saying it was intended for Prinny if only he had behaved toward the Beau with more civility." Further words failed her; she wept copiously.

That the travails of Lord Byron and Beau Brummel were responsible for Rosemary's dolor, none of her audience mistakenly believed, not even the youngest who was looking forward with great glee to the moment when Fennel threw back his bedcovers to find beneath them a toad fresh from the country. An ingenious lad, young Hysop had managed to transport the creature without attracting the notice of either his sisters or his mother. This oversight was not entirely due to Hysop's cleverness, however—Hysop was still a Millikin, and while he claimed no less intelligence than his siblings he certainly could claim no more, for all his ingenuity. Hysop's mother and sisters had en route to London paid him little heed, being thoroughly preoccupied with the tantalizing question of just why Rosemary should believe disaster was imminent, as expressed in her last letter to her family.

It was a question that remained as yet unresolved, in spite of—or perhaps due to—the barrage of inquiries fired upon Rosemary from the moment her mother and siblings had set foot in Chalmers House. That moment had not been a great many past, the interim having been filled with the disposal of the luggage and profuse expressions of the family's delight with the grandeur of their surroundings. The twins, Amaryllis and Camilla, had little enough to say, both being very shy and awkward at fifteen; but their silence had been more than compensated by Hyacinth, seventeen, and Violet, sixteen, both of whom were eagerly anticipating their own debuts.

It was Hyacinth who silenced Rosemary's sniffles now, with a most acute comment that if Rosemary didn't stop her snivelling her cheeks would grow all blotched, which Hyacinth doubted that Lord Chalmers would fancy in his wife, because in Hyacinth's experience gentlemen did *not*. At this strong indication that yet another of her sisters was in a fair way to becoming an accredited heart-breaker, Rosemary ground her teeth.

That action was not lost on Rosemary's mother, who sat beside her on the needlepointed sofa. Marigold raised a languid hand and voiced a husky, lazy request for silence. She was instantly obeyed, as always. Marigold Millikin, at nine-and-thirty, was a frail and ethereal and enchanting creature who looked much too young to possess a daughter already turned twenty. To give credit where it is due, Marigold never tried to deny either her age or her offspring; instead she claimed that her health had been ruined by the production of those offspring, six in eight years. Since this statement was most often made, in the most uncomplaining of tones, to the offspring themselves, who were resultantly guilt-stricken and anxious to atone for their appallingly inconsiderate impatience to be born, Marigold generally managed to indulge almost her every whim. In one matter alone was she balked: few gentlemen wished to marry an impoverished widow with six lively offspring; and Marigold wished very much to marry again. Granted, one of the offspring was already off her hands and another would soon follow suit; but Marigold was

183

fast running out of patience. She knew her children, none better, for they all bore a great resemblance to herself; no sooner would she rid herself of the last of them than some other would return home in disgrace, as it looked very much like Rosemary wished to do.

"That is much better!" she said, as the silence stretched to screaming-point. "The rest of you will now refrain from interruption while Rosemary tells me all." She paused expectantly.

"I am undone!" Rosemary replied, most emotionally. "It's not to be wondered at, when Chalmers makes me read things like *Take Your Choice* and lectures me on things like soup kitchens for the poor. He does, I assure you! Just this morning over the breakfast cups he was telling me about some English Jacobins who have taken to meeting secretly and plotting revolution and drinking toasts to the strangling of the last king with the guts of the last priest. Which is quite enough to spoil anyone's appetite! And so I would have told him, had not he received a note and gone out, looking very angry."

That a discussion of such distasteful matters over the breakfast cups might impair one's appetite, Marigold would concede. Nonetheless she did not perceive why Rosemary should consider her husband's failure to enter into her sentiments as the crack of doom. Nor did she understand why Rosemary was cradling in her arms so hideous a cat. Would Rosemary please explain?

"It's the kitchen cat. I didn't even know we had one until Chalmers accused me of having no regard for the dignities he'd bestowed upon me, which I do!" Rosemary cuddled the cat, which did not appear to especially appreciate this singular mark of esteem. "*I* cannot be blamed because the man is a nipfarthing. As if that were not enough to bear, what must Fennel do but go frolicking among the muslin company, and Angelica sneak off for clandestine meetings with an ineligible *parti*, and Lily fly into the boughs because she'd meant Angelica to marry Kingscote! Lud, it's not *me* that'll make us food for scandal. All *I* did was—"

"Vinaigrette!" moaned Marigold, and stretched out a frail hand. "An ineligible *parti*, the muslin company, *Angelica*? I beg you will compose yourself and explain, Rosemary!"

No more than any of her siblings was Rosemary in the habit of thwarting Marigold who, languid as she was, had a very forceful way with a hairbrush. As coherently as she could, Rosemary explained first Lily's relationship with Lord Kingscote, which she considered the least exceptionable affair, and consequently the least likely to send her parent into convulsion fits.

Nor did it; Marigold laughed. "Kingscote marry Angelica?" she echoed. "The ugly duckling? Lily is a pudding-head, although she *does* mean well. Now what is this about Angelica and an ineligible *parti*?"

Again Rosemary explained. "I never heard such a farrago of nonsense!" gasped Marigold, after Rosemary had revealed that Angelica had come by her just deserts. "That thankless girl! I trusted her to look after the rest of you!" She applied herself to the vinaigrette.

"I'm sure Angelica did her best!" soothed Rosemary, lest her mother succumb to one of the spasms to which she was prone, and to which she would doubtless fall prey before Rosemary's account was done. "Perhaps it is not so bad as it may look."

"No?" mocked Marigold, faintly. "Shockingly irregular conduct? To think that Angelica, whom I have trusted, should exhibit such a deviousness of mind—oh! Was there ever such a sorry thing?"

"Now you've done it!" hissed Hysop, who was leaning against the back of the sofa. "Mama's on the fidgets again, and it's all your fault, Rosemary. I must say, it's awfully paltry of you to send her off when we've just got here. It would serve you right if she *did* go off in an apoplexy!"

At this dire suggestion Rosemary blanched, not only because she was sincerely devoted to her parent, but because Rosemary feared Marigold's premature demise would result in the permanent attachment of her younger siblings to Chalmers House. Though Rosemary was also sincerely devoted to her siblings, she did not think she could bear to be constantly in the company of four younger sisters who promised to be at least as lovely as she. Therefore Rosemary applied herself to Marigold's revival with more than ordinary energy.

If brutal, Rosemary's methods were effective; never before had Marigold been roused so quickly from a shocked swoon. She winced, pushed Rosemary away, sat up and touched her stinging cheeks. Then she put forth an opinion that Rosemary had grown positively demented during her short absence from the bosom of her family. For this, Marigold could only blame Rosemary's husband; a lady of delicate sensibilities must be overset by the discovery that the man of substance whom she'd married was in the habit of cheeseparing.

"No, no!" Once more Rosemary caught up the long-suffering cat against her breast. "It is all *my* fault! If Chalmers wished to keep me without money for common necessaries, I should have abided by his whim instead of being so wildly extravagant. Because if I hadn't run counter to his advice, he wouldn't have given me all those terrible trimmings, and in our last turn-up he wouldn't have turned me—ah! Er, turned me so furious!"

Marigold greeted these excessively fatiguing dramatics with a visible shudder; Hysop stated his opinion that Rosemary had made a rare mull of the thing. He further suggested that his sister might go on easier if she could but decide whether Lord Chalmers was a devilish ugly customer or a great gun. To this kindly meant advice, Rosemary responded with an eloquent gesture toward the door. "Jupiter!" grumbled Hysop, as he departed. Though he had not yet decided what to do with the friendly little grass-snake he'd also smuggled in from the country, he thought it might enjoy a brief sojourn in a baroness's boudoir.

Next to be dispatched were Hyacinth and Violet, Amaryllis and Camilla, at Marigold's command. Then Marigold turned to her remaining daughter, whose tears were making damp splotches on the cat's head, a proceeding of which the cat obviously took a very adverse view. "Now we may speak without roundaboutation," said Marigold. "I have the distinct impression that you have been indulging in shocking wrongheadedness. Don't get in the sullens; you will put me all out of humor with you!"

Damply, Rosemary regarded her mother. Impossible to resent Marigold's selfish viewpoint that no one was entitled to indulge in thunderstorms but herself; impossible, in fact, to resent any of Marigold's various little megrims, even while realizing Marigold's primary concern was and always would be herself. She looked the merest girl in her cambric high gown and Spanish robe, with her hair drawn back from her face into a crown of curls atop her lovely head. She was also looking unusually sympathetic. "Oh, Mama!" wailed Rosemary.

Marigold winced at this inelegant turn of speech, but did not protest. On rare occasions Marigold was capable of expenditures of great energy. Those occasions invariably centered on matters of the heart. Since she had been prohibited by an unkind fate from enjoying such matters herself, Marigold might as well turn her energy to her daughter's muddled marriage, even though it was a very poor second-best. Therefore she said: "My sorry little Rosie! You are *éprise*?"

"*Éprise!*" moaned Rosemary. "Mama, if you only knew—"

Marigold laughed, archly. "But of course I know, my foolish child. Am I not a widowed lady with six children? You were not delivered down the chimney, my pet! Perhaps I should have warned you, but I did not think any of my girls would shrink from—you certainly were not brought up to consider—well, there it is and we must make the best of it! Unless he is of an unnatural—"

"No, no!" Rosemary turned bright red with embarrassment. "I do not—he has not—Chalmers is always very fit and proper and you do him a great disservice by inferring he is not! It is merely that I have been imprudent. Chalmers seemed so cruelly unfeeling—oh, I know it is no excuse—but he is in such very easy circumstances, and so well-connected, and I was grown by no means insensible to him—in short, I have been very indiscreet! Though not so indiscreet that I deserve Chalmers should accuse me of attaching a disagreeable stigma to his name, or scold me for my profligacies!"

With each of her daughter's words, Marigold had grown more ashen. "Rosemary! You didn't—you couldn't! None of my daughters would be so very commonplace! Have you no consideration of my mother's heart, my sensibilities? Apparently you have not! It is a source of great heartbreak."

Rosemary, not certain what her mother was fussing about,

said cautiously, "I'm sure I'd *like* to mend my fences! If it were possible. Chalmers has no heart-strings *to* touch so it avails nothing to try and make him sorry for failing to provide properly for me."

"Provide properly?" Marigold sank down further on the couch. "You shameless child!"

Bewildered, Rosemary could but persevere. "I've tried flinging myself upon his mercy, and hanging round his neck in tears; I even professed myself very fond of him—and what did *he* do but turn me over his knee!"

Perhaps, decided Marigold, there was some excuse for her daughter's shocking misconduct; to be precise, her mate's brutality. Marigold personally approved a slight exhibition of manly strength—or she had used to do so in the days before a large young family left her too encumbered to enjoy anything very much—but she could not expect so delicately nourished a damsel to likewise savor so masterful an attitude. "My poor Rosie! This is a very shocking thing indeed! I make no doubt that in your situation anyone would take a distempered freak. After all, he offered you *violence!*"

"*Violence?*" Rosemary still hugged the hissing cat. "Lud, Mama, I didn't mind *that*. Indeed, had I known how to go about it, I might have intimated that I would have liked very well to—"

Appreciating something was one matter; to frankly admit that appreciation was quite another. "God bless my soul!" ejaculated Marigold, and swooned.

Into the *brouhaha* attendant upon this development walked Fennel, some moments later, narrowly avoiding collision with a fast-moving object that appeared to be a cat. He arrived just in time to see Rosemary abandon the vinaigrette, drop the wrist which she'd been chafing, grasp a flower-vase and empty the contents over her mother's head. "By Jove!" said Fennel, and turned back to the door. "She ain't going to like that, Rosemary!"

Already his sister had grasped his arm and was drawing him toward the couch. "You must help me, Fennel; Mama is very nearly in convulsions and I don't know what to do. Beside, I wish *very* particularly to talk with you!"

To Fennel these latter words had a most ominous ring. Before he could inquire why Rosemary was sounding fit to murder him, Marigold had opened her eyes. She gazed soulfully upon Rosemary and announced that her daughter's startling display of vulgarity had plunged her into grief.

"Vulgarity?" Rosemary tried with all her might to understand, and failed. "Because I admitted to a partiality for my husband? And I had thought *Chalmers* was wonderfully stiff-necked!"

"Not your husband!" gasped Marigold, in fading tones, as she dabbed delicately at the water which dripped down her brow. "Your profligacies! 'Twould be easily enough understood if you'd taken Chalmers in dislike, but if you have a *tendre* for him—Rosemary, this simply will not do!"

"Oh, I say!" uttered Fennel, who was much quicker than Rosemary to achieve insight. "It was bad enough that you should be the first of the family to try and outrun the constable, but it ain't at all the thing to go about having *affaires*, Rosemary."

This, to a lady who had never even briefly contemplated playing her unkind husband false, was too much to bear. "I may have pawned the sapphires, and fallen into the clutches of a moneylender," she said bitterly, "but *I'm* not the member of the family who indulges in *affaires*. In fact, I may be the only member of the family who does not! What with you and Angelica and maybe even Lily—"

Fennel cleared his throat. "About Lily—"

"Never mind Lily!" Rosemary snapped. "Fennel, what have you done with my sapphires? Don't bother to deny that you've taken them! You wished to pawn them yourself to buy off your dragon, and I wouldn't give them to you, and now they're gone!"

"*What* dragon?" inquired Marigold, who now lay prone on the couch.

"Just the mother of a fine vulgar miss with whom Fennel has been frolicking!" Rosemary gazed irritably upon her brother. "Ingrate! To thusly use me even after I offered to explain to her why it would avail nothing to bring against you a breach of promise suit!"

189

"A *what*?" Marigold struggled upright on one elbow, the better to observe the fracas due to become shortly underway between these two of her offspring, and to insure that one did not murder the other.

"You're a fine one to call the kettle black!" responded Fennel. "*I* ain't badly dipped. Rosemary, does this mean you won't intercede with the dragon on my behalf? Because I told her you were wishful of speaking with her and I'll go bail she shows up this very day!"

"How *dare* you ask it of me?" cried Rosemary. "After you've stolen my sapphires!"

"But I *didn't* steal them," Fennel responded patiently.

Marigold's children had underestimated her when they predicted a knowledge of their predicaments would inspire her to convulsion-fits. Certainly Marigold was tempted toward that very thing, but thirty-nine years of experience had taught her that there were certain situations in which convulsion-fits availed their enactor nothing but a headache. Therefore she swung her dainty feet to the floor, sat upright, and set out to be eminently practical. Her first step in that direction was to inform Rosemary, who was exhibiting a histrionic ability that had doubtless been inherited from her mama, that she believed Fennel to be speaking the truth. "Had he stolen your necklace, he would hardly show you his face," Marigold explained. And then she frowned at her son. "Just why *did* you, Fennel?"

Though impressed by his parent's forebearance, Fennel had little hope that she would long remain self-possessed. Still, there was no hope for it, were he to clear himself of the suspicion of theft. Therefore he dropped into his mother's lap a singularly splotchy piece of paper that he'd all this time held in his hand. Marigold perused it, shrieked, and swooned.

"What the deuce?" gasped Rosemary, upon whose bosom Marigold had collapsed.

In pursuit of his parent's vinaigrette, which had dropped to the floor, Fennel bent down. "Lily's been snooping again," he muttered, from beneath the sofa. "As near as I can make it out—well, *you* know Lily will never win honors for her penmanship!—Angelica sloped off with your necklace!"

190

Silence greeted this announcement. Cautiously Fennel peered over the sofa arm. In the face of such continual catastrophies, Lady Chalmers had taken her only logical recourse. Following the excellent example set by her mama, Rosemary had fainted dead away.

Twenty-Two

And so it was that Valerian Millikin and Simon Brisbane, upon arrival at Chalmers House, were conducted to a drawing room most remarkable not for six-paneled doors with classical motifs in the carved panel borders, the richly decorated ceiling of white plaster nor the massive cornice that ran around the room, not for the sash windows nor wainscoting nor the gilt suite, but for what appeared a preponderance of corpses strewn around the chamber. One was stretched out gracefully on a sofa upholstered in needlework, another sprawled half on the sofa and half on the floor; yet another lay wholly on the floor and partially beneath the sofa.

The latter body stirred, rose, brushed ineffectually at its dusty knees. With this sign of life, the butler recalled his position and his purpose and announced the visitors. "You might help a fellow!" complained Fennel, as he waved the vinaigrette in the direction of the prostrate ladies. Then the impact of the butler's introduction struck. "By Jove! Valerian Millikin! You're Angelica's brother, ain't you? And mine, think on it! Dashed if I ain't pleased as punch to make your acquaintance!" Energetically he grasped and pumped Valerian's hand.

Valerian was a great deal less enthusiastic about this reunion, or so it appeared to Simon Brisbane. The deeper Simon was plunged into this situation, the more difficult he found it to understand. What had his so-called Miss Smith to do with this young man who was greeting Valerian so effusively? In search of enlightenment, Simon listened closely to the young man's utterances, which unfortunately were not of a nature to ease anyone's puzzlement, containing many vague references to elopements and sapphires and other mysterious things.

"Ah!" said Valerian, who had after all been made aware of the background of these disclosures, and consequently was able to make sense of Fennel's absurdities. "The pea-goose!" He glanced at the lady strewn half on the sofa and half on the floor. "That, I conjecture, is what's-her-name. No, no, do not revive her! I have no time to indulge in further introductions! It is imperative that I speak with Angelica immediately."

"You and I don't know how many others!" Fennel's brow wrinkled. "But you ain't been listening, or you would have heard me say Angelica has eloped. Have I said Rosemary's sapphires have been stolen? Well, they have, right out from under Rosemary's nose. She accused *me* of sloping off with them, and I don't deny I considered it, but I decided 'twould be a shabby thing to do. Rosemary's already in the River Tick! But there are no flies on Lily, and she saw Angelica filch the necklace, and left us a note." His frown deepened. "I wonder where Lily's gone off to! There's no keeping pace with the little minx! Maybe she's set out to try and save Angelica from landing us all in the briars."

Simon Brisbane possessed great tolerance, as befit a gentleman of his vast experience; but he could not remain silent while slurs were hurled at Miss Smith. *He* might consider her a designing female, the slyest creature in existence, but he would not permit anyone else to heap aspersions upon her integrity. "Poppycock!" said he.

Thus reminded of the presence of a stranger, Fennel cast that individual an appraising glance. He approved the many-caped greatcoat and pantaloons, the Hessian boots and curly-brimmed beaver hat; he even approved the gentleman's sentiment. "You are acquainted with Angelica, sir? She is the best of *all* my sisters—even though she has taken to acting skitter-witted of late. We had grown used to depending on her for assistance in escaping from our little muddles, but this time she left us at *point non plus*. You look surprised! It's true, upon my honor! 'Tis a long story, and one I should not tell you—unless, sir, you already know about the sapphires?"

"Sapphires?" Simon felt more and more remorseful about his misjudgment of Miss Smith. Confronted with one of the siblings whom Angelica had sought to spare further hardship, Simon began to more fully comprehend Angelica's nobility. "I don't know anything about any curst sapphires, but if Angelica wants such baubles I'll see to it she's given them!"

"Zounds!" By this vigorous open-handedness Fennel was extremely impressed. "Dashed if that ain't generous! Especially when she's run off with an ineligible *parti*!"

"You err!" murmured Valerian, looking diabolical indeed. "Allow me to introduce you to Angelica's ineligible *parti*." Fennel's mouth dropped open. Before Valerian could make further unappreciative comments regarding Fennel's powers of deduction, lazy husky tones fell upon his ear.

"Gracious!" Marigold rose in a very graceful manner from the sofa and drifted even more gracefully across the room. "Is it —does my imagination play me tricks—can it be *Valerian*?"

In the most dispassionate of manners, the eldest of the Millikin siblings gazed upon his stepmama. Marigold was looking every bit as lovely as he remembered her, in spite of damp splotches on her gown and various pieces of foliage clinging here and there to her person. She returned the scrutiny, then averted her gaze so that her long lashes lay tenderly against her cheeks. "Oh, Valerian, it has been so many years! I am very sorry—I behaved *very* thoughtlessly— I beg you will forgive me!"

The scheming Marigold, in comparison with her stepson, was a rank novice in the fine art of deviousness. Too, she was a feather-head and Valerian possessed a sharp shrewd wit. Though Marigold was unaware of these factors, Valerian was not. As he plucked away her foliage and dabbed at her damp gown with his handkerchief, he decided he could afford to be

193

generous. "I suppose I must straighten out this tangle since I'm here; it's clear as noonday that your brats are going on in a very bad way. But you needn't think that because I get you clear this once you may rely on me to put all square!"

"Valerian!" Marigold looked very, very frail. "How can you speak so to me?"

"Easily, ma'am!" Belatedly aware that his stepmama might misunderstand his ministrations, which quite naturally derived only from the very proper concern of a physician for a patient and had nothing at all to do with the fact that the patient was a lovely lady only five scant years older than himself, Valerian put away his handkerchief. "Depend upon it, these very great calamities of which Fennel has been telling me can be laid at your door."

"*I*?" Marigold clutched her breast. "You are very stern, Valerian! Have I not for all the years since your father's death sought to raise my family alone and without assistance? Which I do not scruple to tell you is a thankless task and one that fatigues me to death! When I consider that Rosemary and Lily and Fennel—to say nothing of Angelica, the ungrateful chit!—Well! I am sure I *deserve* to go off in an apoplexy!"

"You may do so with my blessing!" Valerian retorted. "Don't be grumbling yourself into a fit of the sullens; I shan't coax you out of them! And don't be spouting any more fustian about raising your brats alone, because I know very well it's Angelica who's dealt with them. You've taken a very shabby advantage of her."

"You are cruel!" Marigold cried feebly. "Cruel! Angelica promised your papa on his deathbed that she would look after us! It's not as if she had anything better to do—after all, she *is* the ugly duckling of the family!"

With this blatant misapprehension, Simon had to disagree. "Rot!" said he.

This untimely interruption had the effect of distracting Marigold. She contemplated Simon, his broad shoulders and narrow waist, his well-shaped calf and dissipated face. No less than her daughters did Marigold revere a handsome gentleman; no slower of comprehension, she also immediately ecognized a hardened rakeshame. With that comprehension all similarity between Marigold and her daughters ceased; Marigold wasn't thrown into a pelter at finding herself in conversation with a noted profligate. Quite the contrary, Marigold thought she would like to pursue the conversation. She looked coy.

If Marigold was impressed by Simon Brisbane, and she was, Simon was not similarly stricken with admiration; he believed Marigold at least partially responsible for his Miss Smith's devilish stratagems. Said he, with quirked brow: "You don't *look* consumptive!"

"Consumptive!" Marigold voiced protest.

Another voice came to them then, faintly from the couch. "Fennel!" cried Rosemary, as she struggled to a sitting position. "Mama! We must go after Angelica and my sapphires. Chalmers will be home at any moment! What can I say to him? I think I shall go mad."

Immediately Fennel was at his sister's side. "There, there!" he soothed. "Say Angelica took them! Which reminds me that this gentleman is Angelica's ineligible *parti*!"

Rosemary propped herself up on one elbow and craned her neck, the better to observe the gentleman who had dallied with the ugly duckling of the Millikin family. Damnably attractive, undeniably dissolute—this rakehell had trysted with *Angelica*? "Good God!" said Rosemary.

Though Marigold's reaction was similar—to wit, stunned disbelief—she expressed herself much more eloquently and with a great many such phrases as "bound for perdition" and "the road to ruin." Perhaps, suggested Marigold, the anxiety Angelica had suffered over Rosemary's little problems had deranged her mind. Conversely, Marigold could think of no good reason why a rakeshame should choose an ugly duckling as the object of his philandering. Since he had done so, queer as it might seem, Marigold trusted that the rakeshame would make amends. Her little Angelica was of good birth and hitherto untarnished character; she must not be made to suffer for what had chanced. Marigold was fully conscious of the incongruity of such a match—Mr. Brisbane was obviously a bachelor of the first water while Angelica was at her last prayers—but Mr. Brisbane should have considered the consequences before he took a spinster off the shelf for purposes of dalliance.

"I trusted her!" Marigold concluded, with a despairing gesture as eloquent as any Mrs. Siddons had ever enacted on or off the stage. "I left my darling children to her care. What must she do but abandon all to dally with you, sir? Though I cannot conceive why you wished to do so, it is obvious you did—which is *thoroughly* reprehensible!"

"This is a tempest in a teapot!" responded Mr. Brisbane, when she paused so that he might defend himself. Since Marigold seemed disinclined to utter any practical remarks, and Valerian seemed disinclined to do anything more practical than thoughtfully watch Marigold, Simon abandoned them. Perhaps the other two members of the party might achieve a greater degree of lucidity.

"Heavy work, ma'am!" remarked Valerian, as Marigold stared in bewilderment at Mr. Brisbane's retreating back. "I can't imagine what possessed you to make such a cake of yourself—not that it's the first time! You were always one to fuss over trifles."

"*Trifles!*" Marigold turned an anguished face upon her stepson. Absurd to think of him so; they were almost of an age. In fact, Valerian had grown into a very personable man. A physician, was he not? And probably as poor as a church mouse. Still, Marigold had always considered other things more important than mere wealth. And had there not been a well-heeled godfather? But first things first. "A man of nefarious reputation trifles with your sister and you say I make a piece of work over *nothing*? He may have offered her a slip on the shoulder for all we know!"

"Oh, yes!" Valerian responded cheerfully. "He did! You needn't go into high fidgets, because first Angelica boxed his ears and then she kicked him in the shin."

"She *what*?" Marigold gasped, then swooned. Since she did so right into her stepson's arms, this act failed to attract the attention of the other occupants of the room.

Valerian's attention it did attract, though not in the precise manner Marigold had planned. He clasped her shoulders, set
196

her away from him, and said: "I am going to release you, Marigold, so you may either cease your posturing or fall upon your head, I don't especially care which!" He suited action to word.

Presented with so unpalatable a choice, Marigold opened her blue eyes, which were damp with tears. "You were not used to dislike me so much, in the old happier days!"

"I wasn't?" Valerian crossed his arms upon his chest and looked interested. "As *I* recall the old days, I thought you were highly capricious, prone to oddities and absurdities and eccentricities! But you don't like plain-speaking, do you? Now I'll warrant you'll threaten to fall into a lethargy."

Marigold, who had been contemplating precisely that, rapidly reconsidered. "I am entirely crushed," she said sadly, "that you should hold me in such very low esteem."

Valerian might have been a devious individual, dispassionate and detached; but he was no more than human and therefore did not even briefly contemplate turning aside temptation. "I might give you," he said speculatively, "an opportunity to change my mind."

Whatever Marigold had expected of Valerian, it was not that manner of response. Caught by surprise, she blinked. Then her blue eyes narrowed, she smiled enchantingly, she stepped forward and laid a fragile hand on Valerian's coatsleeve. "I am flattered!" she breathed. "To think that all these years—Valerian, I had no idea!"

Nor had Valerian, and the notion made him laugh aloud. "You'll catch cold at that!" he wheezed. "Oh, you're first-rate, I don't deny it, but you're not in *my* style. So stay your distance, if you please, because I have other fish to fry!"

And because Valerian was human, at last he had erred. No less than had her daughter Lily did Marigold savor being told she was not in the style of every living gentleman. Valerian had entirely too high an opinion of himself, Marigold decided; he needed to be brought down several pegs. Therefore she did not remove her hand from his sleeve but stepped still closer and said humbly: "I am truly sorry, Valerian, that I spoke so freely. It will give you a disgust of me; it must bring me under the gravest censure; you will be surprised by my boldness. I

197

have no excuse—save that I hoped you might—but that you do not, I perfectly see!"

"Were your vision so perfect, you would see I don't like you above half!" responded Valerian with devastating candor. Marigold looked stricken. Since Valerian clearly recalled her playacting abilities, and since he was most appreciative of her repertoire, he softened this set-down with one of his rare and beautiful smiles. "I also recall that you are the most complete flirt! You always did try and outjockey me."

Marigold was not of sufficiently energetic constitution to persist against unbeatable odds. Too, she was not insensible to the effect of Valerian's smile, with the likes of which she had never before been gifted. "Yes, and you would never let me win, which is deuced unhandsome of you, you scamp! What would it hurt if just once you let me get the better of you? Since you will not, let us consider the imbroglio that your sisters have brought about. I hope you are prepared to give me some advice, because I am of too delicate a constitution to tolerate any more disastrous developments!"

Although it was not his custom to hand out advice, Valerian decided to make an exception. He wished to see his favorite sister happily settled; and to that end he would make any sacrifice, even though life would seem very flat once he'd tidied matters up and was no longer subject to these continual alarms. Thought of alarms prompted him to put forth an opinion that since Marigold was patently unable to control her offspring, she should remarry. The offspring, Valerian believed, would go on a great deal easier with a man's hand on the reins. Thereby reminded that Marigold's hand still rested on his sleeve, Valerian patted it.

This simple act had a startling effect on the participants. Valerian looked shocked. Marigold, who had a great deal more experience with that malady of which the symptoms were giddiness and palpitations and an oppression on the chest, looked rueful and roguish and altogether delightful. "Now *this*," she murmured, "truly is a bolt from the blue!"

Indeed it was, and it had not escaped attention that Valerian Millikin and his stepmama were staring at each other with mingled wonder and dismay. "How can you all gnore what has happened?" wailed Rosemary. "Angelica has -loped, my sapphires have been stolen! We must do some-hing! Let us call in Bow Street!"

Valerian's mind had not ceased to function, even though he had been struck all of a heap. He pointed out the folly of such a course, which would not only insure that the world knew of Angelica's elopement, but might additionally involve her imprisonment for theft. At this particular moment—while Simon voiced a strong curiosity as to with whom Angelica had -loped—yet another caller was ushered into the room. Simon greeted his henchman with an oath.

"I am lamentable sorry for it, Master Simon!" apologized Durward, his long nose atwitch. "I don't know how he did it, but Sir Randall diddled me. It's my belief he's gone off to meet with the young lady, and I've a good notion where!"

Valerian roused from the entranced state induced in him by Marigold's ethereal person and huge blue eyes and heady perfume, and retreated from her several paces. "Angelica and Sir Randall? Don't go leaping to conclusions, Brisbane!" But Simon and his henchman were already through the door.

"My sapphires!" wailed Rosemary, and surged to her feet. "The dragon!" uttered Fennel, and pulled her back down on the sofa. "Where are you going?" cried Marigold, following Valerian to the door.

"To find Angelica!" snapped Valerian, who was feeling a trifle fuzzy-headed, and who was consequently out of charity with the inspiration of his distress.

Marigold, who was feeling no less fuzzy-headed, had no wish whatsoever to be separated from the source of her distress until she could decide what was best done about this bizarre development. She wrinkled her pretty nose and sniffled, all the while gazing imploringly at her stepson.

Valerian knew very well that he was being outjockeyed, but suddenly to be outjockeyed by a conniving stepmama whom he didn't like above half seemed much less terrible than the alternative possibility that she might burst any moment into tears. "Have it your own way, then," he muttered. "But this doesn't change anything!"

Twenty-Three

Lady Chalmers and her brother were not left long to savor their solitude; scant moments after the eldest of the Millikin siblings had departed, in company with his stepmama, in the wake of Durward and Simon Brisbane, the youngest of the Millikins ran into the drawing room. Hot on his heels were Violet and Hyacinth, the twins Amaryllis and Camilla. Overwhelmed by superior forces, Hysop took refuge behind the needlepointed sofa.

Rosemary gazed upon her siblings, who were all gazing upon her with varying degrees of concern. "I think," Rosemary said sadly, as she dropped her face into her hands, "that I shall put a pistol to my own head."

Dead silence greeted this remark. Since the Millikins were by nature very voluble creatures, that silence struck Rosemary as very strange. Even stranger were the footsteps that echoed in the silence, as if booted feet strode across the floor. On due reflection, Rosemary recognized those footsteps, as familiar as her own. Bravely she raised her face from her trembling hands.

As she had guessed, the footsteps belonged to her spouse, who was looking yet again like a thundercloud. "Never have I see a more affecting scene!" he said, with harsh sarcasm. "I conjecture I am to take it to heart that I have laden you so heavily with reproaches you are fit to blow your own brains out! I am the greatest beast in nature, I suppose, because I wished to prevent you squandering my fortune! You may think me cruelly unfeeling, Rosemary—you may think me anything you wish!—I begin to despair of our ever reaching agreement!"

"Oh, I say!" remarked Fennel, in whom the Millikin lack of *nous* was accompanied by a tendency to tread fearlessly where angels dared not. "That's coming it rather too strong, Chalmers! Had you not kept Rosemary without money for common necessaries, she wouldn't have run aground! It was very stupidly done of her, I don't deny that, but the deuce! Ain't *you* ever been a trifle scorched?"

This appeal to fellow-feeling went very wide of its mark. Lord Chalmers, having never had deep doings, had never been dipped; and he had no compassion to waste on those who were so foolish as to fall into debt. Rosemary sniffled. Lord Chalmers cast her an acerbic glance. In so doing, he noted the various wide-eyed siblings grouped artistically around his wife. Chalmers was not especially appreciative of beauty, even of a bedazzling surfeit of Millikins. He suggested that his wife's siblings were embarrassingly *de trop*.

"No, no!" With one hand Rosemary clutched Fennel, with the other Violet. "I beg you, do not leave us alone!"

This plea was not without effect. The Millikins all looked astounded that Rosemary should fear to be closeted privately with her spouse; but no one looked more astounded than Lord Chalmers himself. Could Rosemary *truly* think him the greatest beast in nature? What basis had she for such grievous misjudgment? And then Lord Chalmers recalled that at the termination of their last *tête-à-tête* he had turned his wife over his knee. As a result of that recollection and his consequent suspicion that he had been a thought high-handed, Lord Chalmers looked even more thunderous. He reached into his pocket, extracted a handful of glittering gems and dropped them into his wife's lap. "Jupiter!" breathed Hysop, from the hearth.

"The sapphires!" Rosemary had gone corpse-white. "How—why—oh, dear! I don't imagine you'll believe that *I* didn't pop them! At least not this time!"

Lord Chalmers had opened his mouth to respond that he knew very well, despite Rosemary's peccadilloes, that she had not pawned the Chalmers sapphires. According to the owner of the shop where the necklace had been taken—a discreet individual who had no sooner recognized the stones than he'd sent urgent word to Lord Chalmers, who had immediately set out to buy back the gems, after which he had made some most enlightening calls upon various tradesmen to whom his wife owed long-overdue sums—the necklace had been brought in by two most disreputable-looking men. "*This* time?" he echoed.

"The deuce!" sighed Rosemary.

"Now you've truly put your foot in it," commented Fennel, while his younger sisters and brother watched keenly this enactment of marital drama. "I'll tell you what it is, Rosemary: you'd best make a clean breast of it!"

"Yes, do!" invited the baron, regarding his wife with an unloving eye. "I am a busy man, Rosemary; this whole affair has put me to a great deal of inconvenience."

"Oh!" Conscience-stricken, Rosemary clutched the sapphires to her bosom. "You *have* suffered a revulsion of feeling—not that you ever did care a fig for me! All I wished to do was make a stir in the world and set myself up in the latest mode—I had no notion that it would cost so *dear*! But it did! And then I was under the necessity of keeping you from finding out just how very badly I was scorched, because you already thought very poorly of me. I tried very hard to make a recover, but it did not serve. Now you will publicly denounce me, and it is no more than I deserve! I am the first of the family to try and outrun the bailiffs; I might as well also be the first to be dragged into the divorce court!" Upon saying which, she burst into tears.

With no little consternation, Lord Chalmers eyed his sobbing wife, ringed about with sisters who patted and soothed. "Good God, Rosemary!" he said, rather feebly. "I didn't say anything about divorce!"

"No," wept Rosemary, "but you will when you hear about Mr. Thwaite!" After this dire utterance, she lapsed into total incoherency.

It was left to Fennel to render up such explanations as seemed advisable. He contemplated his brother-in-law's choleric countenance and decided only the whole truth would suit.

"You ain't going to like this!" said Fennel, with a flash of his occasional perspicacity. "Rosemary may be a chowder-head but you *are* devilish high in the instep! It stands to reason she was afraid to tell you about her fix—moreover, she trusted Angelica to see her clear of it. But what must Angelica do but take a maggot in her head and filch the sapphires herself—you look confused!"

Whatever degree of confusion Lord Chalmers may have exhibited was but a drop in the bucket to the turmoil that he felt. He had scant reliance on Fennel as a lucid source of information, but Fennel was obviously the most lucid individual in the room. Lord Chalmers requested politely that, if explanation Fennel meant to render, he should start at the beginning. Fennel professed himself happy to do so.

Fennel started with his own arrival in London, proceeded through the pawning of the sapphires and Rosemary's attempts to redeem the gems, and concluded with his own fruitless visit to Mr. Thwaite in Newgate Street. "You mustn't think *too* bad of Rosemary!" Fennel concluded. "She don't mean no harm, it's just that she has more hair than sense." He cleared his throat. "And I'll take leave to tell you that Rosemary hasn't defied you from a want of affection, Chalmers! To say the truth, she's been wild with horror of the notion that you should cast her off—and it beats me why she should dread being accused by you of boldness if she admitted she was *éprise!*"

If Lord Chalmers was aghast at these disclosures, and he was, he was no more aghast than Rosemary. "Fennel!" she shrieked, and sank back on the sofa, deprived almost of consciousness.

That Lady Chalmers did not, in this most apt of all moments, take refuge in a swoon was due to the advent of the butler. That individual stood stiffly in the doorway and announced with disapproval that A Person sought converse with her ladyship. Before her ladyship could respond, the visitor in question pushed aside the butler and stepped into the room. Fennel recognized that plump and garish figure, the equally garish and most improbably colored hair, the avaricious eye. Fervently he wished that he might sink through the floor.

Though the arrival of Mrs. Holloway had a debilitating

effect on Fennel, Rosemary was vitalized: her days to play the baroness were numbered, after all. Lady Chalmers stiffened her spine, folded her hands in her lap, and inquired with a nice condescension what Mrs. Holloway required.

Mrs. Holloway was not easily intimidated, and the sapphires that rested also in Rosemary's lap had not escaped her greedy eye. Nor was she a woman to waste time with polite absurdities. She reiterated her intention, did not Fennel come across with the ready on the spot, to bring against him a breach of promise suit. Said Fennel, squirming under his brother-in-law's lowering eye: "Nothing of the sort! No promises were made, my word on it! It was just a flirtation!"

"*Flirtation*?!" Mrs. Holloway placed her fists on her ample hips. "A seduction, more like! I disremember when I've been so lamentable put-about. That my poor Phoebe should be led astray by a harum-scarum young man—I mean to see she's not a penny the worst of it!"

Lord Chalmers may not have been beloved of the muslin company, but he had taken Mrs. Holloway's measure on first glance. "And several pennies to the better, I perceive!" he murmured. "That *is* the purpose of this visit?"

"No, no!" protested Rosemary, as Fennel mumbled in a nettled fashion about rosy cheeks and cherry lips and promises he'd never made, and his siblings looked on in unabashed fascination. "Do not concern yourself, Chalmers! This, er, lady is under the impression that Fennel has his own money, that the family is well off. I asked her to call so that I might explain to her how it is the opposite."

Mrs. Holloway was no pigeon for anyone's plucking, and so she announced. Perhaps the Millikins had no money, but Lord Chalmers was rich as Croesus, in proof of which Lady Chalmers was sitting in her drawing room with a sapphire necklace in her lap. Why Lady Chalmers should do such a bizarre thing, Mrs. Holloway could not imagine; but were Lady Chalmers to fork over those sapphires Mrs. Holloway would be on her way, with no more said.

"No," cried Rosemary yet again, and clasped the sapphires to her cheek. "This necklace is not mine, but a family heirloom! Someday it will be worn by the wife of my eldest son!"

To this simple statement, Lord Chalmers reacted with unfeigned surprise. "Rosemary! You're not—"

Rosemary blushed bright red. "I do not mean to argue with you, Chalmers—indeed I have vowed that I will not—but I rather think I am!"

A man of direct action when it occurred to him that action there should be, Lord Chalmers tumbled several of the younger Misses Millikin from his pathway and sat down beside his wife. "Rosemary!" he clasped her hands in his own. "Why didn't you *tell* me?"

"Because," murmured Rosemary, staring at his cravat, "I thought you would be happier if you divorced me. I am selfish and extravagant and headstrong; you had warned me about running into debt and I didn't listen. But you also said it was a dead bore to be forever living in each other's pockets, and you were so often away from home I thought you had a, er, well! Because it didn't seem reasonable to devote that much time to government! And then when I tried to confess my sentiments, you turned me—oh, you know what you did!" She sniffled.

Lord Chalmers applied his handkerchief to his wife's damp cheeks, gently. "Yes! I have regretted it ever since!"

"Pooh!" Rosemary was adorably abashed. "I don't regard it, I assure you! But, Chalmers, does this mean you *will* forgive me?"

"Anything!" Lord Chalmers drew Rosemary into the circle of his arm. "I begin to see that I have been a perfect boor."

"Oh, no! Never that! Although it *was* very dreary of you to make me read that wretched book and to talk to me about things like the suspension of habeas corpus and legislation against seditious meetings—but if that is what you want of me I shall try not to mind!"

"Let us make a pact!" said her lord, craftily. "You will tell me when you wish to spend my money—and yes, I will pay off your debts; I am not an unreasonable man!—and I will *not* complain to you about the state of the nation!"

"Oh, Chalmers!" Rosemary said blissfully, and then: "But I do not want to be reconciled with you if it is only because you want an heir!"

Despite his aforementioned lack of intimacy with the

muslin company, Lord Chalmers was also aware that in certain situations a simple action accomplished more than a hundred words. In plain view of the assembled company, Lord Chalmers embraced his wife. "Jupiter!" breathed Hysop, and departed post haste to remove the friendly little garden snake from Rosemary's boudoir.

Mrs. Holloway was not so easily inspired toward flight. Sight of the newly discovered marital bliss of Lord Chalmers and his wife reminded Mrs. Holloway of her own daughter's unhappy plight, or so she informed her audience in most colorful terms. Fennel, by now accustomed to hearing himself referred to as a gay deceiver, stared when Mrs. Holloway referred to his starched-up brother-in-law as a well-breeched swell. Lord Chalmers, with admirable composure, settled his wife back amongst the sofa cushions, rose, and invited Mrs. Holloway to step into the hallway. Scenting victory, she did so.

Only a few moments had passed, during which the younger Misses Millikin congratulated Rosemary on her reconciliation with her spouse and Fennel anticipated with relish what Rosemary's spouse would have to say to him about Mrs. Holloway, when Lord Chalmers reentered the drawing room. His cool eye alit immediately on Fennel. Fennel squirmed. "It *was* only a flirtation!" he protested. "I didn't pretend to Phoebe's hand—or anything else! No matter what the dragon claims!"

"Mrs. Holloway will claim no more, at least to or about you; I have bought her off." Lord Chalmers resumed his position on the sofa. "Do I not recall, Fennel, that you yearn after a captaincy in the Hussars? I thought so! I will make you a bargain: return to your university and apply yourself to your studies and I will see you have your captaincy."

"By Jove!" breathed Fennel. "Done!"

"Oh, Chalmers!" Rosemary gazed rapt upon her spouse. "You are so *very* good!"

"I have," Lord Chalmers responded ruefully, "much for which to atone. Had I not neglected you, you would not have had to fret yourself—what the *devil* is that child about?" This query concerned Violet, who had dropped to her hands
206

and knees and was scrabbling beneath the sofa. Even as Chalmers spoke she emerged, waving a smudged piece of paper.

"Oh!" wailed Rosemary. "I quite forgot! Angelica stole my sapphires, you know; and Lily set out after her. Angelica has been meeting with an ineligible *parti*, Chalmers! I know I should have stopped it, but Lily persuaded me Angelica should be allowed *some* fun, and how was I to know she would elope? I mean, *Angelica*? It is the queerest thing!"

So it was, as further attested by the babble of melodious female voices that broke into immediate speech. Angelica embarked upon a liaison with a hardened rakeshame? The ugly duckling of the Millikin family courted by a man of the world? One if not both participants in this affair were quite lunatic!

It was Lord Chalmers who restored some degree of decorum to his drawing room. He was not surprised to learn that Angelica had pawned the sapphires, due to the odd antics he'd observed in her of late; he was not even especially surprised that Angelica should have taken to clandestine meetings, for she was despite her practicality a Millikin. Nonetheless, Lord Chalmers was very much surprised, and no less indignant, that Angelica should have grown so inconsiderate that she eloped with her ineligible *parti*, thus subjecting the mother of all his as-yet-unborn sons (of which, for those readers with a fondness for statistics, there were destined to be three) to needless stress. He twitched the letter away from Violet.

The sapphires, Angelica, a flight to Gretna Green—"Ah!" said his lordship, enlightenment achieved. "It's not Angelica who's eloped, but Lily!"

Twenty-Four

The hour was considerably advanced when Valerian Millikin and his stepmama, Simon Brisbane and Durward arrived at a certain cemetery on the other side of town. Their progress had not been rapid. A repetition of the tale told Simon by Angelica in explanation of her venture into the working class caused Marigold to stop dead in her tracks—a consumptive parent sewing seams by candlelight? Marigold had thought Lily was the member of the family to indulge in air-dreams! —and Simon's additional explanation of his assumption that Marigold's numerous offspring had been born on the wrong side of the blanket caused her to swoon. Though Marigold's vapors were not of long duration, due to Valerian's threat to leave his stepmama lying in the street, Simon again had cause to regret the inclusion of Millikins in his small search party. It seemed incredible to him that the lady who had in response to a simple declaration of improper intentions boxed his ears and kicked his shin should then engage in robbery and flight. Surely Miss Smith could not have eloped with Simon's aggravating parent? She could not have so thoroughly deceived him! It must be a farrago of nonsense, in which case Simon was growing momentarily more worried. Where was Angelica, and why? Was she safe? Simon thought that, were he fortunate enough to find her, he would wring Angelica's neck.

It appeared, as Simon stepped through the cemetery gates, trailed by Valerian and Durward and an owl-eyed Marigold, that he was to be granted his wish. Familiar feminine tones smote his ear. They issued from the direction of an elaborately sculpted crypt. Simon gestured for silence.

Cautiously the small party crept forward, paused in the shadow of the crypt. Not only Angelica's voice came clearly to them now, but three others, all raised in angry debate.

"The hornies!" said one such voice, gruff and menacing. "You laid an information against us, missie—you must have or the Runners wouldn't be on our trail! Or was those sparklers you gave us stolen? If so you must be dicked in the nob! I take it *most* unkindly that you should try and queer our pitch!"

"Stolen sparklers!" came another voice, no less gruff but much more refined, a voice very well known to Simon Brisbane, who upon hearing it experienced mingled exasperation and relief. "Bow Street? What *have* you been up to, Miss Smith?"

"Do not play the innocent, Sir Randall!" begged Angelica. "It must be evident that I know all! Or if not precisely *know*, then suspect, even though it does boggle the imagination! Had not these horrid men made the situation clear to me, I *wouldn't* have suspected, ever; they promised to keep silent only if I paid their bribe. You are perfectly safe! No one will ever know!"

Of the eavesdroppers, only Marigold was tempted to interfere. Leaving Valerian and Simon and his henchman raptly listening, she crept forward and peeked around the side of the crypt. Angelica was in converse with a plump and cherubic-looking gentleman whom Marigold assumed was Sir Randall, while two of the most disreputable individuals in existence belligerently looked on. "Suspect *what*, Miss Smith?" Sir Randall inquired patiently.

Angelica frowned and pressed her fingertips to her temples; her life had taken on all the aspects of a most unpleasant nightmare these past several hours. First had been the encounter with Mallet and Bimble and the strong intimation that they would wait no longer for their money; then had come the note from Sir Randall, insisting on this rendezvous. Angelica

209

had stolen her sister's necklace, handed it over to the resurrectionists, rushed to meet Sir Randall—despite all her efforts to free herself from the quicksand into which she had unwittingly stepped, she sank momentarily deeper into the morass. "This is hardly a moment," muttered Sir Randall, "for air-dreaming, Miss Smith!"

Nor was it, with Mallet and Bimble looming over them like two harbingers of doom. "I had thought at first," Angelica said sadly, "that you were prone to undertake your own resurrection work, which though hardly the thing was understandable! Surgeons *do* need specimens; that much I perceive! but then Mallet and Bimble intimated to me that it was very much worse, that it lay within their power to see you in gaol, that you might repeat some horrid offense. They said they would keep silent only if I paid them. But when I tried to ask Simon for money he thought I wanted it for myself! Which left only Rosemary's necklace." Angelica drew breath. "Truly, Sir Randall, I do not care *what* you've done—rather I care, but it doesn't signify—I mean, I'm devoted to you! So you perceive we must do as Mallet and Bimble wish or they won't keep quiet as oysters! Because even if it *isn't* true, you would still be ruined."

Sir Randall pushed his spectacles up to the bridge of his nose, the better to observe the resurrectionists. Unabashed, those worthies suggested that some provision be made for their welfare before the advent of Bow Street. "Else," added Mallet ominously, "the game will be up!"

"Dear me, how *very* tiresome!" Sir Randall set about polishing his spectacles. "I fear that you have committed theft for nothing, Miss Smith."

Angelica stared at her ex-employer. "You mean you haven't—you didn't—but then *why*?"

"Because," responded Sir Randall, with an unfriendly glance at the resurrectionists, who were looking even more hostile, "these scoundrels recognized a flat! They hoodwinked you, my dear."

"Aye." Mallet grinned evilly. "I'm thinkin' it wouldn't go very good with missie here, guv'nor, was we hobbled—acause we'd have to say how we came by those sparklers. 'Twould be a right rare pity was missie to end up in quod!"

This threat to her own well-being Angelica ignored. "I don't understand! Why did you have me meet you *here*? It is a very nice cemetery, as cemeteries go, or so I suppose it is because I am not a connoisseur of such sites! Still it seems a strange choice of places to meet if you're *not* embarked on your own resurrection work."

"Not at all, Miss Smith!" Sir Randall indicated the crypt. Angelica read the plaque attached thereto. "Gracious! Your wife!" she gasped.

"I was in the habit of discussing things with her," Sir Randall replied. "Old habits die hard, my dear, even habits my son deems morbid. It is nothing of the sort; I enjoy speaking with my dear wife as much as I ever did, especially since she is no longer in a position to argue with me!"

"But," she protested, "Durward!"

"Ah, yes!" Sir Randall beamed paternally. "I fear I have been a *trifle* underhanded, my dear! In short, I arranged to meet you here today deliberately so that you might encounter Simon—Williams was to drop a hint to Durward, you see."

Angelica saw nothing, which was not surprising, due to the blinding headache she had developed apace with Sir Randall's disclosures. "What makes you think I wish to encounter Simon?" she inquired irritably.

Sir Randall had no opportunity to answer this very silly question; several things happened at once. Mallet growled and reached for Angelica, with obviously fell intent; Marigold screamed; Simon leapt to his feet. There was a brief flurry of bodies and a cacophony of shrieks. When the dust settled once again, Simon was seen to have planted Mallet a facer, and Marigold had triumphantly wielded the shovel with which she had rendered senseless Bimble, who sprawled at her feet.

"Well done!" applauded Valerian, who had in the midst of the melee settled himself quite comfortably on a broad tombstone. "The question now is what's to be done with them. We can't leave them to be picked up by Bow Street or the brutes *will* drag Angelica into it. Stealing what's-her-name's sapphires, forsooth!"

Durward's long nose twitched. "If I may offer a suggestion, sir? I fancy I may have hit upon a solution!" This he explained. Since it involved conveying Mallet and Bimble into the country in the manner of the goods in which they dealt, that is coffins, Durward's solution should have induced the most unscrupulous of resurrectionists to mend his ways.

Durward's solution met with unanimous approval; he retired to fetch the coffins and a cart. Marigold hefted her shovel experimentally, assured herself that her victim was not likely to regain consciousness for some time, stared censoriously at her stepdaughter. "Ungrateful girl!" she said, and launched upon an explanation of this condemnation, very dramatically delivered, thick with references to ugly ducklings and adders teeth, unsteadinesses of character and descents into profligacy. "I never heard of anything half so shocking!" concluded Marigold, unfairly and with considerable untruth. "You needn't try and tell me you didn't throw out lures, my girl; *I* wasn't born yesterday!"

"That much," said Simon irritably, for he was trying to carry on a sensible conversation with the object of Marigold's strictures, "is obvious!" Marigold's mouth dropped open. Simon led the ugly duckling some slight distance away.

"It was very kind of you," murmured Angelica shyly, to her escort, "to rush to my defense! Can it be that you do not *like* my stepmama?"

"Your stepmama," responded Simon, who hadn't the slightest wish to discuss Marigold, "is a pretty widgeon. So are your sisters, if Lady Chalmers is any example. Which reminds me that they are no longer to be your responsibility!"

"No?" Angelica blinked. "But I promised my papa—"

"On his deathbed! Poppycock! I doubt that your father meant they should take eternal advantage of you."

It was a novel experience to hear her dazzling siblings spoken of in such unappreciative tones—so novel that Angelica misdoubted her ears. Diffidently she pointed out that it was the way of the world: creatures so blessed with beauty as the Millikins could not help but take advantage of those less fortunate.

"Fishing for compliments?" inquired Simon. "I find you quite lovely, my darling, much more so than your stepmother
212

and your sister. All that yellow hair is distinctly commonplace! And now—"

"Now," interrupted Angelica, who knew very well what Simon wished to say and even how she would respond, but who wished most ignobly to prolong as much as possible her moment of triumph, "I owe you any number of apologies! I spun you the most appalling taradiddles, but—"

"My love, I know." Simon smiled to see the expression with which Angelica greeted this endearment. "What I have not pieced together you may explain to me later. *Now*—"

"Will you answer me just one question?" Angelica asked meekly. "Why did you set spies on your father if he's done nothing dreadful?"

"My father," responded Simon, as he took matters into his own hands and Angelica into his arms, "is a curst nuisance. He has no more sense of self-preservation than that tree! Left to his own devices he will neither eat nor sleep—he can spend an appalling amount of time in such activities as observing the animals in the Royal Exchange, which may in itself be unexceptionable, but not when in so doing he disappears for an entire week! It was after he'd laid on his belly by that damned fishpond of his for days—during which it rained and after which he came down with an influenza!—that I introduced Durward into the household."

"Oh!" Angelica's voice was very small. "I suspected you of the most dreadful things!"

"And I you, my love." Simon's gaze was warm. "We shall forgive one another, I think. Even if you do *not* forgive me, I shall not care, so long as you marry me."

"Oh,!" said Angelica again, her cheeks pink. "If that is truly what you want, I think I would like it very well—and *then* will you explain to me what is an orgy?"

"Better!" Simon's voice was harsh. "I'm a man of few words, my love—I will *show* you what an orgy is!"

This avowal, delivered with much more vigor than was necessary to reach ears scant inches away from the speaker's lips, occasioned much comment. Between kisses Angelica confessed rather incoherently that she had some time past confided in her eldest brother a wish to meet a gentleman most impenetrably taciturn; Valerian broke off a discussion with Sir Randall about the skeleton of a giant currently on exhibit in a raree-show to modestly admit his small part in the romance as well as Sir Randall's own; Marigold, who had already been put out of humor by Simon's comment that she was common-looking—Marigold made up in acuteness of hearing for what she lacked in brains—was by this intimation that her spinster stepdaughter was to enjoy pleasures forbidden her stepmama sent straight up into the boughs.

"Shocking!" she cried. "Scandalous! Never did I think to hear my own stepdaughter express a taste for depravity!" To Angelica's protests that she wished to know what an orgy *was*, not to engage in one; Simon's averral that Angelica would wish very much to engage in an orgy, once she knew what it was, enlightenment which he would provide immediately the knot was tied, Marigold paid no heed. "My health is ruined!" she announced dramatically. "Now I am to be deprived of my sole means of support."

By this effusion, Angelica understood Marigold referred to herself. Long the means by which the Millikins were saved from the consequences of their worst excesses, Angelica could not abandon them, no matter how great her wish to do precisely that. Nor could she inquire of Simon if he had reflected soberly upon the drawbacks of marriage to a female so encumbered as herself. Yet to fail to point out that unpalatable fact was wholly reprehensible. The ethical ramifications of the situation made Angelica's head ache.

Not surprisingly, Angelica's throbbing brow recalled her enfeebled state of health. She put forth to Valerian her opinion that syrup of poppies and a hot brick did absolutely nothing to relieve dizziness and palpitations and an oppression on the chest. "Nothing will relieve it!" Valerian responded, in funereal tones. "What ails you, Sis, is love!"

In that case, if she were in love with Simon Brisbane, which seemed the most logical explanation of everything concerned, Angelica could not in good conscience repress mention of her encumbrances. Said Simon, who had grown very weary of hearing about all the drawbacks to his marriage: "Leave the brats to your brother! He'll deal with them!"

In response to this startling notion, Angelica stared up into Simon's dissipated face. "You jest! *Valerian*?"

"Valerian what?" inquired that individual, from his tombstone.

Simon drew Angelica's hand through his arm and led her back to the others. During their conversation Durward had returned and again departed, complete with coffins, resurrectionists and cart. "I was explaining to your sister," Simon said in brisk no-nonsense tones, "that you are to take on the responsibility of the younger members of the family."

When Valerian had advised Simon to adopt a high-handed attitude, he had not meant that attitude to be applied to himself. So Valerian might have stated had not Marigold thrown her arms around his neck. "Oh!" she cried. "I wish you would! Pray say you will! I should be most extraordinarily grateful! Because no matter what anyone may say about you, Valerian, they cannot deny you *cope* excellently!"

"Balderdash!" Valerian sought half-heartedly to free himself. "Have you forgot I don't like you above half?"

Marigold relaxed her death grip and stepped back sufficiently far that Valerian could see how enchantingly she smiled. "Dear Valerian! What has *liking* to do with anything?"

Very little, it appeared: confronted with a deliciously tempting female only five scant years older than himself, Valerian sought what seemed a logical alleviation of his dizziness and palpitations and the oppression on his chest. Said action, which consisted of embracing his stepmama in so enthusiastic a manner that he very nearly tumbled off his tombstone, must not be construed as remedy for the malady to which all Millikins were prey; so far was it from providing relief that it resulted in the addition to the previously-enumerated symptoms of a bell-like ringing in the ears.

Sir Randall readjusted his spectacles and murmured ironically: "Physician, heal thyself!"

"Gracious!" Angelica stared dumbfounded at her dispassionate, indifferent, shrewd elder brother, who was currently looking none of those things. "I hesitate to cast a damper—but is this precisely *legal*?"

Valerian raised his head from his stepmama's golden curls,

215

which smelled like heaven mingled with rather more earthly delights. He had not yet lost all his wits, however; to the notion of an existence shared with Marigold, he said, horrified: "Legal? I devoutly hope not!"

This highly unflattering rejoinder, Marigold let pass. She was, after all, a lovely lady who possessed a son-in-law so influential in government circles that he could if necessary ensure the passage of an act of Parliament to enable a lovely widow to marry her own stepson. Marigold did say, however, and very much belatedly: "Mercy! Where is *Lily*?"

Twenty-Five

Miss Lily Millikin suspected that she had not been altogether wise. It was all very well to plot an elopement while under the influence of the grape, and to embark upon it in a noble spirit of self-sacrifice; but Lily's motives had in the cold light of day begun to seem less valiant than absurd. If Angelica's preference was for a hardened rakeshame, and a diabolically attractive one to boot, she was not likely to settle for a hundred Kingscotes. Life was a sadly mismanaged business, decided Lily, who would have preferred Lord Kingscote over a thousand rakeshames.

Alas, it was not to be, on that point she would hold firm. At least she had with this elopement insured that there would be no marriage between them; with it she had ruined her good name. Young ladies of quality simply did not go wandering unchaperoned about the countryside. Moreover, Lily was not only unchaperoned, she was unaccompanied except by servants. It was not at all her idea of what an elopement should be. In fact, Lily decided, it was all very queer.

This escapade had begun ordinarily enough, with the note left in properly dramatic style for her family, and the secretive rendezvous; but from that point onward events had turned positively bizarre. Within the carriage, which was remarkably comfortable for a job-coach, had waited no anxious lover, no ardent buccaneer. Lily had traveled what seemed a very great distance, with naught but her thoughts for company. At length the carriage had drawn up before a country inn. Lily was handed down from the coach, conducted reverently by no less august a personage than the innkeeper into a private room, informed that "himself" would be with her in a wink. Lily was left alone to await the arrival of "himself" and to ponder that individual's identity. A brief exploration of her surroundings revealed little of interest: the tiny room was snug, with shuttered windows and a cozy fireplace, a low ceiling and a sawdust-covered floor—and a locked door. Lily collapsed onto a wooden chair.

What kind of man would leave her to travel alone to heaven knew what destination? Could the buccaneer fear to show his face by daylight? Was he not a man of substance and breeding, but a common criminal? And if so, what would be *her* end?

As Lily pondered these matters, growing momentarily more lachrymose, the door once more opened. The landlord entered, followed by two maidservants. Each carried a heavy tray. The contents of those trays were arranged temptingly upon a table. Then the landlord crossed to a certain window, threw open the shutters, tipped Lily a wink, and once more left her to solitude.

With some astonishment Lily eyed the table—laden now with, among other things, pigeon-pie and spurling, capons and collard head, a tansy-cake and what looked to be a bottle of ale. Surely the innkeeper could not credit so small a person as Lily with so large an appetite? On one score, anyway, he had judged very well. Lily hefted the bottle of ale.

Came a noise behind her and Lily spun around. Gracefully

through the window leapt her buccaneer. Gone was the elaborate costume of the masquerade ball; he wore this day a riding coat of blue superfine and pale salmon marcella waistcoat, green kerseymere unmentionables, but Lily didn't for an instant doubt his identity. Still he had not discarded his mask.

With something less than enthusiasm, Lily contemplated her courtier, who returned the compliment. Miss Millikin had attired herself very fashionably for her elopement in a spencer of sardinian blue, a neckscarf of white with blue stripes, a carriage dress of white poplin with a deep flounce, yellow shoes, a glorious bonnet with a small crown and helmet front, trimmed with wreaths of blue flowers and two white feathers, tied in a rakish and ribbon bow under her pretty chin. "You are out of charity with me, Lily?" inquired the gentleman, with laudable perspicacity.

"I have begun to think that I have been very silly," responded Lily, with immeasurable dignity. "It was most foolhardy to go running off with a man I do not know—or *do* I know you, sir? Sometimes you seem oddly familiar. I daresay it is only my imagination, which is *very* good! And although I have decided that you do not mean to ship me off to join some sultan's harem, I think it would be an excellent idea if you would send me home."

The gentleman appeared neither surprised nor dismayed by this request, due partially to his full face mask, and partially to the air of sublime unconcern with which he moved around the room to unfasten Lily's bonnet's ribbons. "A harem? My dear child!"

"I am *not* a child, and I am perfectly aware that white slavery rings exist!" Lily allowed herself to be divested of her bonnet and her spencer and her neck-scarf, then accepted a well-laden plate. "I know it is very shabby of me to try and hedge off now, when you have gone to such trouble, but if you should not object I would like to be taken home."

"Yes, but I *do* object," said the gentleman, not unreasonably, as he made great inroads on the pigeon-pie. "Are you angry because I did not accompany you here? I am sorry for it but there are reasons why I could not. I left very explicit
218

instructions that you should be made comfortable in my absence."

"Oh, I was! Every attention was given me." Gloomily Lily pushed away her plate; beseechingly she addressed her companion. "Do try and understand—it is horrid to contemplate an alliance devoid of sentiment! If I cannot marry Kingscote, and obviously I cannot, then I will marry no one. It is very bad of me; I am fully conscious of the shocking advantage I have taken of your kindness; this is the most awkward of businesses—but take me home, that's a good fellow!"

"I fear, Miss Millikin, that I must disabuse you on a couple of points." The buccaneer immediately proceeded to do so. It was not kindness that had inspired him to accede to Lily's suggestion of an elopement; he was not at all good. Furthermore, Lily did not seem to realize that her good name was besmirched beyond whitewashing. In short, the gentleman concluded, as he helped himself to tansy-cake and washed it down with ale, she was hopelessly compromised.

"I *do* know it!" responded Lily. "The fact that I have ruined myself was one of the things that decided me to go back to London. Even my family cannot expect Lord Kingscote to accept spoiled goods. He will cry off, and we shall both be spared unhappiness." Her blue eyes filled with tears. "I shall never, ever marry! And so I am very much obliged to you, sir, and very sorry that I have put you to a great deal of inconvenience, but that is the way with these fits of folly!" The buccaneer appeared to have been struck very forcibly by these remarks. Lily looked at him askance. "You would not want to elope with a woman who is going mad for another man, surely?"

"Why not?" inquired the buccaneer, with a fine insouciance. "Think you to play fast and loose with *me*? If so, my child, you had best think again. You have in a manner of speaking made your own bed, and now you must lie in it! In a word, you are mine to command!"

"Oh!" Lily clasped her pretty little hands. "I think I should warn you, sir, that I am not a biddable female. And I *am* a respectable female, although you would never credit it from my conduct, for I have behaved like a shocking loose-screw." She took a deep breath. "This is all fudge, you know! You may be very far gone in infatuation—certainly you *act* like you are!—but ours is only the briefest of acquaintances and you cannot be hankering after me so very terribly. Even if you were, sir, it would be to no avail. Truly I do not wish to cut up all your hopes, and I wish even less to be *disagreeable* —but nothing you can say or do will induce me to look more kindly upon your suit!"

This prettily delivered set-down, the buccaneer took in very good part. "Nothing?" he repeated, and drew Lily into his arms.

"Nothing!" Lily asserted once again, though with a note of doubt. "It would be most ungentlemanly of you to try and take advantage of me!" It soon became obvious, alas, that the buccaneer was no gentleman. "Oh, dear! Sir, I wish you would not—I will not trust myself to express—if you do not cease that this very instant I shall lose all sense of decorum! This is a very poor sort of amusement, sir—I mean, I like it very well of course; I would not wish you to think—oh!" Speech having failed her, she burst into tears.

This had not the effect Lily anticipated; the buccaneer did not release her but instead picked her up bodily, crossed the room, and sat down near the fireplace in the most comfortable of the small chamber's chairs. Nor did he allow Lily to remove herself from his lap, as she tried half-heartedly to do. "This is *most* indelicate," she said, as she abandoned the struggle for freedom and nestled against his shoulder. Then she expressed a feeble wish that she might somehow contrive to check his starts.

"You cannot!" he replied, against her hair. "Nor shall you wring my withers, so you may cease from further tears. I am a man of *very* violent passions, and I indulge them with great latitude."

"Heavens!" said Lily faintly, though without any appreciable effort to remove herself from the vicinity of such a brazen rogue.

"Quite." One of his arms encircled her slender shoulders, the other hand stroked her curls. "You perceive me absolutely enraptured." And then he proceeded to entertain the inspiration of his rapture with professions of ardor and protestations of loyalty unto death. She stood without rival, he proclaimed; she was the very woman calculated to suit his tastes.

Unfortunately this last comment recalled to Lily the gentleman by whom her own feelings were engaged, and the extreme reprehensibleness of her feelings, for she had entirely forgot her true love for the past several moments, which was behavior outrageous even in a Millikin. Lily tried once more to free herself. "Pray let me go!" she wailed.

"No." The buccaneer's tone was almost angry and Lily suffered a sudden surge of alarm. "Have I not said already I do not mean to let you go? I am a man of wild and ungovernable passions, if you will recall. You are the woman for whom I have a marked preference, the woman who has by act if not by word promised to favor me. Now you think you may say a mistake has been made and bid me quit you? I would not have thought you so missish!"

"I am *not* missish!" Lily protested indignantly. "Were I missish I would hardly allow you to embrace me. You will say I had no choice, but I *could* have swooned!"

"Ah!" The buccaneer's arms tightened around her. "Then you are *not* indifferent to me?"

"What I am," snapped Lily, who was discovering in herself a great many erroneous notions about romance, "is tired and cross and very weary of these transports! I have erred; I admit it. I have grievously misled you; I admit that too! There isn't the least use in you working yourself up into frenzies, or enacting me threats. Certainly I must count myself honored, and I do, but these dramatic flights will avail you nothing. It distresses me beyond measure to refuse you but I must. Now we shall say no more about it and you will take me home!"

"Disabuse yourself of that notion, my child," retorted the buccaneer. "And refrain from enacting me further displays of bravado. Why are you suddenly turned so timid, Lily? I have no wish that you should be afraid of me."

"Gammon! When you have practically abducted me? Not that you were wholly to blame for that, since it *was* my idea. But I thought that you would accompany me and when you did not I realized—" Lily gulped. "Sir, it is true that I am not indifferent to you, which is no doubt very depraved in me since I do not even know your name! And it is also true that I liked kissing you; indeed I have never liked it so well! But I have never kissed Lord Kingscote, you see, and so I do not know how that would be, and now I never will, because nothing could be more revolting to propriety than this dreadful scrape. It would serve me very well if no one ever spoke to me again. Oh! I did not mean to wound you," she added, because the buccaneer's chest had begun to shake alarmingly. "Pray do not do violence to your feelings! You must not take it as a reflection on yourself that Lord Kingscote would suit me to a cow's thumb!"

"But I do!" gasped the buccaneer. "I must!" He succumbed to a fit of merriment.

While her captor was thus indisposed, Lily sat up. The sound of the buccaneer's laughter struck a chord of memory. Nor, now that Lily pondered the matter, was the buccaneer's laughter all that seemed familiar. The gentleman's height and build, the color of his hair . . . Abruptly she tweaked the mask aside. "What the *devil*?" Lily inquired.

"You must thank Fennel," said Lord Kingscote, clasping her hands. "He intimated subtly that you felt my courtship lacked romance. In point of fact, he intimated it *so* subtly that it took me some time to catch his drift. When I did so, I took immediate steps to remedy the situation. I trust, Lily, that I did not act too late?"

Lily had been too grossly misled to allow Lord Kingscote to wriggle so easily off the hook. Yet she would not pretend an indignation she did not actually feel. "Wretch!" said Lily merely, with an arch glance and a fine flutter of eyelashes.

By this gentle indication that Lily would take his deception in good part, Lord Kingscote was encouraged to draw her once more against his chest. "I trust also," said the duke, "that you will forgive my masquerade? I feared that you had got in the habit of thinking me elderly." Here Lily interrupted with an opinion that eight-and-thirty was the best of all ages to be. Her failure to previously realize this fact she attributed to a shocking lack of perception on her part, perhaps because of her scanty prior acquaintance with wealthy peers, which she begged Lord Kingscote would excuse. "Gervaise!" said he.

"Gervaise," repeated Lily, "I like it very well that you should wish to embrace me, but I fear I cannot breathe! Thank you! Do you mean you went to all this trouble just to please me—the carriage, the masquerade?"

"I did," confessed Lord Kingscote. "I will admit I expected to feel very foolish, but instead I enjoyed myself excessively."

"Gervaise!" whispered Lily, overwhelmed. "You *do* love me!"

"Pea-goose!" responded her lord to be, and kissed her once again, after which he transported her not to Gretna Green but to his mother's house, no great distance away. For the sake of romance, Lord Kingscote had greatly exaggerated the consequences of Lily's solitary journey. Since no one knew of the misadventure except Lord Kingscote's loyal servants, no voice was raised in protest on the occasion of Lily's triumphant wedding ceremony in St. George's, Hanover Square.

Thus did the elder Misses Millikin achieve their fondest wishes, and Fennel as well. But what of Hyacinth and Violet, Amaryllis and Camilla, and young Hysop? What, indeed, of the lovely Marigold? Lest the reader fall into the common error of leaping to assumptions, this much may fairly be said: nothing in this world is predictable, and the Millikins less than most—but that's another tale.

Let COVENTRY Give You
A Little Old-Fashioned Romance